THE
CREPES
OF WRATH

A PENNSYLVANIA DUTCH MYSTERY
WITH RECIPES

Tamar Myers

NEW AMERICAN LIBRARY

NAL
Published by New American Library, a division of
Penguin Putnam Inc., 375 Hudson Street,
New York, New York 10014, U.S.A.
Penguin Books Ltd, 27 Wrights Lane,
London W8 5TZ, England
Penguin Books Australia Ltd, Ringwood,
Victoria, Australia
Penguin Books Canada Ltd, 10 Alcorn Avenue,
Toronto, Ontario, Canada M4V 3B2
Penguin Books (N.Z.) Ltd, 182–190 Wairau Road,
Auckland 10, New Zealand

Penguin Books Ltd, Registered Offices:
Harmondsworth, Middlesex, England

Published by New American Library, a division of Penguin Putnam Inc.

First New American Library Printing, January 2001
10 9 8 7 6 5 4 3 2 1

LIBRARY OF CONGRESS CATALOGING-IN-PUBLICATION DATA:

Myers, Tamar.
    The crepes of wrath : a Pennsylvania Dutch mystery with recipes / Tamar Myers.
        p.   cm.
    ISBN 0-451-20225-2
    1. Yoder, Magdalena (Fictitious character)—Fiction. 2. Women
detectives—Pennsylvania—Fiction. 3. Pennsylvania Dutch—Fiction.
4. Hotelkeepers—Fiction. 5. Pennsylvania—Fiction. 6. Mennonites—Fiction. I. Title.
PS3563.Y475 C74 2001
813'.54—dc21   00-058215

Printed in the United States of America
Set in Palatino
Designed by Leonard Telesca

In loving memory of my mother,
Helen Yoder
1908–2000

AUTHOR'S NOTE

The crepe recipes found in this book are from *Waffles, Flapjacks, Pancakes, Blintzes, Crepes, Frybread from Scandinavia and Around the World*, published by Penfield Press, 215 Brown Street, Iowa City, Iowa 52245.

1

I woke to find a woman's face pressed against the pane of my bedroom window. Her features were grotesquely misshapen. I screamed and pulled the covers over my head.

After a few seconds, during which my heart had stopped beating, curiosity overcame terror. I said a quick prayer before peeking. The face was still there, illuminated by the dial on my alarm clock.

Instead of screaming again, I pulled on my blue chenille robe, slipped my size eleven feet into fuzzy pink bunny slippers, and padded over to the window. When I jerked it open, Thelma Hershberger fell to the floor with a loud thud.

"This better be good," I growled.

Thelma struggled to her feet. "It's a matter of life and death!"

"Yours?" I asked hopefully.

I know, it's terrible to feel that way, un-Christian even, but I can't stand the woman. Thelma is the local postmistress, and on occasion delivers the mail—along with every bit of sordid gossip she can possibly dig up. Unfortunately, a lot of it is about me. If it hadn't been for the fact I didn't want my mail to end up in her attic, or dumped in some farm pond, I would have booted her back out the window with the toe of my fuzzy bunnies.

Thelma wastes no love on me either. "Did you know you sleep with your mouth wide open?"

"I'm quite aware of that, thank you. And you have no business invading my privacy. I ought to have you arrested."

She rubbed her left shoulder. "I rang your doorbell six times, Magdalena. Why didn't you answer?"

"I was asleep." I glanced again at the clock. "It's only three A.M., for crying out loud!"

"So it is." Thelma pushed past me to sit on my bed. "Well, I couldn't risk being followed."

I stared at the dumpy little woman. She has eyes the size of jelly beans, a bulldog's nose, and her lips, if indeed she ever had any, disappeared ages ago.

"Followed? By whom?"

"Remember Lizzie Mast?"

Of course I remembered Elizabeth Mast. How could I not? In addition to being the world's worst cook, she was a member of my church. Beechy Grove Mennonite Church in Hernia, Pennsylvania.

Just last week I was supposed to see her at the Mennonite Women's Prayer Breakfast, an annual event. I remember that morning well. Lizzie was late, and those of us already in attendance prayed mightily—that Lizzie would not show up at all.

We weren't being mean, mind you, just practical. Elizabeth Mast was the salt of the earth—a kind Christian woman with the soul of a saint, and the hands of a pioneer. Her fingers were quite capable of applying a healing poultice, of making tiny straight stitches, or of planting a prize-winning flower garden, but they were incapable of frying an egg. I still have one of last year's eggs, which I use as a coaster here on my desk at the PennDutch Inn.

Our prayers were answered and Lizzie didn't show up. Imagine our guilt later that day when we learned Lizzie had been found dead. The cause of her death had yet to be shared with the public, and rumors abounded—thanks to the likes of Thelma. The most widely believed, and sensational, rumor was that Lizzie had committed suicide. At any rate, one thing was for sure: the poor woman was *not* following Thelma Hershberger.

"Don't be ridiculous," I snapped. "Lizzie is dead and you know it."

Thelma rolled her eyes. "Of course she's dead. That's why I'm afraid of being followed."

"There's no such thing as ghosts." I don't believe that statement, having seen my grandmother's ghost on more than one occasion, but that is the official party line.

The postmistress snorted. "I'm not talking about Lizzie. I'm talking about whoever killed her."

"Say what?"

"Lizzie Mast was murdered."

"Murdered? Why, that's ridiculous. That woman was practically a saint."

"Stop calling me ridiculous." Thelma hopped to her feet. "If you don't want to hear the rest, Magdalena, just say so."

I gave Thelma a gentle shove, and she landed on my bed in approximately the same spot she'd been sitting before. "Spill it, dear. Tell me why you think Lizzie was murdered."

"Because I was there."

I sat on the bed beside Thelma. "You were a witness?" I asked incredulously.

"Well, I didn't see it actually happen, if that's what you mean. But she told me herself that something awful might happen to her. In fact, she was pretty positive it would."

"What exactly did she say? No, wait. Start at the beginning."

Thelma took a deep breath. "It was a Tuesday morning, the day before your prayer breakfast, and I was doing delivery. Hank Stutzman, who usually handles that route, was feeling poorly. He claims it was the flu, but I know for a fact he stopped at the Bigger Jigger up in Bedford the night before. But since he'd covered for me so I could attend the breakfast, I decided to cut him some slack. Besides, Sara Kirschbaum said—"

"Please," I said through gritted teeth, "start at the beginning of *Lizzie's* story."

Thelma glared at me, no mean feat considering the size of her peepers. "Okay, but don't interrupt again. As I was about to say, I delivered Lizzie's mail Tuesday morning. She had postage due on a letter, so I rang her bell. She answered it—on the first ring, by the way—and invited me in for some tea.

"While the water was boiling, she opened the letter. Right

away I could tell by her expression that something was terribly wrong. I asked her what it was, but she wouldn't tell me. Then when she was fixing the tea, I got myself a look."

"Why am I not surprised," I mumbled.

"Magdalena, do you want to hear the rest of this, or not?"

I gave my right cheek a perfunctory slap. "I do."

Thelma smiled smugly. Her half of my bed was the catbird's seat.

"I know you're anxious, so I'll get right to the point. There were only six words on that letter, and they were cut out of a magazine and pasted on. Like a ransom note."

"You don't say!"

She nodded vigorously. *"Don't tell Anyone or you Pay.* That's what it said. It didn't even say 'you'll,' it said 'you.' What kind of grammar is that? Anyway, Lizzie caught me reading it and she burst into tears. I asked her what it was all about, but she wouldn't say. Not at first. But finally I got her to open up a little. Just a little, mind you." Thelma folded her pudgy hands and sat back, as if through with her recitation.

"Don't keep me in suspenders!" I wailed.

"You mean 'suspense,' don't you?"

"Whatever!"

"Look, Magdalena, if you're going to be sarcastic—"

"I'm not! *Please,* go on."

"Well, if you insist. Now where was I?"

2

"You were going to tell me what Lizzie said!" I screamed.

Thelma blinked. "Oh yeah, no matter how much I coaxed her, Lizzie wouldn't tell me who was threatening her. Only that she had seen something she wasn't supposed to see."

"*What?*" I wanted to shake Thelma Hershberger until her jelly bean eyes rattled loose in their minuscule sockets.

The woman clearly enjoyed my discomfort. "I was getting to that," she said slowly. "Honestly, Magdalena, you need to be more patient."

I immediately prayed for patience but, finding it not forthcoming, prayed for a paralyzed tongue. That prayer was answered long enough to prompt Thelma to speak.

"If you must know, she wouldn't tell me that either. Finally—well, I have a job to do, you know. It wasn't my fault if I left her there crying. Besides, I think her husband was somewhere around. Out back, I think, in his workshop."

"So," I said, taking it all in, "you think Lizzie was murdered because of something she saw, and that letter was a threat—wait just one minute! You also think that the killer—assuming there was one—saw you deliver the letter, and because Lizzie invited you in for tea, the killer—again, assuming there was one—jumped to the conclusion that Lizzie had taken you into her confidence."

Thelma nodded.

"Whew!" I said. "That is a scary thought. Have you told the police?"

"You mean Melvin Stoltzfus?" It was Thelma's turn to sound incredulous.

I nodded reluctantly. Rumor has it our Chief of Police was kicked in the head by a bull—while trying to milk it. This rumor, I believe, was started by his mother. At any rate, Melvin is so out of touch with reality that he once mailed a gallon of ice cream to his favorite aunt in Scranton. The only reason he has the position is because no one else in Hernia is willing to work for what we pay him.

"What about the sheriff?" I suggested.

Thelma gave me a pitying look. "Lizzie Mast died within the city limits, as you well know."

She was right. Thanks to Hernia's ambitious founders, most of whom were my ancestors, the city had annexed large tracts of farmland. But despite a recent influx of urban refugees, we don't number even two thousand souls and most of that farmland is still intact. Her point, however, was that the Bedford County sheriff was not about to get involved in a case that was outside his jurisdiction.

"So what are you going to do?" I asked foolishly.

"Just what I'm doing now. I'm coming to you for help."

"Why *me*?"

"Don't be coy, Magdalena. Everyone knows you do the real police work for Melvin."

"Somebody has to!" I wailed.

"Exactly. And I'll only say this once, so listen up. You always do an excellent job."

I beamed. It was true, after all.

"But there's one thing I don't get," I said. "Why did you wait a week to tell me this? And why at three in the morning?"

The jelly bean eyes became mere slits. "Don't you ever listen, Magdalena? I said I didn't want to be followed, and the reason I waited until tonight was because I was trying to talk myself out of believing it."

"But you saw the note—"

"The word was '*pay,*' " Thelma said vehemently. "It wasn't 'die.' "

"Okay, okay, simmer down." I said that for my benefit as much as hers. "Has anything happened since to make you think the note—" I clamped a bony hand over my mouth, and then just as quickly removed it. "Good heavens, you haven't received one too, have you?"

Thelma shook her head. "But I feel something."

"What?" The facetious side of me wanted to ask her if it was tiredness she was feeling.

"I feel like I'm being watched."

"That's it?"

"Isn't that enough? Today I couldn't shake the feeling, as much as I tried."

"So you came to me." I yawned. "Look, it's the middle of the night, and I have to teach Sunday School in six hours. But I'll speak to Melvin first chance I get, and if I don't learn anything from him, I'll try to wheedle it out of the coroner. But I wouldn't expect to hear anything until Monday."

"Fair enough." Thelma is surprisingly spry for a portly woman in her middle years. She hopped off the bed and, without further ado, let herself out the window.

I returned to bed feeling guilty. I know it wasn't my fault Lizzie died, and the cause of her death was still unknown, but I was sure it was somehow my fault. It's because I'm a Mennonite, you see—an Amish-Mennonite to be precise. My ancestors were Swiss Amish who adopted the Mennonite faith in my grandparents' generation. I am related by blood to virtually every Amish person alive, and perhaps half the Mennonites as well. Due to this excessive inbreeding I am, in fact, my own cousin. Give me a sandwich, and I *am* a family picnic. My point is, this restricted gene pool has produced a few interesting mutations, the most notable of which is the guilt gene. As a result, I am capable of feeling more guilt than a Baptist, Catholic, and Jew combined.

Still wallowing in this guilt, I awoke later that morning with a splitting headache and had to skip out of my Sunday School class. Fortunately I am an innkeeper and my occupation allows me to pass a good deal of guilt on to my guests, and I was expecting a new batch that afternoon.

Just for the record, passing guilt on to complete strangers is a skill, something not to be tried by the novice businesswoman. And I am a businesswoman above all else. When my parents died—squished in a tunnel between a milk tanker and semitrailer filled with state-of-the-art running shoes—I inherited the family farm. That was a dozen years ago. Since then I turned a struggling farm into a thriving, full-board inn.

At any rate, when the front door opened that delightful Sunday afternoon in June, I knew I had my work cut out for me. The couple standing there, unnecessarily intertwined, were quite obviously in show biz. I've dealt a lot with the Hollywood set before, and let me tell you this, for a goodly number of them, scruples is merely the name of a party game. As for sincerity, well, most of those folks have never heard of *that* S word.

But like I said, business is business. "Velcommen to zee Penn-Deutsch Inn," I said in my best fake Pennsylvania Dutch accent, and with as much cheer as I could force under the circumstances. "My nammen eez Magdalena Yoder and I am zee ownah of zees fine establissment."

The couple disentangled. The male half, a tall young man with square jaw and shoulders, dark glasses, and studio-lightened hair, smiled.

"That's a lousy accent."

I gasped at his impertinence. "It is not!"

He grinned and I squinted. No doubt he wore the shades to protect himself from his own smile. There were more caps in that mouth than at a high school graduation.

"I once played the part of a German guard. My drama coach was really strict about me getting it right."

I glared at this young man. "For your information, I am not German, and this most certainly is *not* a concentration camp."

"I can see that now. Anyway, we're here to check in."

I glanced at my reservations list. "Ah, yes, the Murrays from Beverly Hills."

He extended a well-groomed tan hand. "Archibald. And this is my wife, Megan."

"Gingko! My name is Gingko now."

"Whatever," I said and shook her tiny hand. She was altogether a small woman, pale as cottage cheese, and had waist-length hair the color of starlings. That this doll-like creature was capable of speech seemed incredible to me. I was tempted to spin her around and look for the key in her back. At any rate, the mite's limp hand felt like a dead mouse. I haven't felt a lot of those, mind you, just enough to know whereof I speak.

"Aren't you going to ask for Archie's autograph?" she asked.

"I beg your pardon?"

Gingko turned to her husband. "She doesn't know who you are."

"Of course I do," I snapped. "Archibald Murray. We've just been through that."

She giggled. "Archie's sitcom is the hottest thing since *Seinfeld.*"

I took a sip from my glass of lemonade, which was sitting on the fried egg coaster. "Isn't that nice."

Frankly, I could not have cared less. My branch of the Mennonite faith does not forbid television, but we prefer to emphasize face-to-face conversation, and we do strive to avoid those TV shows that are obscene or profane in any way. In my opinion, there has not been a show worth watching since *Green Acres* went off the air.

Gingko smiled, a mistake if you ask me. Her unnaturally white skin made her teeth seem like an ear of buttered corn.

"Archie is the star of *Two Girls, a Guy, and a Calzone.*"

I shuddered at what possible pagan implications lay behind such a ridiculous title. "And what do you do, dear?"

Archibald Murray rested a manicured mitt on his wee wife's shoulder. "Megan—I mean, Gingko—is a medium."

"Is that so?" The woman was definitely a "small." Even at the 5-7-9 in Pittsburgh, she'd have a hard time finding something to fit.

"She doesn't know what that is, either," Gingko whispered.

"But she has good ears," I snapped. "A medium is somewhere between a large and a small, or else it is—oh, my heavens! You're a witch!"

Gingko struggled from beneath her hubby's heavy hand. "I most certainly am not a witch! I'm a clairvoyant."

"Well, I'm a clarinet." The Bible lists many sins, but being a smart aleck, thank heavens, is not one of them.

"Miss Yoder, clearly yours is not a very evolved soul."

"Well, I never!"

"Ladies, please," Archibald begged, "could we just get on with checking in?"

"But Archie, we might want to reconsider. I'm picking up some weird vibes."

I prayed for a civil tongue. "That's just the refrigerator, dear. When the icemaker comes on, it makes the whole place shake. Now, would you be wanting A.L.P.O.?"

"What is that supposed to mean?"

"It means," I said calmly—after all, money was at stake—"Amish Lifestyle Plan Option. For a mere fifty dollars extra per day you get to clean your own rooms. It adds to the authentic Amish-Mennonite experience."

"You're kidding!"

Archibald gently touched his wife's arm. "Sounds great. Sign us up."

I nodded. You'd be surprised how much folks will pay to be abused, as long as they can view it as a cultural experience. I decided to test the actor's limits.

"For another twenty-five dollars you get to help in the kitchen. Wash dishes, clear tables, that sort of thing."

"Sure, why not."

Gingko stamped a foot barely larger than my thumb. "Archie! She's conning you."

I smiled serenely. "And for an even hundred you get to muck out the barn and clean the chicken house. But it will cost you extra to gather eggs."

Archibald grinned. "Can I milk?"

"Sorry, dear, but that puts you over the top."

"Ah, man! Can't I just pay more?"

I sighed. "Okay, a hundred fifty above the standard rate and

I promise to load you down with so much honest work your head will spin."

"Thanks, Miss Yoder, you won't regret this."

"I'm sure I won't, but you—"

The door to the inn flung open, slamming into the doorstop. "Yoder!" the intruder barked.

3

I shuddered. It was Melvin Stoltzfus, Hernia's Chief of Police. I'd been unable to get hold of him, but had left a message. For a split second I regretted it. The man is both a menace and a mantis.

I don't believe in evolution, but if I did, I'd also believe that mankind evolved from insects, not apes, and that Melvin is the missing link. He has bulbous eyes that operate independently of each other, virtually no lips, and a neck as big around as my wrist. His thorax is bony and protrudes through his shirts in suspicious little bumps, and recently I've come to suspect that his baggy pants hide an extra pair of legs.

Of course Melvin's peculiar physique would be none of my business, were he not married to my sister, Susannah. But he *is* married to my only sibling, and although they have yet to breed, it breaks my heart to contemplate the fact that someday I may find my nieces and nephews in the rose garden eating aphids.

I glanced under my desk for a can of bug spray and, finding none, smiled pleasantly. "Yoder is my name. Please don't wear it out."

"Very funny. Yoder, you said we need to talk."

"We do. *Privately.*"

"Yoder, either we talk now, or I leave."

"I'm in the middle of conducting business," I hissed.

"Then I'm out of here." He turned and headed toward the door.

"Wait! It's about Elizabeth Mast."

"What about her?"

I eyeballed the California couple, but Melvin didn't get my drift. He headed for the door a second time.

"She was murdered," I wailed, "wasn't she?"

Melvin stopped abruptly and turned in his arthropodan tracks. "Don't be stupid, Yoder. Nobody killed her. She died of a drug overdose."

"Drugs?" That was not the Lizzie Mast I knew.

"Her system was full of it."

"Antacid?" I asked incredulously.

"Guess again."

"Just tell me!"

"It was Angel Dust," Gingko said.

Melvin's left eye focused on Gingko while his right eye remained on me. "How did *you* know?"

"I had a vision," Gingko said.

In a rare instance of ocular solidarity, Melvin's right eye joined the left. "What did you say?"

"She's from California," I hastened to explain. "The land of fruit and nuts. Her name is Filbert."

"It's Gingko!"

"Whatever."

"Let her speak, Yoder."

Gingko smiled smugly. "I'm a psychic medium. My specialty is clairvoyance, although I'm pretty good at clairaudience and clairsentience. A couple of times I've even channeled."

Archibald nodded so vigorously his sunglasses slipped. He pushed them back into place with a pampered pinkie.

"Yeah, she channeled James Dean. Man, that was awesome."

"Give me a break," I said.

Melvin waggled a finger at me presidential style. "Yoder, I'm warning you. This is official police business. Let them talk."

"Talk away," I said blithely. "Chitter-chatter to your heart's content. Pretend I'm not here."

They did just that. I pretended not to listen, but how could I not? It was my inn, for Pete's sake, and they were talking about a dear friend of mine. Okay, so maybe not a *dear* friend, but still, a woman who was responsible for one of my most intimate experiences. After all, the only time I'd ever hugged a toilet bowl was after eating one of Lizzie's concoctions.

Gingko seemed delighted to pretend I wasn't there. "I had the vision just now when you came in," she told Melvin. "Some visions can last a long time—sometimes an hour or more—but usually they're just fleeting impressions. This was the quick kind."

"What exactly did you see?"

"Colors mostly. Bright swirls of color—like in a really good painting. But I saw a lady too. She was lying on her back on a purple cloud and holding a jar filled with phencyclidine."

"That's the scientific name the coroner used!" Lacking antennae, Melvin scratched his head with a fingernail. "But how did you know that's what it was?"

"She probably knows from personal experience." I slapped a bony hand over my mouth.

Gingko glared at me. "I had a *sense* that it was Angel Dust. Maybe it was the cloud, or the way the woman was lying. Visions give you impressions, but they don't spell everything out in black and white."

"How convenient," I muttered.

Much to my surprise, Melvin ignored my remark. "Miss— uh—"

"Mrs. Archibald Murray."

Melvin's eyes swelled to twice their usual size. He turned to face his prey.

"*The* Archibald Murray? The star of *Two Girls, a Guy, and a Calzone?*"

Archibald's blinding grin would have been answer enough. "Yeah, that's me. It's probably these shades," he said, reading Melvin's meager mind. "Had that laser surgery everyone's been getting, so I have to keep them on a few days. Hey, you're not going to spread this around, are you?"

"Well, I do know the folks at the *National Intruder*," I said and instinctively held a hand out, palm up.

The actor paled to the point his chompers looked dingy. "You do?"

"I've had *real* celebrities stay here."

"Don't worry," Melvin said quickly, "she won't say a thing. *Will* you, Yoder?"

"Is that a threat, Melvin?"

"No threat, Yoder. I'm just remembering that you have a fondness for speeding and—"

"My lips are sealed," I wailed.

"Good. Now where was I? Ah, yes, can I have your autograph, Mr. Murray?"

A grateful Archibald was happy to comply. Although I have plenty of paper at my desk, Melvin insisted that the television star sign his name on the police chief's back. His *bare* back—or should I say carapace?

When the embarrassing spectacle was over, when Melvin was quite through making a horse's cousin out of himself—because believe me, it got a lot worse than that—Melvin turned back to Gingko. To her credit, the girl was still there.

"Mrs. Murray, did you see anything in your vision that told you how the lady died? Did she eat the Angel Dust? Was it on purpose?"

Gingko shook her head, and the long black hair rippled down her back. "She didn't do it on purpose. And I don't think it was just an accident. You know, like a normal overdose. No, I had another feeling altogether, like—well, like it was murder."

"Aha!" I practically shouted.

Melvin turned to me. "Yoder, maybe we do need to talk."

A lesser woman—say, the Magdalena of a decade ago—would have railed at Melvin for giving credence to a California kook while discounting his country cousin. But I have grown over the years and know when to zip my lip. Especially if doing so helps fill my coffers.

"You bet your bippy we need to talk. But first let me check these folks in."

Much to my surprise, Melvin waited patiently while I took down credit card information. He didn't interrupt once! Kind soul that I am, I rewarded him by allowing him to sit in my chair while I escorted my guests to their upstairs room.

My inn has both an elevator and an impossibly steep stairs, and the Murrays chose to use the latter. No doubt they were on a health kick. I, on the other hand, believe that we are born with a finite number of movements; use them all up and we die. Therefore, I have learned to get my exercise from jumping to conclusions and rolling my eyes. I took the elevator.

I was gone only a few minutes, but it was long enough for Melvin's uncharacteristic patience to evaporate. He pounced on me as if I were a juicy aphid.

"Yoder! Where the hell have you been? I haven't got all day."

"You do if it's your job." I proceeded to tell him about Thelma's predawn visit.

The mantis looked more miserable than menacing by the time I was through. "You know I've decided to run for the state legislature. Running a campaign is a lot more time-consuming than I thought. The last thing I need right now is a murder case."

"I'm sure Lizzie Mast felt inconvenienced too."

He blinked at me. "Yeah. But Yoder, I've been thinking—"

"There's a first time for everything, dear."

To his credit, he plowed right through. "So anyway, Yoder, it's occurred to me that—well, maybe I could use your help."

"I don't do exorcisms."

"Very funny. You're not making this easy, you know."

"Sorry. Perhaps that was a little harsh."

My apology seemed to throw him. He looked around the room, as if searching for my evil twin.

"Yoder," he finally said, "I'd like you to help with this case."

"What?"

"You heard me, Yoder. I need your help."

"Why me?"

"I'm busy, Yoder."

"I said, 'Why me?'"

"Don't make me say it, Yoder."

"Say it!" I grabbed a broom from behind my check-in counter and waved it at him. It was a mock threat, of course.

"Well, you've helped me before and you were. . ." He mumbled something unintelligible through clenched mandibles.

"Speak up, dear, I'm losing interest fast."

Melvin sighed. "You were good, Yoder. You were damn good."

"Don't swear in my inn, Melvin," I said sternly. Then I smiled. "I *was* good, wasn't I?"

"Enough, Yoder."

"Okay, but understand that I don't really know the Masts that well. Lizzie came to our prayer breakfasts and occasionally to church, but her husband almost never came."

"Just do your best, Yoder. That's all I'm asking."

"What exactly is it you want me to do?"

"You know, ask a few questions."

"Easier said than done." From what I'd heard about Joseph Mast, he was on the taciturn side. "Anything else?"

"Look around for me. Keep your eyes open, that kind of thing. The coroner said Lizzie had enough of that stuff in her to keep half of California high for a week. I want to know how it got there."

"I see. In other words, you want me to handle the entire case for you, don't you?"

Melvin squirmed. "Unofficially, of course. When you solve it—"

"You mean, *if*, don't you?"

He hesitated. "You're smart, Yoder. Don't make me say that twice."

Like I said, I've learned when to quit. "Okay. Let's say I solve it. So then what?"

"I get the credit."

"Of course. I'm sure it will be a big boost for your campaign. But tell me, what do I get out of this?"

Melvin looked like a sheep who'd been asked an algebra question. "Uh—well—"

"Never mind, dear, I'll do it."

"You *will*?"

I nodded. Even if Melvin hadn't asked for my help, he would have gotten it. Solving Lizzie's murder—and it had to be just that—was the least I could do for her. Even then, how could I possibly forgive myself for praying that the woman would stay away from church, while at the very moment she lay dying?

No matter what it took, I was going to solve Lizzie Mast's death.

4

I had my back to the door a moment later when I heard it open. Just for the record, I prayed for patience. Unfortunately that's my least-answered prayer.

"Go away, you bothersome bug, or I'll whack you with this broom."

"Is that a traditional Pennsylvania Dutch welcome?"

I whirled. Standing just inside my door was the tallest woman I'd ever seen. I'm five foot ten, skinny as a rail, but this big-boned gal loomed over me. I couldn't help but gasp.

"Hi. My name's Darlene Townsend," the woman said and extended a hand the size of New Jersey.

I allowed my hand to be swallowed by hers. "I'm Magdalena Yoder, and welcome to the PennDutch Inn." Too late I remembered my charming fake accent.

Miss Townsend's raised eyebrows nearly brushed my ceiling. "Funny, but you don't sound like you did on the phone when I made the reservation."

"How do you mean?"

"The woman I spoke to had an accent."

"I'm bilingual. The accent comes and goes." It was only a pseudo-fib. I'm the daughter of bilingual parents, and I've heard Pennsylvania Dutch spoken my entire life. What did it really matter if I couldn't speak the lingo?

Darlene smiled. She had soft brown eyes in a pretty face framed by a bob of auburn hair.

"I'm bilingual too."

"Oh, what other languages do you know?"

"FORTRAN."

"You're Fortranese?" I asked pleasantly. Ever since the breakup of the Soviet Union, it's been hard to keep track of all those little countries.

Darlene laughed heartily. "That's a good one. Confidentially—and I don't mean to brag—I'm somewhat of an expert on UNIX too."

I held the broom protectively in front of me. "Your sex life is none of my business, dear."

The giantess laughed again. "You're a real hoot, Miss Yoder. I can see that I'm going to enjoy my week here."

Keeping the broom between us, I maneuvered behind the counter and checked my reservation book. I was indeed expecting a Darlene Townsend, but her mailing address was Philadelphia, not Fortran. She'd stated in her letter that she was an athletics instructor at a private girls' school and was looking forward to a working vacation. The work—if you can call it that—was to recruit girls who could play basketball.

"How will you be paying?" I asked suspiciously. No Hernia teacher could afford a night at my inn, even excluding A.L.P.O.

Darlene handed me a platinum credit card.

"Would you like an authentic Amish experience?" I asked.

"Does that involve a broom?"

I chuckled grudgingly. "Yes, but not on the behind. For a bit more money, you get the privilege of doing chores." I showed her a list of fees.

Her dark eyes sparkled. "What a clever idea! Sign me up for everything."

No doubt I beamed. There is a sucker born every minute, and I definitely have a sweet tooth.

"You're a wise woman, dear. You'll enjoy the Amish experience."

As if on cue, the front door opened and in stepped a real live Amish man. This was not planned, I assure you, but the timing could not have been better.

I recognized the man as Jacob Troyer. There are perhaps seven Jacob Troyers in the county, but none so handsome as the man standing in my lobby. The standard Amish beard, sans mustache, and inverted bowl haircut detracted little from his symmetrical classical features. Tall, dark, with broad shoulders, this Jacob was better looking than most of the movie stars I'd had as guests over the years.

Amish garb varies within the denomination according to sect and region. Jacob's dark gray pants, long-sleeved white shirt, and black suspenders were typical of workday attire for a local man in his twenties. As does every good Amish man, Jacob wore a hat at all times. Local custom dictates felt hats during cold weather, straw hats in summer. A simple black band is permissible, although some of the older generation view it as "proud."

The Jacob Troyer in question didn't have a clue that he was gorgeous, and his straw hat was unadorned. He smiled bashfully when he saw us.

"Miss Yoder?"

"Please, call me Magdalena."

"Yah. Miss Yoder, may I borrow your telephone?"

Our Amish are strictly forbidden to own telephones, but they may use the telephones of the English, as they call outsiders, to conduct their business. There is a public phone in nearby Hernia that is constantly in use.

"Is everything all right, dear?"

He blushed at my careless use of the endearment. "Yah. My Gertrude's sister in Ohio is having a baby. Twins, they say. Gertrude is a twin herself. Anyway, I am supposed to call an English woman there and see if the babies have come, but the phone in town is not working."

"Well, you're certainly welcome to use mine. In fact, I was just about to show my guest to her room. You'll have plenty of privacy."

He blushed even deeper. "Thank you, Miss Yoder."

"That's Magdalena," I said firmly.

"Yah, Miss Yoder."

"Never mind." I turned to Darlene. "Well, dear, shall we go upstairs?"

The big girl trotted gamely after me, but left her suitcase behind. I made her turn around.

"You carry your own suitcase, dear. That's part of A.L.P.O., remember?"

"Who *is* he?" Darlene whispered when she caught up with me.

"Down, girl," I said gently. "He's a married man. The Gertrude he mentioned is his wife."

Darlene sighed. "All the good ones are taken."

"You can say that again."

"You ever been married?"

"Once—to a bigamist, so I guess that doesn't count. But I'm seeing someone now."

"Is he as dreamy as that Amish man?"

"Even dreamier," I said, sounding for all the world like a schoolgirl.

That so excited Darlene she nearly dropped her suitcase. "Details," she demanded. "I want details."

Unlike Darlene, I wasn't about to share my life with a perfect stranger. I can, however, be very good at small talk. We chatted amiably about men and life in general as I showed her around. She was pleased with her room, which she called "charming," but when I suggested she might want to give the toilet a good scrub before using it, she yawned.

"It was a long drive from Philadelphia," she said. "I think I'll take a nap first."

"Suit yourself, dear. But I expect the powder room off the lobby to be spic and span by supper."

She yawned again. "Will do."

I returned downstairs to await the arrival of my remaining guests, as well as to check on the handsome Jacob Troyer. Alas, the lobby was empty.

A good Magdalena would have spent the time wisely, perhaps reading the Bible. It was, after all, Sunday afternoon. Instead, I sat on my chair and twiddled my thumbs. When I got bored with that, I reached down my dress to play with my pussy.

*   *   *

My pussy is a purebred chocolate point Siamese named Little Freni. She was a gift from Gabriel Rosen, the dreamy man I've been seeing. The day I got her, Little Freni crawled up my dress and climbed inside my bra which, as you should know, has lots of wasted room. Little Freni took an immediate liking to her surroundings, and now spends most of her time next to my heart.

You may think it a strange place to keep a kitten, but I assure you, I am *not* the only woman to harbor pets in her underwear. My sister Susannah, Melvin's wife, has been toting a dinky dog around in her bra for years. That pitiful pooch, which my sister calls Shnookums, is not nearly as cute as Little Freni, and has a nasty temperament.

At any rate, Little Freni preferred to nap that Sunday afternoon. I tried getting her attention by dangling a rubber band down my dress, but my pussy would have none of it.

"Just play for a few minutes," I coaxed.

Little Freni purred contentedly, too lazy to open her eyes.

I gave up my quest for a playmate and stroked her silken head. "You're so soft," I whispered. "I could pet you all day."

"Ach!"

The short, stout Amish woman standing behind me was my cook, Freni Hostetler. It is she after whom my kitty is named. Freni is my mother's double second cousin, once removed. Or something like that. After Mama died in that tunnel, Freni has been like a mother to me. At seventy-five Freni is the same age Mama would have been, and every bit as cantankerous.

The woman threatens to quit at least once a week, and actually does quit about a dozen times a year. On several occasions I've taken the liberty of firing her. But since I can't boil water without directions, and Freni despises her live-in daughter-in-law, Mama's replacement and I are doomed to each other's company until the day she can no longer stand on her feet, or I decide to retire. But don't get me wrong, I am immensely fond of the stubby woman with the wire-rim glasses and perpetual frown. She is, in fact, my dearest friend; it's just that we don't get along.

"Good afternoon, Freni," I said pleasantly. "I was just talking to your namesake."

"Ach! Such an insult to have an animal named after me."

"There are those who would consider it an honor."

"Yah, you would know about honors," Freni said, making no attempt to hide the bitterness in her voice.

The dear little woman was referring to the recent birth of her grandchildren—triplets. The two male children were named after their father and grandfather, but the girl was named after me. The proud parents, Jonathan and Barbara, named the baby after me because I was instrumental in saving her life. It was not because Barbara was trying to slight her mother-in-law. Alas, there is no convincing Freni.

"How *are* the little dears?" I asked cheerily.

Freni frowned. "She picks them up every time they cry. Is that any way to treat a baby?"

I shrugged.

"Of course, you would not know."

Boy, did that strike a nerve. I am acutely aware that I will never give birth to a child, that I will forever be as barren as the Gobi Desert.

"As a matter of fact, Freni, I read in a magazine that a baby can never be held too much."

"Ach, maybe that is true of English children." Freni waved a plump hand, signaling a change of subject. "How many vegetations this time, Magdalena?"

"Excuse me?"

"Ach, you heard me!"

I smiled slowly. "You must mean vegetarians."

"Yah." My kinswoman is culinarily challenged. For her, the four food groups are fat, sugar, starch, and meat. She has only recently begun to make a distinction between meat and vegetables, and still finds some foods, such as cheese, hard to place. Since the Amish normally serve a slice of cheddar with apple pie, she had, until recently, just assumed that cheese was a fruit.

"Freni, dear, only three of the guests have arrived, and I'm sorry, but I forgot to ask them."

Freni shook her head and muttered something unintelligible in her native Pennsylvania Dutch.

"Look, Freni, just play it safe and plan on serving lots of vegetables. But leave the ham hocks out of the green beans, in any case. City folks don't like joints on their plates."

Freni made a face.

"And if it turns out we do have some vegetarian guests, don't—"

The front door opened and in walked two more guests. Freni's eyes lit up like lightning bug tails. I instinctively grabbed for her apron straps, but the woman is remarkably agile for someone her age. She got to them first.

"Are you vegetarians?" she demanded.

The pair giggled. They were the cutest little couple you have ever seen. Each was barely five foot tall, and plump as a goose the day before Christmas. They both had snowy white hair and wire-rim glasses not unlike Freni's. The man was beardless, and I am a believing Christian, but with the slightest bit of encouragement I could easily have believed they were Mr. and Mrs. Claus on a summer vacation.

Freni stared the couple into silence. "Well? Are you vegetarians or regular people?"

"Please excuse her," I said, and tried to push Freni aside, but she seemed to have taken root. Perhaps my floors were even dirtier than I believed. "This woman is my cook and is trying to take a head count."

The couple giggled again. Freni stared harder, but that only sent the couple into spasms. At last, my plucky little cook flapped her arms in disgust and barreled off to the kitchen. The vagaries of a wood-burning stove are within her ken, but the English will forever be an enigma.

I, on the other hand, have more experience with the ways of the world. I singled out Santa.

"Shame on you," I said sternly. "You have just upset that nice little Amish woman."

The man blinked and searched for a speaking voice. "Uh, uh, we certainly didn't mean to."

"Well, you did. All she wanted to know was whether or not you ate meat. You didn't have to laugh at her."

He turned the color of the real Santa's suit. "We weren't laughing *at* her. It was a private joke. You see, my honey bunch and I were just discussing how we were going to explain the new diet we're on."

I felt the makings of a headache. "Which diet might that be?"

"We're carnivores."

"I beg your pardon?"

"We eat only meat. I hope that won't be a problem."

"Only *meat*?"

"The rarer the better," Mrs. Claus chortled.

I grimaced. "Surely you're joking."

"Oh, no," Santa said. "We've each lost ten pounds on this diet."

"When's the last time you saw a fat tiger?" Mrs. Claus asked.

"Well, never, but on the other hand, not that many tigers pass through Hernia."

"Good one." He extended a pudgy paw. "I'm Keith Bunch, by the way, and this is my wife, Honey."

"You're serious?"

"We are now."

I took a nervous step back. "You're not part of some Satanic cult, are you?"

That brought guffaws. "Oh, no," Honey Bunch said after a great deal of wasted time. "We're just two old retirees out to see the country."

"Retirees? Surely you're aware of my rates."

"We were both lawyers. Personal injury cases."

"Well, in that case, I have some wonderful news for you," and went on to explain A.L.P.O.

The Bunches thought the plan delightful. They signed up for every chore and even offered to make their own meals. I told them the latter was not only unnecessary, but inadvisable. The Good Lord Himself would have a hard time distributing loaves and fishes in Freni's kitchen.

"But what about our special cake?" Honey asked.

"What special cake?"

"Tomorrow is our fifty-fifth wedding anniversary," Keith said, putting his arm around Honey.

She nodded vigorously. "It's a very simple recipe really. You just take a rolled rump roast—two if they're small—and cover it with liter pâté. If the roasts are small, you see, you stack them one on the other with a layer of pâté icing between."

"I want green icing," Keith said and giggled.

I gagged. Thank heavens I was just steps from the powder room, and the delightful Darlene Townsend would be cleaning it later that day. When I was quite through being sick, I plastered my best hostess smile on my face, for I had yet to get a credit card or check from the plump pair.

Unfortunately the couple paid in cash. *Green* cash. I streamlined the transaction and hustled their bustles into the elevator. No impossibly steep stairs for litigious elves with a fondness for flesh.

Alone once more, I made a mental note to prescreen my guests. In the old days, when I catered almost exclusively to the rich and famous—and often infamous—my primary concern was money. Well, the Bible warns us about greed, doesn't it? Over the years I've had to pay dearly for flagrantly fleecing the fortunate. On several occasions I've almost lost my life, and I've lost my dignity more times than Dennis Rodman. In the future I would at least ask a few basic questions of potential guests— like what flavor icing do you prefer?

I was lost deep in thought, Little Freni snuggled peacefully against my meager bosom, when the last of my expected guests arrived. I didn't even hear the door open, and nearly jumped out of my cotton hose when I glanced up and saw them standing there.

"Gracious sakes alive!" I clutched my chest, waking Little Freni.

"Sorry, we didn't mean to startle you."

Mercifully I remembered to switch to my fake German. "Velcommen to zee PennDeutsch Inn. My nommen ist Magdalena Yoder und I see by my reservations list zat you must be zee Hansons. Zee Herr Doktor Hansons, yah?" I looked closer at the book. "Ach, zee Herr und Herren Doktors."

Dr. Margaret Hanson and her husband, Dr. George Hanson, exchanged amused glances. They were an attractive, well-dressed African-American couple, the kind of folks I love having as guests.

I scrambled for more words to mangle. "Vat vell it be today, zee Visa or zee MasterCard?"

Their looks of amusement turned to pity.

Honesty may be the best policy, but unfortunately it is often my last resort. I sighed miserably.

"Okay, so I'm not a native Pennsylvania Dutch speaker, and maybe I'm only a Mennonite, but I *am* a native of Pennsylvania and all my ancestors were Amish, so I have a right to pretend to speak like them, don't I? That isn't so weird, is it? I daresay you English are not without your foibles."

The doctors raised their eyebrows in tandem.

"English is a generic term for 'outsiders,' " I hastened to explain. "People not of the faith. You aren't Mennonite, are you?"

They shook their well-groomed heads.

"Now, your names, address, and phone number are the only things I have on your reservation card, so I hope you don't mind if I ask a few simple questions."

I waited an appropriate length of time for them to respond, and when they didn't, I barreled on. "You two wouldn't by any chance be carnivores, would you? Or practicing mediums?"

The doctors exchanged worried glances.

"I know those might sound like silly questions to you, but you wouldn't believe the day I've had. It started at three in the morning with the postmistress tapping on my window like a giant raven. Then one of my guests had a vision of the world's worst cook lying on her back on a purple cloud. Minutes later my brother-in-law, the praying mantis, asks me to help him solve a murder case while he runs for public office. As if that weren't enough, Santa and his wife ask me to make them a meat cake for their anniversary. Thank heavens the world's tallest woman is friendly, although whom she expects to recruit in Hernia is beyond me."

Dr. Margaret Hanson glanced nervously at the door. "Uh—I think we may have left something in the car."

"Ah yes, the car." Dr. George Hanson put his arm protectively around his wife's shoulder.

"Don't go!" I wailed. "I'm really a very normal woman."

At that precise moment, my one-pound bundle of joy wailed

piteously from the depths of my bosom. As you may know from personal experience, Siamese cats have loud, clear voices, and can sound uncannily like a human baby.

The doctors stared at my chest.

"She's hungry," I hastened to explain. "Either that, or she has to use the litter box."

Dr. Margaret Hanson smiled kindly. "Miss Yoder, have you taken your medications for the day?"

"*What?* I'll have you know I'm as sane as the next person!"

As if on cue, the front door opened and in swirled my sister, Susannah. Behind her trailed fifteen feet of filmy fuchsia fabric. Over her head was a cardboard carton with a square hole cut out to frame her face. Black knobs had been drawn on either side of the box and a pair of bent metal rabbit ears were taped to the top.

"Hey, Mags, how do I look on TV?"

5

How to Make Crepes

Basic Crepe Batter

4 eggs
2¼ cups milk
¼ cup melted butter

⅛ teaspoon salt
2 cups flour

Combine all ingredients in a blender and blend well. Scrape sides and blend again for 10 seconds. Or you may mix all ingredients together in a mixing bowl with a whisk or mixer.

Crepes can be made in a greased 6-, 7-, or 9-inch skillet or special crepe pans. If you use a crepe maker, follow the manufacturer's directions since some require the crepe to be cooked on both sides, and others just browned on one side.

If you are using a skillet, grease it with oil or butter if it is not a nonstick pan. Heat the skillet first, then pour 2 or 3 tablespoons of batter into the skillet, tilting the skillet quickly so that the batter covers the bottom of the pan before it sets. Return the skillet to medium-high heat and cook until the bottom is brown, about 1 minute. Turn the crepe carefully with a spatula and cook the other side for about 30 seconds. If the crepe tears, patch it with a little batter and continue cooking.

MAKES ABOUT 32 CREPES.

6

"Go away," I whispered.

"What?"

"Not now, sis," I hissed. I made shooing motions that I hoped were discreet.

Perhaps Little Freni's loud mewing was making it hard for her to hear. Susannah paid no attention to the Hansons and prattled on.

"Mags, I'm so excited! My sweetykins is going to run a political ad and he wants me to be in it. I know it's for Melvin's campaign and everything, but there's always a chance someone from Hollywood will see it and want me to star in a movie. So I was talking to Sherri Hall, who's been on TV and in a movie—if you count that video she made for her dentist on how to brush your teeth—and she said you're supposed to wear bright colors. Do you think this is bright enough?"

"You look like a boil in need of lancing," I said charitably. I was still whispering, of course.

My baby sister squealed with glee. "Oh, Mags, I knew you'd say that, which means this outfit is perfect! Now about my makeup—"

"Susannah, if you go away right now, I'll donate one hundred dollars to Melvin's campaign."

"Hey thanks, Mags! But do you think this eye shadow—"

"Two hundred bucks if you leave without another word."

Susannah may be eccentric, but she's not stupid. She clamped one hand over her mouth, but then in a move that defied centuries of inbred reserve, gave me a one-armed hug. I was so touched by this gesture that I overcame my own inbreeding, and hugged her back.

While this sisterly scene might sound touching to some, it was not amusing to Little Freni, who stopped meowing and began hissing like cold water dribbled on a hot stove. Of course, this excited Shnookums, the dinky dog Susannah carries around in her bra. I'm quite sure the miniature mangy mutt would have yipped and yapped himself into a frothing frenzy, had he not accidentally piddled.

Susannah shrieked, turned white as a crock of farmer's cheese, and fled the inn. To her credit, however, she said nothing.

I smiled warmly at the Delaware docs. "I've never seen that woman before in my life."

Dr. George Hanson's eyes narrowed. "Thank you, Miss Yoder, but we'll be finding accommodations elsewhere."

I pulled Little Freni from the nether reaches of my lingerie and placed her on the counter. "You see, there really was a kitten in there. And she was hungry, that's all." I reached under the counter and withdrew her saucer and a box of semisoft kitty chow. I poured a serving of chow on the plate, and Little Freni immediately began to wolf it down.

Dr. Margaret Hanson put a restraining hand on her husband's arm. "I think I'd like to stay, George."

"You can't be serious."

"Oh, but I am. This really is a very charming inn, and I couldn't help but notice as we drove in that there is a very large pond across the road." She addressed me. "Are there fish in that pond?"

"More fish than in a Starkist factory."

"Would my husband be permitted to fish there?"

"It's actually a requirement."

Dr. George Hanson frowned. "I didn't bring my tackle. Besides, I don't have a Pennsylvania fishing license."

"No problem. I have oodles of bamboo poles, and you don't need a license. That's a private pond."

"Hmm. I haven't fished with a bamboo pole since I was a kid. What kind of fish are in that pond, and what would I use for bait?"

"There are bluegills and bass, and Little Freni here and I will dig all the worms you want. Won't we, Little Freni?"

Little Freni burped.

Dr. Margaret smiled, but her husband appeared unconvinced.

"My cousin Hiram caught a six-pound bass," I said quickly. That may have been a slight exaggeration, but isn't that what fish stories are all about?

Dr. George Hanson glanced at the door, and then back at me. "Well—"

"And if you get tired of fishing, George, it would make a lovely spot for you to set up your easel and paint."

Dr. George Hanson looked back at the door. Apparently what he saw outside was more tempting than I was off-putting. He excused himself to fetch the luggage while his wife completed registration. I was so relieved I decided not to even mention A.L.P.O.

"You made the right decision. You won't regret it. You'll love Hernia, and your stay at the PennDutch in particular."

Dr. Margaret Hanson looked at me, her large brown eyes filled with compassion. "I'm sure we will."

I felt the need to babble. "Lots of famous people have stayed here. Streisand, Spielberg, even the Clintons. I don't usually let guests pick their rooms, but in your case I'm willing to make an exception. Of course, I'll have to shuffle folks around a bit, but that's really no problem. So which would you like, the bed Babs slept in, or the bed Bill claims he *didn't* sleep in?"

She cleared her throat, softly, like the lady she was. "Miss Yoder, I would be happy to counsel you. We could begin tomorrow morning, say around ten?"

"*Counsel* me?" I said loud enough to make Little Freni stop eating. "You want to counsel *me*?"

She didn't even blink. "Yes, I'm a psychiatrist. My husband is one as well, but he's chosen to retire. So, is ten o'clock all right?"

"You're kidding, right?"

"We could make it in the afternoon if you prefer."

"I mean about the counseling!"

"I'm quite serious. I think you could benefit from my serv-ices."

"But I'm not the one who's crazy," I wailed.

"My usual fee is one hundred twenty-dollars an hour. How-ever, given your—uh" —she glanced around my tidy, but sim-ply furnished inn—"special circumstances, I'm willing to waive my fee."

"You mean you're willing to shrink me for free?"

The doctor laughed pleasantly. "I prefer to call it counseling, or therapy, but yes, I'm willing to do it for free."

"Then ten it is," I said, causing ten generations of ancestors to turn over simultaneously in their graves.

Big Freni—Freni Hostetler—was rolling pie crusts when I caught up with her in the kitchen. The woman has rolled enough dough to pave a road from here to California, yet she still manages to cover herself from head to toe with flour. Stout as she is, that Sunday afternoon she resembled a polar bear cub.

"Freni!" I exclaimed. "It's the Sabbath! You shouldn't be mak-ing pies."

My kinswoman wiped the flour from her glasses with a flour-covered sleeve. "Ach! The Good Lord Himself picked corn on the Sabbath. Is baking pies so different?"

"It was His disciples who picked the corn, dear. And they were hungry. You know we serve sandwiches to our guests on Sunday evenings, and all you need to do is set things up. Why aren't you at home with your family?"

"Family shmamily. This morning I told Barbara to bundle up the little ones for the buggy ride to church. Can you guess what she said, Magdalena?"

I shrugged.

"That's exactly what Barbara said! Nothing!" She wiped her glasses again, leaving a fringe of discarded dough hanging from her right earpiece.

"But it *is* June, dear," I said gently. "The low temperature this morning was near seventy. Your grandbabies wouldn't have gotten cold."

"Yah, but in my day we dressed the little ones properly, and we did not have all the sickness like we do today."

There was no point in arguing with a woman who firmly believes that the common cold is caused by air temperature, and not a slew of viruses. Still, Freni was obviously suffering emotionally, and there just might be something I could do to help.

"Freni, have you ever considered seeing a shrink?"

"Ach!"

"There's nothing in the Bible against it, you know. And we just happen to have one staying at the inn. Tomorrow morning I'm getting shrunk myself."

Freni looked me up and down, the strip of pie dough flapping with the movement. "Yah, you can afford this shrinking. Barbara too." Then she had a thought, and suddenly I could see her beady eyes burning brightly behind the dirty lenses. "How *much* can my Barbara shrink?"

"Not that kind of shrinking, dear! I mean a psychiatrist."

"Ach, Magdalena, how you talk. Your mama would be ashamed if she could hear you. There are no psychiatrists mentioned in the Bible."

"It doesn't mention glasses either, but you're wearing them."

Freni is adept at changing the subject to avoid losing an argument. "So how many carnivals do I cook for?"

"That's carnivores, dear, and that's what I came to tell you. There are two of those, one vegetarian, and the rest said they'll eat anything. Oh, except that Miss Townsend says she hates lima beans. Now *there* is a gal who could use some shrinking."

Freni nodded. "Yah, I saw her in the parlor earlier. She is even taller than my Barbara." Freni clucked like a hen who had just laid an egg. "A sin if you ask me."

"What?"

"*That's* in the Bible, Magdalena. David and Goliath."

It was time to dodge like the master, above whose floury face I loomed. "Well, I'm off to visit Joseph Mast. Will you watch Little Freni while I'm gone?"

"Ach!" Freni appeared perturbed by my request, but I know

she has a fondness for my bundle of fuzz. A namesake is a namesake after all, even if it's not a proper grandchild.

I extracted the mite from her cozy quarters and set her gently on the floor. Freni, like many Amish women of her generation, does not wear brassieres, and even if she did, there would be no room for a hankie, much less a kitten.

"Any pies ready that I can take to him?"

"So soon?"

"Well, I suppose I could wait an hour or so. When will these pies be done?"

"Not the pies, Magdalena. I mean it is so soon that you court this man, his wife dead now just a week."

"*What?* I am not off to court, as you so quaintly put it, Joseph Mast. For your information, Melvin asked me to look into Lizzie's death."

Freni mumbled something unintelligible. I didn't even know which language she used.

"Come again?"

Patches of Freni's cheeks shone pink through the white mask. A godly woman, she tries not to pass judgment, but like me, she sometimes fails. This time, however, she was a saint.

"That's okay," I coaxed. "You and I are family."

"I said, there is nothing suspicious about that woman's death. It was her cooking. If you ask me, Lizzie Mast committed suicide. Accidental suicide."

I tried not to laugh. "Bad-tasting food isn't necessarily lethal." And then because Freni is both family and friend, I let the cat out of the bag. "It was drugs, dear. Illegal drugs."

I'm sure Freni blinked behind her coated lenses. Her mouth opened and closed wordlessly.

"Something they call Angel Dust," I said. "It's a very powerful drug I've read about in the newspapers."

"Ach, but that is impossible. Lizzie Mast was the salt of the earth."

"Who often used too much salt," I said and clamped a hand over my irreverent mouth.

"Yah, she was a terrible cook, but our Lizzie would never do such a thing!"

"You mean take drugs? Just a minute ago you said you thought she might have killed herself. That's a lot worse than taking drugs."

Freni removed her glasses and vigorously wiped them on her apron. Her action served only to rearrange the smudges.

"Yah, but I was only joking!"

"You were not."

"Maybe half-joking."

"I'll grant you that. After all, Lizzie Mast didn't have the easiest life."

"Ach, no children and married to Joseph."

"And you had the nerve to think I liked the man!" Joseph Mast had a reputation for being strange. Strange and silent.

"Some women get desperate," Freni said, and trained her beady little eyes on mine.

"I resent that remark. I am perfectly happy being a single woman." I sighed. "Anyway, I better get this visit to Joseph over with. Not that talking to him will do any good. I'll be lucky if he says two words."

Freni popped her glasses back into place. "*Three* words. The man will only say three words at a time."

"Whatever. Freni, dear, can you keep a secret?"

"Ach! That you should ask such a thing, hurts me here." She pounded her ample bosom with a floury fist.

"I mean it, Freni. This has to stay between you and I."

"Yah, yah," she said irritably. I have never kept a secret from the woman, and no doubt she found my caution offensive.

"Well, I don't have any proof, but I do have reason to believe that Lizzie's death may not have been accidental. It may have been murder."

Freni's bosom got another floury pounding. "Ach!"

I told her about Thelma Hershberger's nocturnal visit. Freni listened intently, but began shaking her head before I was halfway through.

"Ach, that woman," she said, interrupting me, "she is the vein of my existence."

"Do you mean 'bane,' dear?"

"Yah. Such gossip she spreads. Most of it lies. My Mose,"

Freni said, referring to her husband of almost fifty years, "he says that Thelma Hershberger makes up these stories because she does not have excitement in her life. Can this be true?"

I shrugged. What did Mose, or any Amish man, know about excitement? Was roofing a barn exciting? How about birthing a calf?

"So you think this warning note might not have existed?" I asked.

"Yah, that is what I think!" Freni's vehemence was a tip-off that Thelma's tongue had crossed her path on at least one occasion.

"So what did she say about you, dear?"

"Ach, not me! The babies. She says they are slow."

"Slow? That's ridiculous! They're not even crawling yet. How can she call them slow?"

Freni rapped her head with her knuckles. "In the koph! She says they are slow up here."

"What nonsense! Those are the brightest little babies I've ever seen."

Freni beamed. "Yah, they are true Hostetlers."

I opened the back door to the kitchen, but Freni's stubby fingers caught my sleeve. "These illegal drugs you spoke of—this Angel powder—that's what they do in the city, Magdalena. Not in Hernia."

"Au contraire, dear. It's everywhere these days."

"But only among the English, yah?"

"Not *only*," I said.

"But our people—*my* people," she said, narrowing the field further, "what do they know from drugs? Who teaches them such things?"

"It's a national sickness, Freni. I don't know how Amish youth get started. Maybe they encounter drugs during *rumschpringe*."

Freni recoiled. "Ach!"

But it seemed as logical an explanation as any. Rumschpringe literally means "running around." When Amish youth enter their late teens they are given a great deal of personal freedom. Parents turn a blind eye to youths with boom boxes strapped to their buggies, nighttime excursions to movie theaters and other centers of sins, and in some cases, even the ownership of automobiles. Of course, the cars are carefully hidden in a barn by day so as not to shame the family. A few brave souls dare to leave the community altogether and, dressed in worldly clothes, head for the big cities. For better or for worse, some never return.

The Amish elders recognize the rebellious teenage spirit and their wisdom is to allow this spirit to express itself before adulthood. When an Amish person reaches his or her twenties, they are expected to settle down. The defining moment is baptism, whereupon the applicant renounces the ways of the world and agrees to be submissive to the *Ordnung,* the rules of the church. This is expected to be a lifelong commitment. Often those who, for one reason or another, simply can't conform elect to become Mennonites. This was the case for both sets of my grandparents.

My Mennonite faith has no counterpart to rumschpringe. In many instances, we are far stricter with our young folk than are the normally conservative Amish. On the other hand, we have more latitude as adults. The choice for us is not as dramatic. In fact, there are those who say we sit on the fence, with one foot in tradition, the other in the world. Only rarely does one of our number fall off the fence and into the Amish community. To the contrary, we tumble with some regularity into other Anabaptist denominations and, in some extreme cases, like that of my sister, become Presbyterians. But to my knowledge, even Susannah has managed to stay clear of drugs.

"Well," I said, "I'll just have to poke around. If Joseph Mast isn't forthcoming, I'll try my Amish contacts, *such* as they are." I gave Freni a meaningful look. "Maybe one of *them* has heard of some kids recently back from the city."

Perhaps the grimy glasses prevented Freni from picking up on my expression. Perhaps she was one of the many who, strange as it sounds, can't hear as well when their vision is impaired. Or perhaps she was just being Freni, i.e. stubborn. At any rate, she made no offer to help.

"So," I said patiently, "have you heard of any young people back from 'outside'?"

Freni thumped her rolling pin on the table with such force that specks of plaster drifted down and dusted her dough.

"You want drugs?" she demanded. "Then try that English couple who bought the Berkey farm last year."

"You mean the Hamptons?"

Freni shrugged. "Who knows from funny English names? But I see them in Miller's Feed Store all the time. Her with a young woman's face on an old woman's body, and him—ach, he wears perfume! Now I ask you, Magdalena, what do English like that want in our store?"

"It isn't *our* store, dear, it's the Millers'. And maybe the Hamptons want garden supplies, shovels and rakes, that kind of thing." I paused to consider any hidden agenda she might have, perhaps some rumschpringe gossip she was sitting on, but just aching to tell. "Freni, dear, you haven't heard anything about the Hamptons giving parties, have you?"

Just a month before, a tourist couple up in Bedford had held an impromptu party in their hotel room. The guests were all Amish teenagers. Booze was the drug of choice on that occasion, and young Ben Bontrager had been hospitalized for alcohol poisoning.

At any rate, Freni refused to answer my question. Her only response, if you can call it one, was to pound my table with her rolling pin and grunt as she pushed it across the dough. No doubt it was going to be the thinnest pie crust on record.

I sighed. "Well, at least we'll get more pies this way. Just remember to skimp on filling too."

Not a peep.

I gave up and headed out to do my job. But I hadn't even got all the way through the door when I bumped heads with the most gorgeous man God ever created.

7

I know, one doesn't normally refer to men as "gorgeous." But there is no other word that so aptly describes Dr. Gabriel Rosen. "Handsome" would be barely adequate if I was describing just his physical appearance. Gabe makes most men look like old nags that have been ridden hard and put away wet. He has thick dark wavy hair, chiseled features, straight white teeth, and his body—well, it would be a sin to describe it in any detail. Not that I am at all familiar with it, mind you!

Anyway, my whole point is that there is more to Gabe's looks than just the outer layer. It is the twinkle in his eyes that bumps him from handsome up to gorgeous. Imagine, if you would, two perfectly formed roses, one unscented, the other fragrant. Gabe is the fragrant flower. His manly smell stirs the juices of my soul—okay, so perhaps that is a bad analogy. Just trust me on this one—Gabe is gorgeous.

At any rate, the doorway bump wasn't painful. It was, however, embarrassing.

"I'm so sorry," I said, assuming full blame.

"No reason to be sorry. It's kind of fun bumping into you."

"You're fun to bump too."

Gabe grinned. "You're a real hoot, Magdalena, you know that?"

"You should hear me holler."

He winked. "I'd love to."

I blushed to the tips of my stocking-covered toes. "Did you want something, Gabe? I mean, I was just leaving and—"

"I want to ask you out."

"What?" I jiggled a pinkie discreetly in my left ear. It's been known to give out on me in times of stress.

"You heard me. I want us to go out."

I tried the other ear for good measure. "Out where?"

He laughed. "Out like on a date. Where doesn't matter to me, just as long as it's with you. How about the movies? Surely there are theaters in Bedford."

Just so you know, Dr. Gabriel is also an outsider. He moved here from New York City about a month before the Hamptons arrived. Although he is only my age, Gabe is retired, and was seeking a quiet place in the country where he could try his hand at writing novels. Mysteries, to be exact.

"Of course there are movie theaters in Bedford." I bit my lip nervously before continuing. "But you see, I don't go to movies."

"Not ever?"

I shook my head miserably. Many Mennonites do go to movies, but I belong to one of the more conservative branches. Besides, what was the point in seeing those people act on a screen, when I could see them up close and personal here at the inn?

"Do you bowl?"

"Once. They paid me not to come back."

"Hmm. Well, we could just go out to eat. Any suggestions?"

"How about a picnic?"

"Your farm or mine?"

"Actually I was thinking of Stucky Ridge. You ever been up there?"

"Can't say that I have."

"I think you'd like it. It's that mountain just south of town. There's a little cemetery up there where all the founders of Hernia are buried."

Gabe chuckled. "Supper with a bunch of stiffs! Well, it may help supply atmosphere for the chapter I'm working on."

"There's more up there than just graves. Why, there's a nice little park with picnic benches and great views of Hernia and the valley. You'll love it, I know. Even teenagers like it up there."

"Ah, the make-out zone."

"That's not what I meant!" I wailed.

He winked. "Well, you seem pretty anxious to get me up there. What say we leave here at six?"

"Today?"

"That was my plan. But of course, we could always make it some other time."

A bird in the hand is worth two in the bush, Mama always used to say. Unfortunately she never said anything about dates. But since neither my hand nor my bush had seen a date in a long time, I decided I'd better jump at the chance.

I glanced at my watch. It was already close to four o'clock.

"Today will be just fine, but I was just on my way to see Joseph Mast. You know, the husband of the local woman who died last week." I paused. Surely it was all right to tell Gabe that I was investigating the Mast case, but in the end something held me back. "So, anyway, it may take me a while. Can we make that six-thirty?"

"Super. Oh, and don't bring anything. This is my treat."

"You sure? I could at least bring some lawn chairs, maybe a blanket."

"A blanket would be nice," Gabe said, and winked again.

This time I not only blushed, I felt my knees go weak. "I'll bring two chairs."

"Then I'll bring the blanket. A good picnic always involves a blanket somehow."

I hobbled to my car while I still could.

I'd left Little Freni at home, which was just as well. The Masts never had any children, but they seemed to have every kind of animal imaginable. Don't get me wrong, they didn't live on a farm either, but a double lot on the west side of Hernia. Alas, our zoning laws are lax. The Masts had a llama, three goats, and a miniature horse that barely came up to my knees. That was just for starters. In order to reach the front door, I had to negotiate my way through a pack of panting pooches, a bevy of bickering bantams, and a gaggle of garrulous geese. There were lesser creatures as well, and I fear I may have stepped on a few, if the squeaks and hisses (and occasional crunch) were any indication. I didn't dare to look down. I hate seeing a perfectly good pair of shoes ruined. It was no wonder Melvin foisted the job on me.

At any rate, Joseph didn't answer the door when I knocked, so I trudged around to the rear of the house. The man was a carpenter—a very good one, I hear—and sure enough he was in his shop busily sanding a curved piece of wood. He was, of course, not alone. A fourth goat perched on a stool next to the workbench and regarded me with surprisingly human and somewhat lustful eyes, and in the corner a brightly colored parrot hung upsidedown from a wooden bar.

"Hello," I said cheerily. "I'm Magdalena Yoder. Remember me?"

"Yup." Joseph, a stout man with red hair, a galaxy of freckles, and wire-rim glasses, hadn't even bothered to look up from his work.

"I'd like to express my condolences again, if I may. Your wife was certainly one of a kind, and I'm sure you miss her a great deal."

"Yup."

I cast about for a way to ease into my investigation. "Nice day, isn't it?"

"Yup."

"But we could always use more rain."

"Yup."

"So what is that you're building there?" I pointed pointlessly at the work in progress. "An ark?"

"Nope."

"Say, Joseph—I hope you don't mind me calling you that—I didn't really know your wife all that well, but I just wanted to say she was—uh, well, she was exceptional."

"Yup."

"One of a kind, you might say."

"Yup."

I was obviously not thinking fast on my feet. It was time to assume a position more conducive to intracranial activity.

"Mind if I sit?"

"Nope."

"I was talking to the goat."

Joseph grunted.

I turned to the beast. "Now be a dear and hop off that stool. You have four feet to my two."

The goat grunted.

"Move it, Billy!"

"Name's Amanda," Joseph said.

"Wow, a multisyllabic word!" I slapped my own cheek—gently of course. "So it's a she?"

He nodded. "Nubian nanny."

"How original." Joseph grunted again.

Clearly the pleasantries were over. It was time to get down to business. Quite justifiably I gave the goat a gentle push.

Amanda was not so polite. She butted my bosom with her knobby head, and I nearly fell over backward. The thud of bone hitting bone was sickening.

Now I know there are some who might think that a mature woman should let a rude ruminant remain roosting. I, however, firmly believe that the Good Lord intends us to use our attributes to the best of our individual abilities. Having said that, I don't mind sharing that I backed up ten paces, set my purse carefully down on the sawdust-littered floor, lowered my head, and charged the recalcitrant nanny.

I may be skinny, but I outweighed the goat. Amanda flew through the air with the greatest of ease, knocking the parrot off her wooden trapeze. The parrot squawked as she fluttered to the floor, stirring a great cloud of sawdust.

"Darn!" I said, which is bad as I can swear. "Now my purse is all dirty."

At first I thought the parrot was laughing at me. It could not have been the goat, because as soon as Amanda hit the floor of the workshop, she bolted in a bleating blur. Then slowly I realized the high-pitched laugh was coming from Joseph Mast, the recently bereaved husband.

"What's so funny!" I demanded, arms akimbo. That posture happens to be a distinctly un-Mennonite one, but I didn't care. I was in an English frame of mind.

Joseph laid down his sandpaper. "You are what's so funny! No one's ever gotten the best of Amanda before."

I stared at the man.

"Sit down," he said, nodding at the vacated stool. "You've earned the right to sit there."

I sat. "So you can talk?"

He laughed again. "It's true that I'm shy around strangers. And most folks are strangers. But any woman who can put Amanda in her place is no stranger to me."

I eyed the parrot, who was waddling through the dust, headed in my direction. "Does she bite?"

"It's a he. His name is Benedict, and he's a scarlet macaw. And yes, Benny could snap your finger in half like it was a carrot stick." Joseph reached down and, extending his own, apparently impervious finger, invited the parrot to hop on.

"Aren't you afraid he's going to hurt you?"

"He could. But I got him as a fledgling and hand-weaned him. Benedict and I have been buddies for twenty-two years."

"That long?" I asked incredulously.

He lifted the parrot back up to his swinging perch. "Macaws can live to be one hundred. Now Amanda, she's the amazing one. She's lived twice as long as your average goat."

"Oh great, make me feel guilty. Ousting a geriatric goat no longer seems like such a remarkable feat."

"Well, it is in her case. She defines the word 'stubborn.' You see, my wife, Lizzie"—he paused to wipe away a tear—"never had any children. I guess you might say we filled the void with animals. Anyway, Amanda was our very first pet. Next thing we knew our little family was growing by leaps and bounds."

"Pun intended, I'm sure."

He grinned. "I'm afraid not. At any rate, it was Lizzie's idea to name the animals starting with the first letter of the alphabet. You know, like they do hurricanes."

"Good heavens! Have you made it to Z?"

"Twice. Zeek—that's with two E's—is a French poodle. You may have met him coming around the yard. And Zelda, well, she's a giant Amazon dung beetle we bought through a mail-order catalogue. She helps keep the place clean."

I remembered the crunch underfoot. "Not anymore."

He raised a sparse red brow above the wire frames. "I beg your pardon?"

"Nothing. Mr. Mast—"

"Please call me Joe."

"Joe then. I'd like to ask you a few questions if you don't mind."

He nodded. "Our dearly beloved chief of police, Melvin Stoltzfus, sent you, didn't he?"

"How did you know?"

"Well, you didn't come carrying a cake or a pie, and everyone knows you help out Melvin when he gets stumped."

I flushed with pride. "*Do* they?"

"Don't get me wrong. Most folks don't hold it against you."

"You mean some do?" I wailed.

He had the grace to smile kindly. "Very few. Everyone knows the man is, well, how should I put this kindly—"

"A sandwich short of a picnic?"

"That analogy will do. It's common knowledge he was butted in the head when he tried to milk a billy goat. Apparently his noggin isn't as tough as yours."

"Bull!"

He looked surprised.

"It was a *bull* he tried to milk, not a goat. And he was *kicked* in the head."

"Is that so? Well, that would still do the trick, wouldn't it?"

I nodded in agreement. "So, Joe, may I start with the questions?"

He held up a callused hand. "Yup, but I can save you a whole lot of time. If you're thinking my Lizzie's death was no accident, you're right. What's more, I know exactly who killed her, and why."

8

"You do?"

"Yup. It was the neighbors."

"Your *neighbors*?"

"Amish," he said with surprising vehemence.

"What is that supposed to mean? Your ancestors were Amish, for Pete's sake."

"Yup. But what I mean is the Keims have ten children. *All* sons."

"So?"

"Rumschpringe. You know what that is?"

"Yes, I do, but—"

"The oldest two Keim boys are of that age. Hellions on earth, if you'll forgive my language."

"Just barely, dear. Please elaborate."

"I can't keep their names straight, but the two older ones have a car, a dilapidated bright yellow Buick they keep hidden behind a haystack up in the north forty. Anyway, they tear around in that thing at night and don't give a damn who or what they hit."

"Now that's too much."

"It's the truth."

"I meant your language, dear."

"Sorry. I was in the army."

My eyes widened. Not many Mennonites serve in the armed forces. Both we and the Amish have a centuries-old tradition of being pacifists. This is based directly on scripture, like Matthew, chapter five, verse thirty-nine: "But I tell you, do not resist an evil person. If someone strikes you on the right cheek, turn to him the other."

It is this staunch belief that set the stage for the massacre of some of my ancestors in 1750. True, my great-great-great-grandmother, Mrs. Jacob Hochstetler, wasn't following the Lord's teachings when she refused water to a hunting party of Delaware Indians at the height of the French and Indian War. But when the homestead was attacked that night, it was to my ancestors' credit that they refused to fight back. Granny Hochstetler was stabbed and scalped, an infant daughter scalped as well, and Jacob and two sons were taken hostage.

At any rate, a Mennonite with army credentials is a rare beast. "Were you drafted?" I asked.

"Yup, it was the Vietnam War. I could have gotten a deferment, but some of my buddies from high school were getting drafted, and it didn't seem right for me to get out of serving when I wasn't really a pacifist."

"You *weren't*?"

"Not then. Not at eighteen."

"Are you now?"

He shrugged. "That depends on the situation—so I guess the answer is 'no.'"

That explained why Joseph Mast seldom darkened the door of Beechy Grove Mennonite Church. I took a deep breath and asked a question that was none of my business, but one which I'd been dying to ask.

"Did you ever kill anyone? In Vietnam, I mean."

Red lashes blinked. "Yup."

I waited patiently for him to expound. When he didn't, I reluctantly got back to business.

"So, we were talking about the Keim kids. You said they don't care who or what they hit with that old jalopy of theirs. What exactly did you mean by that? Have they tried to hit you?"

"Nope. But they ran over Queequeg."

"Who?"

"Our pot-bellied Vietnamese pig."

"Oh."

"And Dora."

"Dora!" The parrot's sharp voice made me jump. "Watch out for Dora!"

Joseph smiled sadly. "Dora was an albino ferret. Friendliest thing you could ever hope to meet, although Benedict hated her. I think he thought Dora wanted him for lunch. Anyway, Dora would crawl right up your pants leg if you let her."

I shuddered. "Did the Keims apologize? Did they offer to pay for replacements?"

Joseph picked up the sandpaper and resumed sanding with vigor. "You can't replace friends."

I thought of Little Freni. Big Freni too.

"You're right," I said. "That was insensitive of me. But did they at least offer to compensate you for new animals?"

"Nope."

"That's a shame."

"Yup."

"Oh no," I wailed, "we're not back to single syllables, are we?"

He grinned sheepishly. "Sorry. I tend to shut down when I feel threatened. It's a Nam thing."

"*Moi?* Threatening?"

"Like I said, Miss Yoder, you have a reputation."

I smiled proudly, then gave myself a mental slap. "Please, call me Magdalena. Now, if you don't mind telling me, what did you do after they killed Dora?"

"Dora," the stupid parrot squawked. "Dora lunch. Dora lunch. Dora lunch."

Joseph made a futile attempt to stare his bird into silence. Finally he gave up and turned to me.

"I scattered nails on the dirt road that leads up to their house. The driveway, if you want to call it that."

I gasped. "For shame! You could cripple their horses. And I thought you liked animals!"

"I do. The horses weren't ever in any danger. I sprinkled the nails along the sides of the road. The horses trot down the middle. Anyway, it didn't do any damn good. They changed tires a couple of times, then they just took to driving across the fields." He smiled. "So, I resorted to a more direct method."

"What could that be?" I braced myself for the answer.

"I shot their tires."

"You *what*?"

"Of course they weren't in the car at the time. But they knew I did it. They even told their beloved father that I'd taken potshots at them. Only they didn't bother to tell him about the car."

"He doesn't *know*?"

"Apparently not. The old man—Benjamin—came over, and he was as mad as I've seen an Amish man get. He wanted me to apologize to his sons for shooting at them. I started to tell him about the car and what his boys had done to my animals, but I couldn't get a word in edgewise. He just kept screaming at me in Pennsylvania Dutch. To tell you the truth, Miss Yoder, it was all I could do not to shoot at him."

I pondered this for a couple of minutes while he sanded. It is, of course, quite easy to see the sins of others. And given that I still have almost perfect vision, I occasionally see some of my own. In the end I decided that chastising the carpenter wasn't going to get me anywhere.

"And Lizzie?" I asked calmly. "What were her relations like with the neighbors?"

Joseph blinked, and then wiped his eyes on the back of a freckled hand. "Lizzie was a saint. She baked them a beautiful cake and took it straight over."

I stifled an impulse to snicker. "And?"

"Well, that's what mystifies me. They cut a couple of slices and sent the rest back with one of the young ones."

"Ouch."

He gave me an odd look.

"What I meant is, that was a very rude gesture on their part."

"Magdalena rude!" the parrot trilled. "Magdalena very rude on their part."

The macaw was no match for my glare. He sidestepped to the far end of his perch, tucked his head under his wing, and feigned sleep. Come to think of it, my pseudo-ex-husband often did the same thing.

"Sorry about that," Joseph said. He was actually blushing.

"No problem. Look, you said earlier that the Keims killed Lizzie. Did you mean that literally?"

He nodded. "Yup. It's a gut feeling, and I'm seldom wrong about those. Sometimes in Nam that's all that kept me alive."

"I see. Joe," I said to put him at ease, "the day before your Lizzie died—"

"She was murdered."

"Yes, but the day before that, did she receive a threatening letter in the mail?"

The sparse red brows met briefly while he frowned. "Thelma Hershberger call you?"

"She paid me a visit. Is it true?"

"The woman's a gossip and a liar. Lizzie never got a letter like that. She would have told me. Magdalena," he said, using my given name for the first time, "don't let that woman's lies distract you. Lizzie's killers live right next door."

His tone convinced me he was telling the truth. As *he* saw it. But since we all know there are three sides to every story—mine, yours, and God's—I wasn't convinced of his Amish neighbor's guilt.

"I know you believe the Keims killed your wife," I said gently, "but it doesn't make sense. They're pacifists."

Joseph put the wood and sandpaper carefully down. His blue eyes glittered through the dusty lenses.

"I already told you why. It's because I shot their tires."

"But that's ridic—" I stopped myself just in time. "Well, how do you think they did it?"

"Booby traps," he said. "They're all over the place. Got to watch your step, you know. The war may be over, but Charlie's still got it in for you."

"I don't understand."

"Animals. Get lots of animals. They step on the mines first."

I realized, sadly, that there was little else to learn from Joseph Mast. At least not on that occasion. Perhaps a quick visit to the Keims was in order.

9

It was almost five o'clock. A prudent Magdalena would have waited until the next day. An amorous Magdalena would have driven straight home, taken a scented bubble bath, and put on her best broadcloth dress and a fresh white prayer cap. But alas, I am who I am. That is to say, I carefully navigated the menagerie—took no additional lives (at least none that I am aware of)—and drove to the adjacent farm.

There are many varieties of Amish, the subtleties of which would not be readily apparent to the outsider. But having grown up surrounded by Amish, and myself belonging to a denomination with many divisions, I am able to pick out the differences quite readily. The Benjamin Keim family belongs to the most conservative group of Amish in this part of the state.

The South Fork Amish, as this congregation is known, forbid their members the use of electric- and gas-powered energy sources. Muscle power, both animal and human, is how the Keims get their chores done. Since it was probably milking time, I knew Benjamin and the majority of his sons would be in the barn, their heads pressed up against cows, their fingers busily squeezing the teats of gentle Jerseys. Therefore, I headed straight for the back door of the house.

"Hello!" I called cheerily.

Catherine Keim appeared momentarily behind the neatly

mended screen door. "Yah?" She sounded as wary as a cat at a dog show.

"My name is Magdalena Yoder and—"

"Ach, the detective!"

"I am not a detective," I wailed. "I'm simply asking a few questions on behalf of Melvin Stoltzfus, the Chief of Police."

Catherine simply stared at me. I stared back. I had often seen her from a distance—riding in the family buggy, or shopping at Miller's Feed Store—but had never been privileged to have a close-up look.

The Bible instructs us not to judge others on their physical appearance, and I try not to. We cannot help the looks the Good Lord has chosen to give us. Were that the case, I would have no room in my bra for a feline, my feet would be four sizes smaller, and no Amish man would have to stifle his desire to hook me to a buggy and yell "giddyap."

That said, please allow me the following charitable observations about Catherine Keim. The woman is no beauty. For one thing, she is a good twenty-five pounds overweight. For another, she has teeth like a jackrabbit. And did I mention that her ears protrude straight out from the sides of her head? And as long as I'm being frank, there is the not-so-small matter of her eyebrow. She only has the one—never mind that it stretches from temple to temple.

Having said that, I'm sure it will come as a big surprise to you that virtually everyone I know talks about how beautiful the woman is. "Too beautiful for her own good," they say. "Gorgeous." "Just like the English." "God made the rose, and then he made Catherine Keim." That sort of thing.

Now that I had seen her close up, albeit through the screen door, I knew for a fact that all this profuse praise was unjustified. The woman was *interesting*, I'll grant you that. Exotic even. But what made Catherine so interesting was not her face, nor was it her rather lumpy body. It was her coloring; Catherine Keim was unusually dark-complected for an Amish woman. Her skin was olive, her hair almost black, and her eyes glittered under that single brow like twin lumps of wet coal.

As a result of all this unexplained pigmentation, rumors abound about Catherine's origins. Some say her people came from the Amish community in Paraguay, where they intermarried with the Indians. Other folks claim that she is of Middle Eastern origin. Still others hypothesize that she was left behind by a wandering band of gypsies.

But it just so happens that birth records show that Catherine was born in the environs of Hernia, as were her parents and grandparents before her. No doubt we share the blood of the same limited set of ancestors, only in different proportions. Unfortunately the dark and mysterious stranger who climbed into our family tree generations ago never made it over to my limb, and I was born a dishwater blonde whose locks eventually faded to plywood brown. I'm not jealous, mind you—I just don't think it's fair that everyone goes around calling her beautiful.

At any rate, although I may be able to stare down a parrot, I was no match for Catherine Keim. She stared at me calmly under her brow until I, fearing that I might be late for my date with Gabe the babe, finally cracked.

I looked away. "It is imperative that I speak with you."

She remained silent.

"Well?" I said, demanding some response.

"What does this imperative mean?"

"It means I *must* speak to you."

"About Lizzie, yah?"

"Yah—I mean yes!"

"Then we speak," she said, but made no move to invite me in.

I sighed. It had been a long day and my dogs were barking. A rocking chair and a nice glass of lemonade would have been very welcome. Still, the woman was willing to talk.

"Correct me if I'm wrong, dear, but from what I understand, your relationship with Lizzie was a good one, despite—how shall I put this—some disagreements with her husband?"

"Yah. Lizzie Mast was a kind woman."

"Were you friends?"

She nodded almost imperceptibly. "I have ten sons, Miss Yoder. No daughters. Yah, Lizzie was a friend."

"What did you think of her husband?"

"Ach! Not all God's children are easy to love."

"Apparently he feels the same way. Is it true that your sons ran over some of his animals with their car?"

"Car?"

"*Tch, tch,* Mrs. Keim. Pretending to be innocent is the same thing as lying."

Her olive skin took on rose accents. "It is only a temporary thing, Miss Yoder. The boys are young. This thing will pass."

"I'm sure it will, but does the bishop know?"

The rose accents deepened. "Benjamin says it is best not to bother the bishop with such small matters." She paused. "And one must obey the husband, yah?"

I gave her a meaningful stare through the screen. "That depends on whether or not one's husband is right. If one's husband is a fool, then it would be foolish to obey him."

"Ach, Miss Yoder, you speak so plain."

"I do tend to get right to the point, don't I? But anyway, running over pets is no small matter."

"Yah, I understand, but these animals—these pets—they are all over the place. They come into our fields, even our barn, and eat what is meant for our cows."

"I see. Well, this sounds like a problem that could be solved simply by checking the zoning laws. Surely, at least the larger animals have to be fenced."

"You think that is so?"

"Quite possibly. I could check, if you like."

"You would do that?" The sound of hope in her voice was touching.

"No problem. Now back to Lizzie, if you don't mind. Joseph Mast said she baked a cake—a peace cake, as it were—but that you sent it back. Is that true?"

Catherine mumbled something that even these sharp ears couldn't pick up.

"What's that, dear?"

She mumbled again.

"Speak up, please."

"It is wrong to say what I said."

"Maybe not, dear. Why don't you let me be the judge? After all, I am a Sunday School teacher."

"Yah?"

"Every Sunday at Beechy Grove Mennonite Church. I teach the seventh and eighth grades."

My credentials apparently impressed her. Either that, or she had an overwhelming need to confess.

"Like I said, Miss Yoder, Lizzie was my good friend, but she was—ach, how do I say such a thing—"

"The world's worst cook?"

The screen door flew open, banging my prominent and somewhat probing proboscis. "Come in!" she cried, as if greeting an old friend after a long absence.

I stepped into the Keim kitchen. It was like stepping back into the nineteenth century. The large cast iron stove was fueled with wood. At the sink there was a hand pump that drew its water from a well. Hot water could only be had by heating a heavy cast iron kettle. Some Amish use gasoline- or kerosene-powered refrigerators, but the Keims's sect forbids this. They had, instead, an insulated metal and wood box into which they put ice from time to time. Apparently Häagen-Dasz was not high on their list of priorities.

Catherine motioned for me to sit on a simple wooden chair, one of the eighteen arranged neatly around a massive oak table. She took a chair closer to the door, and I could see by the light that played along her face that I had been right in my initial assessment; no beauty there. But like I said, it wasn't her fault.

"So tell me about Lizzie's cooking," I said.

"Ach, even the pigs wouldn't eat it."

We both giggled.

"But still," I said, switching to my grave voice, "it wasn't very nice to send the cake back. Not after you'd taken a few slices."

Catherine hung her head in shame. "Yah, that was not the right thing to do. My Elam took it back. He is the oldest. He said Joseph was trying to poison us and was using Lizzie to do it."

"That's quite an imaginative boy."

"Yah. I was not home at the time, or I would have stopped him. But then, Miss Yoder—"

"Please, call me Magdalena."

"Yah, Magdalena. So my Benjamin whips Elam. He breaks even a buggy whip. The boy has been punished," she said firmly.

I nodded. The Amish might be pacifist in their dealing with the outside world, but the Biblical injunction not to spare the rod is taken seriously.

"Was that the end of your friendship with Lizzie?"

"Ach, no! It was not her fault she had a crazy husband. She still needed a friend, yah?"

"I don't think Joseph's crazy," I said kindly. "I think he suffers from flashbacks."

Her brow puckered like the hem on a badly sewn dress. "What is this flashbacks?"

"Bad memories, dear. Joseph Mast fought in Vietnam. A lot of those men went through horrible, indescribable experiences. For some, the experiences have been impossible to let go of. Joseph is one of those."

She nodded again. "Yah, these wars the English make, always there is so much suffering."

"You're preaching to the choir, dear."

"What is this choir, Magdalena?" The Amish use neither choirs nor musical instruments in their services.

I smiled and explained.

"Does this choir visit the sick?"

"The pastor does that. And we have teams of volunteers that see shut-ins as well."

"And who visits the lonely, Magdalena?"

"Well, uh—anyone I guess. Why do you ask?"

"Because Lizzie Mast was very lonely and I did not see visitors."

I should have seen that one coming. My guilt quotient soared to dangerous levels. Any higher, and I would find myself washing dishes in a Bedford soup kitchen or changing sheets in the hospice.

"Didn't she have any visitors? Any friends besides you?"

"Two times only do I see someone visit, but I do not think they are friends."

"Oh? Who were they?" Catherine was volunteering more than I'd hoped for.

"Gertrude Troyer—"

"Which one?" I could think of half a dozen.

Catherine glanced around the room. It was a guilty look if ever I saw one.

"The one who is married to Jacob the Handsome."

I winked. "Gotcha. And who was the other, dear?"

"Thelma Hershberger. The post office lady."

"When were these visits?" I tried to make it sound like a casual question, but even to my own ears I sounded like the Gestapo.

Catherine jumped to her feet. "Ach, I have the manners of the English! You must be hungry, yah?"

"I'm ravenous but—"

"The supper is not yet ready but there is some shoofly pie here on the counter"—she scratched her thick dark braids with a finger the color of honey—"ach, it is gone! The boys," she said, turning with a smile. "Jonah has sweet teeth."

"You mean a sweet tooth."

"Yah, at Miller's Feed Store he wants always the candy with the English soldiers on it."

I put my brain into high gear. "You mean *Three Musketeers*?"

"Yah, that is the one. Boys," she said, as if that explained everything.

As if on cue, three little boys tumbled into the kitchen from the adjacent room. One was a toddler, the other two just barely older. Remarkable, all three were towheads.

"Mutter," said the tallest, "how long yet until supper?" He said this in Pennsylvania Dutch.

"When the men are done milking." Catherine turned and glanced at a windup clock on the window sill behind her. "Ach, it is time to start the beans!"

I glanced at the worldly watch on my bony wrist. "Ach!" I squawked. "It's time to get ready for my date! From what I hear, those New York types don't like to wait."

Catherine's brown eyes widened. "Yah?" She seemed quite

willing to delay supper preparations if I was willing to dispense some juicy details.

"Later," I cried, and hustled my bustle out the door.

But the second I saw my car, I knew I wasn't going anywhere. Not for a long time. Maybe even never.

10

Crepe Fillings

Crepes can be served for breakfast, lunch, dinner, or dessert depending on the filling. The combinations are endless, so experiment and enjoy!

For simple fillings, try butter and jam; butter, sugar, and lemon juice; mashed berries and sugar; sour cream and brown sugar; or preserves mixed with rum or brandy. (Don't forget to dust finished product with powdered sugar!)

For a heartier meal, try filling crepes with meats, vegetables, or seafood in a basic cream sauce. Leftover bits of meat and vegetables taste great wrapped in a crepe.

Apple Filling

¼ cup orange juice	2 cups peeled, chopped apples
1 teaspoon cornstarch	2 tablespoons vanilla yogurt
⅛ teaspoon nutmeg	⅛ teaspoon orange extract

Combine all ingredients except yogurt and orange extract in a saucepan. Cook, stirring occasionally, until apples are soft and sauce is thick. Place 3 tablespoons of filling on each crepe and roll up. Combine yogurt and orange extract and top each crepe with the mixture. Makes enough to fill 8 crepes.

11

My car had three flat tires. *Three.* I knew at once that this horrible situation was a result of my sin.

You see, I am a sinful woman. As a matter of fact, since we are all children of Adam and Eve, we are *all* sinners. Of course, some of us are worse sinners than others. To be honest, I would have to say my worst sin is pride which, I understand, is one of the lesser sins. At least it's not as bad as lust, which is a form of coveting, and therefore one of the big ten. Come to think of it, my worst sin is probably a lot less worse than yours.

My people are renowned for their humility. Mama was, in fact, proud of hers. "Magdalena, don't stand with your hands on your hips," she would say. "That's *hochmut.*" Prideful. So I stood with my hands to my sides, neck craned forward, shoulders hunched, like the vultures I'd seen in *National Geographic* magazine photos.

But sometimes, alone in my room, I would puff out my undeveloped chest, arms akimbo, and practice pride. Eventually I got very good at it, if I must say so myself. At my peak I could brag and boast along with the best of them—not that I would, of course, since I am a far better Christian than that.

Then about a year ago everything changed. Inspired by the celebrities that often stay at my inn, I bought a brand-new expensive car. A sinfully *red* BMW. I had to go all the way to Pittsburgh to get that car. I may as well have gone to Sodom and Gomorra. The hubbub that followed that purchase rocked Hernia on its heels.

The very day I came home with that car, Lodema Schrock, our preacher's wife, organized an emergency meeting of the Mennonite Women's Sewing Circle, of which she was the president at the time. This group, incidentally, is the largest, best-attended women's organization in our church, and its members form the bulk of the attendees at the Annual Prayer Breakfast. Lodema—without her husband's knowledge, I might add—not only had the women down on their knees praying for me, but she persuaded them to visit me in pairs, in an attempt to talk me out of my purchase and into repentance.

I don't mind sharing that I so resented this intrusion by Lodema and her ladies that I threatened to transfer my membership from Beechy Grove Mennonite Church to the First Mennonite Church, which happens to be far more liberal. At this point, allow me to humbly explain that I am Beechy Grove's wealthiest member and by far the largest contributor to their offering plates. When the elders heard about my threats, they gave serious consideration to ousting poor Reverend Schrock. The grounds, they said, was his inability to control his meddling wife.

The Reverend is a good man—although his sermons are a mite too long—so I had no intention of actually quitting. I merely wanted to force Lodema into an apology. But the woman is more stubborn than a toddler and a teen combined, and she wouldn't budge. I am only half as stubborn as she, but it was I who had been wronged, so for as long as Lodema remained recalcitrant, I stayed home on Sunday mornings, my purse tightly zipped.

Of course in a town this size, there are no secrets, and soon every congregation in town was vying to get me as a new member. Even Richard Nixon came knocking on my door. I'm not talking about the dead president, of course, but the pastor of the First and Only True Church of the One and Only Living God of the Tabernacle of Supreme Holiness and Healing and Keeper of the Consecrated Righteousness of the Eternal Flame of Jehovah.

His is a small, but devout, group out by the interstate, who really could use the bucks, thanks to abnormally high life insurance premiums they pay on behalf of their pastor. But if you ask me, any preacher who routinely handles live snakes during worship, and any congregation who puts up with such a thing, deserves to pay through the nose.

At any rate, the war between Lodema and I, both pacifists that we are, finally ended. But alas, there was no clear victor. Lodema apologized through clenched teeth, and I resumed giving, but with a somewhat clenched fist. Don't get me wrong though. I still give the same amount of money—ten percent of everything I earn—but I now spread my giving around. Why, just last week I sent a hefty check over to the Hernia Presbyterian Church. (The rumors I've heard that Presbyterians bathe in beer and dance naked in their living rooms better not be true.)

It is Lodema who took the low road. She told everyone in Hernia with two ears (about ninety-eight percent of the population) that two terrible things would happen to me because of my pride. The first, she predicted, would involve my personal life. When my bigamist husband Aaron ran off to Minnesota, she claimed her first victory. The second calamity was supposed to involve the sinfully red car itself.

"Three flat tires," she'd said, "all on the same day. And then something so horrible you'll wish you'd never been born."

I stopped staring at the three flat tires and stared at Benjamin Keim and seven of his stair-step sons who were approaching from the barn. No doubt about it, Benjamin Keim had Yoder blood coursing through his veins. His nose, like mine, required its own zip code, and he had the same watery blue-gray eyes. Same deep folds running from nose to chin, same jowly cheeks. But unlike me, he was a true blond, a trait characteristic of some Yoder clans. In fact, as preposterous as this may sound, generations of inbreeding seem to have produced a dominant blond gene, not only among some of the Yoders, but the Kauffmans, Millers, Troyers, and Hostetlers as well. How else could one explain nine towhead sons in a family all born to a mother as dark as molasses? Only one son, apparently the oldest, was brunette.

"Good evening," I called to Benjamin when he came within earshot. To my credit, my voice was entirely calm.

"Good evening," Benjamin answered. His seven older sons said nothing.

I waited a minute. "My name is Magdalena Yoder."

"Yah, and I am Benjamin Keim." He was close enough to shake hands, but neither of us made the gesture. He, no doubt, would just as soon not press the flesh with a woman of the world, which was entirely fine with me. I abhor the antiquated custom of greeting folks by touching a part of their bodies that has in turn touched every private part; parts upon which the sun seldom, if ever, shines. Once meant to convey the message that one was indeed unarmed, handshaking is now the number one transmitter of colds and flu virus. If Melvin did get elected to office, I would demand that he introduce a bill banning hand-shaking in the Commonwealth of Pennsylvania.

"I see there are Yoders in your family tree," I said to break the ice.

"Yah! My mother was a Yoder."

"So then we're cousins," I said cleverly.

"Yah, maybe so."

"You're probably wondering what I'm doing here, aren't you?"

"Yah, that is so."

"I came to visit your wife."

"Catherine?"

"No, the other wife."

Seven pairs of watery blue eyes, and one pair of dark eyes, widened.

"That was a joke," I said quickly. Alas, no one laughed. "Yes, I came to see Catherine."

"Why do you see Catherine?"

It may have been just my imagination, but it sounded to me like Benjamin's voice had risen half an octave. That is a sure sign of anxiety, if you ask me. And although the seven sons remained silent, they shuffled in the dust like horses just before a thunderstorm.

"We talked about cooking."

That seemed to satisfy him, although it ought not to have. Most Mennonite women are not in the habit of dropping in on virtual strangers to yap about recipes.

"Yah, my Catherine is a good cook," he said. There followed an awkward moment of silence until he added, "So, you will be going now?"

"That was my intention, but it appears that my horseless carriage"—I chuckled pleasantly—"seems to have thrown a couple of shoes."

My mangled analogy apparently confused the man. The creases on his forehead swelled to match the deep folds on either side of his mouth.

"I have three flat tires," I explained.

"Ach!" Benjamin exchanged glances with his two tallest sons. "The nails."

"Yes, nails," I said. "There are at least two nails in each tire. It's a wonder the fourth tire wasn't punctured."

He bent and inspected each tire. Finally he stood, but avoided direct eye contact.

"For this I am very sorry, Miss Yoder. I do not know how these nails got on this road."

"Well, I do!"

Benjamin blinked. "Yah?"

"Why don't you ask your sons?"

"My sons?"

"Yes, your sons. From what I hear, you might want to start with the two oldest."

"Papa!" the oldest boy said with surprising sharpness. "It is time to go into supper. Mutter will be waiting."

Benjamin ignored the interruption. "Elam, who speaks now, is the oldest. And this"—he gestured at a lad who could have been his clone—"is his brother Seth." The latter instantly turned the color of a good beet-pickled egg. Bright pink, but not so dark that the yolk turns color.

I nodded at the introductions. "Now ask them about the nails."

Benjamin turned to his sons. "Tell me about these nails."

The two boys stared at their father, as silent as salt and pepper shakers.

I sighed. "Well, then I guess I'll have to tell you. You see, I really did talk to your wife about recipes, but that was *after* I spoke with your neighbor, Joseph Mast. Boy, did I get an earful over there."

"Ach—"

"I *listened* to him, Mr. Keim. I didn't yell at him."

Benjamin took an anxious step closer. "What did Joseph say?"

"Don't believe her, Papa!" It was Elam again, the dark one. He may have had his mother's looks, but he had the hormone-ridden blood of an eighteen-year-old roaring through his veins.

Benjamin's watery eyes congealed into cold focus. He turned and addressed his other sons.

"Go into the house," he said in Pennsylvania Dutch. "*Mach schnell!*"

All the boys obeyed, including Seth. Benjamin then turned to Elam. "Let Miss Yoder speak."

"But what she says is not true."

"Silence."

"But Joseph Mast is a liar," Elam said vehemently. "And he tried to kill us, remember?"

"I said '*silence*'!" Benjamin's hands remained at his sides, but a thousand snakes couldn't have hissed more threatening than that.

Elam's face darkened as it twisted with rage. "Why, Papa? Why do you always listen to the English, and not to us? Well, I will tell you, Papa. It is because you are a fool."

My mouth opened wide enough to swallow a Philadelphia hoagie. I've lived around Amish my entire life but, until then, had never seen an Amish youth talk back to his or her parents. And even Mennonite children—my sister Susannah excepted—wouldn't dream of calling either of their parents a fool. It says quite clearly in the book of Matthew, chapter five, verse twenty-two, "But anyone who says, 'You fool!' will be in danger of the fire of hell."

Even Benjamin had a hard time believing his ears. He gasped like a guppy in a stagnant bowl, barely able to breathe. Speech was not an option just then. Of course, I felt sorry for the poor man.

"Shame on you!" I said to Elam. "You're supposed to honor your father and your mother."

Elam gave me a look that only a teenager—and my sister Susannah—is capable of giving. I, who have a hard time swatting a fly, wanted to slap that expression off his face.

Benjamin finally found his tongue. "Go to the house!" he ordered in dialect.

"Nein."

"Now!"

Elam didn't budge. "It is the Englisher who should go before she tells more lies."

That did it. That hiked my hackles. My left hand found its hip in the most English of poses, but I waggled my right index finger presidential style.

"I am *not* an Englisher. I am an old-style Mennonite, and you and I just happen to share the same limited gene pool. And while it is true I am more worldly than you, I would never have spoken to my parents that way. Frankly, I am shocked to hear an Amish boy talk back to his father."

"Yah," Benjamin said, "this talk back is not our way. You will apologize now to me and to Miss Yoder."

Elam closed his eyes, the ultimate act of defiance. "Englisher," he said coldly.

"Ach!" Benjamin was beyond despair. "What is a good father to do?"

I used my waggle finger as a poker. Elam's chest was surprisingly bony under his homemade shirt.

"Look, buster, I would leave right now, if I could. Unfortunately I have three flat tires and only one spare. As I understand it, I have these flats thanks to a feud between you and your neighbor. If I had two extra spares, I'd make you change them, since you undoubtedly have a lot of experience in that department."

"Elam, is this true?"

Elam's jaw clenched. His eyes remained closed, as did his lips.

"Go ahead and tell your father." I couldn't help but sneer. "If you don't, I will."

Nothing.

"Suit yourself, you impudent little"—I caught myself just in time. I have never used the B word, but it is one my sister Susannah uses with some frequency, thanks to her brief marriage to a Presbyterian. I was, however, not through. "But the least you can do is loan me your car."

Dark eyes opened just a crack. "What car?"

"The one you have hidden under a haystack."

"Ach!" I thought Benjamin was going to have a heart attack. He was literally clutching his chest.

You might think it strange that an Amish father did not know his sons had a car, but allow me to assure you, the ability of a parent to deceive his or her self is mind-boggling. It far surpasses the child's ability to deceive the parent. I speak from experience—not as the deceived nor the deceiver, mind you—but from close-hand observation.

My sister Susannah had our parents hornswoggled from the moment she hit the P in puberty. As a teenager, she slipped in and out of the house at all hours of the night, smoked cigarettes, drank beer (in preparation for marrying a Presbyterian?), told horrendous lies, even shoplifted, and almost never got caught. And don't think for a moment that I didn't do my duty as an older sister and tell on her. I ratted like a gross of combs at a hairdressers' convention, but to no avail. It was easier for my parents *not* to believe Susannah, and to pay the price of confronting her, than to believe me. *Me*, the faithful daughter. The one who followed the rules because they were there. Because the Bible told me to.

Granted, the Keim boys were of rumschpringe age, and expected to misbehave, but no doubt their parents had visions of them riding around the countryside at full gallop in the family buggy. Or maybe they thought the boys rebelled by going into Bedford, the nearest real city, and ogling the girls who work at Tastee Freeze. At worst—given one's penchant for self-deception—they imagined their offspring requesting permission to visit a Mennonite church on Sunday. After all, our benches have decadent backrests, and our services are a good two hours shorter than those of the Amish.

"Now see what you've done!" Elam's eyes were wide open now.

"*Me?*"

Benjamin let go of his chest. "Ach, Elam, it is you!"

"But Papa—"

"Enough!" Benjamin raised a hand as if to strike his son. Mercifully he did not, but that scene has haunted me ever since.

It certainly made an impact on Elam. He burst into tears and fled into the house, slamming the screen door behind him. The rebellious young man was back to being a boy again.

For some time I stood quietly and allowed Benjamin to compose himself. He was crying as well, and while I am not a sexist in these matters, tears did not suit the man. With the faucets open, a complexion that pale looks like two pounds of high-fat hamburger meat.

"Tissue?" I asked kindly when it was time to get on with things.

He shook his head, and then wiped his face across a sleeve. "Ach, a car!"

"I'm afraid so. Look, I don't mean to be rude or anything, but it's getting really late, and I *have* to be going. I don't suppose you could persuade one of the boys to lend me the key."

That nearly brought on a second near heart attack.

"That's okay," I said, "I'll think of something else. Perhaps you could drive me in your buggy. Just as far as the nearest phone."

Benjamin nodded. "Yah, Joseph Mast has a phone."

"He does have a phone," I agreed, "but he's as stable as a skyscraper made of cottage cheese."

"What means this?"

"Never mind, dear. Perhaps you'd be willing to drive me a little further. After all—"

"Benjamin!" Catherine called from the back porch. "Benjamin!" The stress in her voice was almost palpable.

"Uh-oh," I said, "sounds like there's a crisis brewing inside."

"Yah." Benjamin looked at his wife, back to me, and then at his wife. The poor guileless man was torn between familial duty and the commandment to be hospitable to strangers. It was a painful struggle to watch.

"That's all right, dear," I assured him. "You go on in where you're needed the most. I can hoof it all the way home if I have to."

"Thank you, Miss Yoder." He needed no further urging, and bolted for the house as if his life depended on it.

I started down the long dirty driveway, praying that the Good Lord would send a car my way to give me a lift. Any car, just as long as it didn't belong to Joseph Mast or Lodema Schrock. Then, for some inexplicable reason I burst into a rousing rendition of the old spiritual "Swing Low, Sweet Chariot."

Ask, and you shall receive, the Bible says. It also says something about God working in mysterious ways. Well, let me tell you, these words are all true. I had just set foot on hard pavement, still singing, when the Good Lord sent a sweet chariot to carry me home.

12

Strictly speaking it wasn't a chariot, but an Amish buggy. But it was awfully sweet of the driver to stop, although the fact that I was standing in the middle of the road, arms and legs spread, may have been a determining factor.

"Good evening, Miss Yoder. Is something wrong?"

I recognized the handsome face of Jacob Troyer, the young man who had asked to borrow my phone earlier that day. Sitting beside him on the front seat was his mousy little wife, Gertrude.

For some reason I have always disliked the woman. Perhaps it is because—and experts will back me up on this—we instinctively have a visceral antipathy toward approximately twenty percent of the people we lay eyes on for the first time. At any rate, there is something about Gertrude's scrunched-up face, her tiny eyes, and pinched lips—oh and that ridiculous button nose—that just sets my teeth on edge. It is nothing personal, I assure you, since I had never, until then, actually met the woman, but only seen her around at places like Miller's Feed Store, Yoder's Corner Market, and the county fair. And just so you put it out of your mind, my negative feelings had absolutely *nothing* to do with the fact that such a plain Jane had somehow managed to snare the most gorgeous man in the county, Gabe the Babe included.

I smiled pleasantly at the handsome man and his homely wife. "There's more wrong than you could shake a buggy whip at, but the bottom line is, I need a ride."

"How far?"

I glanced at my watch. Alas, it was already twenty-five after six. Gabe would be well on his way to Stucky Ridge. So what was there to be gained by stopping at the nearest house with a phone? Hernia had no professional mechanics and the garages in Bedford were already closed. Why prevail upon a guest, or an untrustworthy sister, to pick me up, when a leisurely ride through the countryside might actually soothe my soul?

"To the PennDutch," I said decisively.

Jacob nodded, and had a mumbled, and somewhat belabored conversation with his wife. A paranoid Magdalena might well have suspected that said spouse was not thrilled to pick up a hitchhiker. This one in particular.

Finally Jacob turned back to me. "We would be happy to take you home."

The buggy was a partially enclosed two-seater, and logic would dictate that I take the backseat. That, however, simply would not do. After all, I am an older woman, and getting in and out of a buggy is an acquired skill which requires some athleticism. Then, too, it is hotter and stuffier in the covered section, and I had had a long hard day and might doze off, thereby missing my stop—okay, so my real motive for getting the front seat was the opportunity to sit next to Jacob Troyer. But I ask you, is it wrong to indulge in a harmless, and lustless, fantasy? Who would it hurt if I pretended, for mere minutes, to be married to the Amish equivalent of Leonardo DiCaprio?

"Be a dear," I said to Gertrude, "and slip into the back, will you?"

"Ach!" The woman's tiny eyes widened to their limited capacity.

"Yah," Jacob said, "the guest should sit up front."

So I did. And I will confess that was a thrill, trotting down the road at ten miles per hour, haunch to haunch with a hunk. And I will not deny that it gave me pleasure to see the astonished looks on the faces of motorists, or the more shocked and somewhat dismayed looks of the Amish we passed.

Jacob enjoyed it too, I'm sure. The entire way he kept up an animated stream of chatter.

"Are you friends of the Keim family, Miss Yoder? A relative perhaps?"

"Some sort of relative almost certainly, but friends, no. I just dropped by to ask them a few questions."

"Yah? What sort of questions?"

"You may as well know, dear. The police chief, Melvin Stoltzfus, has asked me to help him with the investigation into Lizzie Mast's death."

"Ach!" I heard from the backseat.

Jacob chuckled. "You are becoming a famous detective, Miss Yoder, yah?"

"Yah," I said proudly, and then remembering that pride cometh before the fall, grasped the side of my seat more tightly.

"So, what have you learned already? Did Joseph Mast kill his wife?"

I caught my breath. "My, aren't we jumping to conclusions! Who said anything about Lizzie Mast being murdered?"

Jacob shrugged his broad shoulders. "But everyone knows things. About Joseph Mast, I mean."

"What sort of things?"

"He has a bug in his bean."

I smiled at the quaint Amish way of saying someone was crazy. "The Vietnam War," I explained. "Joseph Mast saw things—experienced things—that you can't imagine."

"Yah," I heard from the backseat, "but did he have to go?"

"He felt he was serving his country," I said irritably. The last thing I wanted to do was defend a war—any war—or its participants, willing or otherwise.

"Mennonites are pacifists, yah?" Jacob said.

"Yes. But there are exceptions to everything, aren't there?"

"Our people do not go to war," the voice from the peanut gallery said.

"I know that, dear. You rely on others to safeguard your freedom of religion."

"Ach!"

"What do Mennonites believe?" Jacob asked.

Before I could answer, an approaching car swerved into our lane, steered sharply toward the shoulder, and then sped off like a bat from you-know-where. During the split second I saw the driver's face, I recognized Lodema Schrock, my pastor's wife. The look of pure envy on her normally smug mug was worth three new tires. It was almost worth a missed date with Gabriel Rosen.

"Now what were you saying, dear?"

"We want to know if you—ach, how do you say—practice infant baptism?" Gertrude had a voice as tiny as her mouth.

"What was that, dear?"

"I asked if you baptize babies?"

"Of course we don't," I said calmly. "We're Anabaptists just like you."

"Do you believe in the Trinity?"

"Absolutely."

"Do you worship Mary?" Much to my surprise, that question came from Jacob.

"Of course not. I don't know that anyone does."

"Do you take baths in beer?" Gertrude asked.

"That's the Presbyterians," I wailed.

"*Yah?*" they asked in unison.

It was time to trot out the truth before they did something wild like trade their buggy for a bathtub of brew. Besides, I had a sneaking suspicion that the beer rumor, if traced to its origin, might land at my feet. "I don't know that they actually bathe in it," I said, "but they are very liberal compared to us."

Jacob shook his head. "I saw a magazine in the back at Yoder's Corner Market. The woman on the cover was"—he looked away—"naked. Was she Presbyterian?"

I had a feeling that if I said yes, he'd become a baby-baptizer in a heartbeat. Clearly lust, not money, is what makes the world go 'round.

"I don't know! She might have been a Lutheran—or a Buddhist even. Besides I've seen magazines like that, and I'm sure she wasn't naked. She was probably wearing a bathing suit called a bikini."

"I've seen pictures of such bathing suits, also. Smaller than a man's handkerchief," our backseat judge said wistfully. "Surely a sin."

"Then don't wear one, dear."

"Ach, but the picture I saw, she was not even wearing a bathing suit."

I shook my head in disbelief. Sam would never stock any magazines like that.

"Well, enough talk of religion," I said cheerfully. "How long have you two been married?"

"Three years," Gertrude said almost fiercely.

"And you have yet to hear the pitter-patter of little feet? I mean, besides your own?"

"The Lord will bless my womb when the time is right."

"Of course, dear. But in the meantime you get to play with your sister's babies."

"Ach!"

"My Gertrude and her sister do not get along so well," Jacob said.

"*Really?*" What an exciting day this was turning out to be. First, I got to butt heads with a goat, then I got to watch an Amish father butt heads with a rebellious teenager, and now, the *pièce de résistance*: the discovery that Amish siblings don't necessarily get along. And twins at that!

"Tell me, dear, does your sister ever drive you nuts—I mean *really* nuts—like you just want to reach out and strangle her? Maybe even reach your hand down her throat and pull out her tonsils?"

"Jacob," the mousy thing whimpered, "I think I forgot to feed the chickens. Can you drive faster?"

Jacob gave the reins a hard slap. "Geeyaw!"

The horse plunged into its traces. Unfortunately we had just entered a stretch of road known locally as Dead Man's Curve, and were headed downhill. Now an Amish buggy can go remarkably fast, and they aren't the stablest of vehicles. I know of several instances where buggies have tipped over, harming the occupants and, of course, injuring the horse. To say that we careened might be putting it strongly, but it was definitely yet another exciting moment. An adrenaline rush, as sister Susannah might have said.

Given the fact I had no seat belt, and little to hold on to, can I be blamed for reaching out and grabbing the nearest solid thing I could find? And can I help it if that thing just happened to be Jacob's knee?

"Ach!" Gertrude squeaked. "Don't touch my Jacob."

I quickly withdrew my hand. "Sorry, dear, I guess I got carried away in all the excitement."

"Yah? Like when you married another woman's husband?"

My cheeks stung. "That isn't fair! I had no idea Aaron was married."

"You, the big English detective," she muttered.

"And anyway, how did you know about my bogus nuptials with a bigamist?" I wailed.

"Ach!"

Even Jacob gasped.

"My mistake of a marriage," I translated. "Does *everyone* in Hernia know?"

"Like Rahab the harlot, some say."

"Who says?" I demanded.

Gertrude twittered. "Like Mary Magdalene, I say. She is your namesake, yah?"

"Now that's hitting below the belt! I certainly can't help my name, and besides, half the Amish women in Bedford County have Magdalena somewhere in their names."

We clattered across the narrow bridge that spans Slave Creek and made a sharp turn to the right on to Hertzler Road. This time, although I nearly toppled from my perch, I kept my hands to myself.

The fact that I risked life and limb did not satisfy Gertrude. She had found my Achilles' heel and would not let go.

"Did you have to confess your sin to the elders?" she trilled.

"That does it! Stop the buggy, Jacob!"

"Ach, but Miss Yoder—"

"That's *Magdalena* Yoder. Stop the buggy this minute!"

Jacob reined the horse to a snorting stop and I clambered down. No doubt I was snorting as well.

"Thanks for the ride." I forced the words out. And then I hoofed it home. Unlike Lot's wife, I managed not to look back.

I can only guess Jacob managed to back up, or else made a dangerous and illegal U-turn, because no one passed me on the way home.

I limped into the PennDutch at half past seven, thanks to the rock I had stepped on. My plan was to sneak through the back kitchen door, fix myself a sandwich to eat while soaking my foot, and then creep off to bed undetected. I know, I own the inn lock, stock, and barrel, and by rights can sail through the front door at any hour I please, but when the going gets tough, and the tough get going—I'm usually at the tail end of the pack—I find the back door more suitable. It was the door I used as a child. Mama reserved the front door for company, and since her personality, plus a little rock salt, could make a fine ice cream, the front door was hardly ever opened.

Given the hour, I expected the guests to be in their rooms, or perhaps in the parlor reading, or maybe even engaging in polite conversation. I certainly did not expect to find one in the kitchen, chowing down like there was no tomorrow.

"Good gracious," I said, "that is an extraordinarily large hoagie." The sandwich in question could have fed a small third world nation, or maybe even a family of five from Ohio.

Darlene Townsend smiled, a ring of raw white onion dangling from her teeth. She scooped it in with a flick of her tongue. "I guess I'm still a growing girl."

I frowned. The woman was already too tall for her own good. "Be careful, dear. Remember what happened to the tower of Babel. The Lord doesn't like it when folks poke their heads into Heaven uninvited."

Darlene laughed. "You're funny, Miss Yoder, you know that?"

"I'm a virtual laugh riot," I said, and hobbled over to the phone. Gabe's answering machine picked up on the sixth ring.

"It's me," I whispered, mindful of someone else in the room. "Something happened that you aren't going to believe, and that's why I didn't show up on the ridge. Call me when you get in."

The second I replaced the receiver in its cradle, the phone rang. I grabbed it.

"Gabe?"

"In your dreams."

"Melvin! Melvin Stoltzfus!"

"That's my name, Yoder, don't wear it out. Look, there's been another development."

"You're dropping out of the race?" I couldn't disguise the hope in my voice. During my long walk home I'd come to the sobering conclusion that I, Magdalena Portulacca Yoder, was not going to save the world. So what if Melvin was an egotistical incompetent? Getting to the bottom of Lizzie's death was his problem, not mine.

"No," he snarled, "I'm not dropping out of the race. I called to tell you that there's been a second murder."

"Oh?" It may not have been my problem anymore, but it was definitely getting more interesting.

"She was hit by a car. There was a witness."

"Who was hit by a car?" My volume must have risen because Darlene was looking at me.

"It happened this afternoon. About five-thirty. She was crossing North Elm when the car came barreling out of nowhere and mowed her down. Well, actually, the car only grazed her, but it sent her flying into that stop sign there at the corner of North Elm and Beechy. Her head busted wide open like a melon."

"Whose head?" I shrieked. "What's the victim's name?"

"You should listen harder, Yoder. I already told you it was Thelma Hershberger."

I gasped. My knees felt weak, and what with my sprained ankle and all, I desperately needed to sit. Unfortunately all the kitchen chairs were out of my reach. Not partial to pride, I slid to the floor. At least I wouldn't collapse and bust my head open like a melon.

"Who witnessed it?" I was more in control now, and spoke softly.

"It was a phone tip. The caller wouldn't say."

"Man or woman?"

"Don't be ridiculous, Yoder. Thelma may not have been my type, but she was all woman."

I let that pass. "What makes you think it was murder and not your standard hit-and-run."

"The caller said Thelma tried to dodge, but the car veered in her direction."

"I see. What about the car? Your anonymous caller get the make, color, and year?"

"Nada."

"Nothing?"

"That's what I said, Yoder."

"Melvin," I said tiredly, "I don't have the energy to put up with your rudeness. My ankle hurts and—"

"Sorry, Yoder."

I was too tired to jiggle a pinkie in my ear. I had to trust that it was working. If Melvin had indeed used his least favorite word, I'd be a fool not to jump on it.

"Apology accepted."

"So does this mean you're going to investigate that, too, for me? Because I'm in the middle of a campaign here, Yoder. I can't have two unsolved mysteries on my hands."

"I didn't know bugs had hands."

Melvin must have been desperate for my help. Although he swallowed loudly several times before speaking, his voice was remarkably calm.

"Can I count on you, Yoder?"

"You can count on me," I promised, and then hung up before he could ask me to do his taxes and dirty laundry. Besides, I owed it to Thelma to track down her killer. She'd come to me for help and I'd let her down.

Ignoring Darlene's scrutinizing gaze, I hauled myself to my feet, labored over to the sink, removed a plastic basin I store beneath it, and began to prepare my foot bath. In my mind there is nothing quite as comforting as soaking your tootsies— wounded or not—in a tub of warm Epsom salts.

"Oh, Miss Yoder, you needn't do that. I signed up for the A.L.P.O. plan, remember?"

"Of course I remember, dear. I'm not planning to wash up after you, I'm planning to soak my foot."

She looked away from her sandwich for the first time. "What happened?"

"It's just a little sprain. I took an unexpected stroll."

"If it's a sprain, then you need to apply ice."

"Is that so?" I continued to fill the basin. A lesson I have learned late in life is it's possible to acknowledge advice without actually taking it.

"You'll be sorry if you apply heat first. Trust me, Miss Yoder, I work with sports injuries all the time."

"I'm sure you do." I carried the basin over to the table, sat down, and plunged both feet into the warm soothing bath. "*Aaaaaah.*"

"Well, it may feel good now, but the swelling won't go away, and that's what causes most of the pain."

I smiled pleasantly and pointed to her sandwich. "You wouldn't mind making me a smaller version of that, would you? Something about one third the size will do."

"No, of course not."

"Thanks. But wash your hands first, dear. Better yet, after you're done washing, put a couple of those zipper bags over your hands."

She gave me the oddest look, but followed my instructions and put together a fairly decent repast in no time at all. Meanwhile I soaked, and although it may not have helped the sprain any, it did wonders for my morale. Therefore, I barely minded when she began talking sports.

"Did you watch the Women's International Basketball Championship this year, Miss Yoder?"

"It wasn't held in Hernia, dear."

"I meant on TV."

"I don't watch television."

"*Never?*"

"Well," I swallowed guiltily, "I used to watch reruns of *Green Acres* on my sister's set, but they took that off the air about a year ago. Since then I haven't found anything worth watching."

"Good one!"

I struggled with a bite of salami. I buy the kind with casings, not only because it is more economical, but because it is made locally by one of our Amish, and exceptionally good. At any rate, Darlene had forgotten to remove the skin.

"Miss Yoder, do you know the names of the girls' basketball coaches at any of Hernia's high schools?"

I finally got the casing out. It was like flossing with a piece of pig gut.

"We have only one high school, dear, and it doesn't have a girls' coach. Miss Betty Quiring is the girls' physical education teacher, if that's any help."

"Quiring?"

I spelled the name for her. "But mind your Ps and Qs around her. She likes to pull ears."

"You mean she makes things up?"

"No, I meant that literally. The woman has a thumb and fore-finger like a vise. When a girl misbehaves, or even just doesn't pay attention, Miss Quiring will pull her ears." I patted my left ear. "She only had to do that to me once."

"She was your gym teacher?"

I patted my bun, which has yet to see a single gray hair. "Thank you, dear, but I'm not that young. Miss Quiring pulled my ear last Sunday in church."

Darlene giggled. "Do you have her phone number?"

Her request reminded me painfully of Gabe. "Yes, I'll give it to you in just a minute. But first, do you know if there were any calls for me, say in the last hour or so?"

She shook her head. "The others ate earlier, and then went out to play horseshoes. Then I think they took a walk. Funny, but they have this instant friend thing going—even the weird one from California. At any rate, I've been inside the whole time and haven't heard the phone ring."

"Thanks, dear." I wrote down Betty Quiring's number, with-out referring to a directory.

"Oh, you know it by heart?"

"I've had occasion to call her in the past. But it wasn't me who made all those prank phone calls between two and three in the morning. Well, not *all* of them, at any rate." What can I say, my conscience got the better of me.

"Like I said before, Miss Yoder, you're a real hoot."

I stood. My soaking water had gone stone cold.

"Well, I'm turning in for the night," I said.

"So early?"

"I like to read. Mysteries mostly. You might want to try Selma Eichler, Mignon Ballard, and Carolyn Hart. Anyway, breakfast is at eight sharp, but since you're participating in A.L.P.O., I'll expect you to report at seven-thirty to set the table."

"No problem."

I dried my feet on a dishtowel, spread it carefully across the dish drainer to dry, and toddled off to bed. I will admit now that it was a stupid thing to do. What sort of mother—and an innkeeper is just that—goes to bed when her children are still out and about? And what sort of lover—for that's how I hoped to think of myself—would fall asleep before she's had a chance to clear up a big misunderstanding?

Magdalena Yoder, that's who.

13

I slept like a teenager, rather than a baby. True, I'm as barren as the Gobi Desert and will never see a baby of my own, but from what I hear, they wake up frequently, requiring attention at both ends. But I've been a teenager, and my sister Susannah was one for almost thirty years. I know from personal experience that teenagers can sleep like hibernating bears, and that's just how I slept.

It wasn't my alarm that woke me from such a sound sleep, but Freni. She was shaking me, hard and persistently, which added to my confusion.

"Not now," I moaned, "I have a headache."

"Ach! Magdalena, how you talk!"

I struggled to a sitting position, scraping enough crust from my eyes to make a small pie. "What is it? Is the inn on fire?"

"No fire," Freni said, still shaking me. "The English are revolting."

I yawned. "*Tsk, tsk*, dear, you really shouldn't be so judgmental."

"Yah, maybe, but now is not the time for sermons. The English are revolting."

"Well, okay, if you insist on a little disparagement before breakfast, that Gingko gal and her actor boyfriend are definitely Hollywood weird, that pudgy pair of carnivores have bizarre eating habits, and—uh—oh, that basketball coach is too tall. Only the African-American couple seem normal."

"Magdalena, get your grip on yourself. I mean this literally. They are revolting downstairs."

I translated Freni's English into American Standard. "Oh! You mean they're rioting?"

"Yah. The carnations say there is not enough meat for breakfast, and the hippie wants wheat germs for her cereal. Then they argue with each other about meat and cancer and"—Freni blushed—"hormones."

"Oh, dear, and they were getting along together famously last night."

"Yah, famous! They argue about that too. The Hollywood man says he is famous, and the black lady says she has never heard of him. Then he says all cyclists are crazy, and that makes the black man mad too, and the tall one tells them all to shut up."

"She did?"

"Yah, but then the hippie calls the tall one a dike, and soon they are throwing food."

"What?" I flung back the covers, burying Freni.

"Ach!" The poor woman floundered about, turning my quilt into a huffing, puffing creature.

I snatched my chenille robe from my bedside chair while my cousin extricated herself. "They'll pay for any damages," I roared and charged from the room.

Thank heavens Freni had exaggerated. The only food flung was one biscuit, which Archibald Murray admitted having tossed at Darlene Townsend, who was sitting opposite.

"Shame, shame, shame," I said, pounding my fist on the table with each word. "Shame on all of you." Fortunately, the table is solid oak, built by my ancestor Jacob "The Strong," and has withstood generations of Yoder families. It, and Grandma Yoder's bed, were the only two pieces of furniture to survive a tornado last year.

"She started it," Dr. George Hanson said.

I glared at him down the considerable length of my nose. "And you call yourself a cyclist—I mean, a psychiatrist! You are all adults, and I expect you to act as such."

"You tell them, Miss Yoder." Pretty boy Archibald was grinning beneath his sunglasses. His teeth were so white, I would need a pair of shades of my own in order to glare at him.

"Be quiet, all of you!" I pounded so hard, the salt and pepper shakers danced. Fortunately, it was not a sin for them.

My guests grumbled into silence, like the children in my Sunday School class.

I pounded the table one more time for good measure. "Now listen up, folks. This is a respectable inn, not a den of iniquity. There won't be any arguing at this table, and the only shouting will come from me. The same thing goes for name calling. Anyone who can't follow these few simple rules of common decency is welcome to pack their bags and leave."

"Then we're out of here," Dr. George Hanson said.

I smiled at the distinguished man. "Fine. But along with the application you submitted, was an agreement explaining that due to my booking system, and the excessive demand for my services, there will be no refunds. Under any circumstances."

"Except death," Freni said.

I smiled at the stout woman at my elbow. She had managed to extricate herself from the quilt, and although her organza indoor bonnet was askew, she looked none the worse for her ordeal.

"Yes," I agreed, "except for death. And none of you look particularly dead."

Like the kids in my Sunday School class, the group grumbled some more, but when they were certain I wasn't going to budge, and that they had better make the best of things, or else have a rotten time, they settled down. Freni calmed down too and, bless her soul, bent over backward to satisfy their culinary needs. She rustled up some stale All-Bran, which she pulverized under a rolling pin and offered to Gingko as a wheat germ substitute. Finding enough breakfast meat to satisfy the Bunches was a bigger problem, until I remembered the scrapple Lodema Shrock gave Aaron and I for a wedding present a year ago, and which was still in the freezer.

Scrapple, for you English, is a mixture of corn meal and bits of meat you would feel guilty feeding your cat. And not because they are choice cuts, mind you, but odds and ends a crow wouldn't pick off the highway. Lodema has never asked for the pan back, which leads me to conclude she was given the delicacy for her wedding some twenty years earlier, and even then, it may have been secondhand.

At any rate, Freni fried the stuff until it was a crisp golden brown, and quite frankly, it smelled almost edible, if not quite delicious. The carnivores were happy to ignore the corn component, and even one or two of the more normal guests ventured a bite. As I've said before, there is no limit to the indignities a person is willing to suffer, as long as one can justify them as a cultural experience.

Peace may have been restored, although not for long. I have a very pleasant-sounding doorbell—it usually means coins for my coffer—but I am not inclined to answer it in my bathrobe. True, I was already holding court in my chenille, but my subjects were strictly B-List, if you know what I mean. I had certainly never heard of Archibald Murray before. Now Pierce Brosnan is another story. The last time he was here—

I shook myself out of my reverie. "Freni, would you be a dear and see who that is?"

Freni mumbled something in Pennsylvania Dutch but trotted off obediently, perhaps even hopefully. Although she has never seen a movie, she has cooked for more stars than Wolfgang Puck, and in her book there is no finer gentleman than Mel Gibson. She claims to be inspired by his commitment to God and family, but just between you and I, there is a bit of lusting that goes on beneath that bonnet of hers as well. Finding Mel at my door would really make Freni's day.

But it wasn't Mel who rang the bell. When Freni returned just seconds later, her arms were flapping like those of a grouse trying to decoy a fox away from its intended victim. I prayed that the fox trailing her would be Gabe the Babe. When I saw who the fox was, I prayed mightily that the prey would somehow get away.

Alas, many of my prayers seem to go unanswered. "Good morning, Lodema," I said pleasantly.

"Harumph!"

"My but that's a pretty dress you have on." The Good Lord doesn't mind a flat-out lie in the interest of peace.

"Don't try and sweet-talk me, Magdalena. I want to know what you were doing up in that buggy with Jacob Troyer."

"Ah yes, that was you who nearly wrapped a Buick around the Kreiders' mailbox. You really should keep your eyes on the road, dear."

"Maybe you should heed your own words. You were staring at that man like there was no tomorrow."

"Ach!" Freni squawked. "Magdalena!"

"I'm innocent," I wailed. "I was just hitching a ride home from Benjamin and Catherine Keim's place."

Lodema pushed horn-rim glasses back up her slippery beak of a nose. "That's a likely story," she said, her voice dripping with sarcasm. "Why would you be out at the Keims' farm?"

"That's none of your business, dear."

Lodema smirked. "Both Benjamin Keim and Jacob Troyer are married. Not that it makes a difference to *some* people."

Freni frowned. She has always been like a second mother to me, although a good deal shorter and not quite as critical as my first.

"Magdalena's sins should stay in her past," she said archly.

"Thank you, Freni." I looked triumphantly around the table, but the cocked ears of my guests indicated they would be happy to hear a litany of my sins, past, present, and future. Mindful that happy guests tip well, and ever generous to a fault, I was about to indulge the group with a few details of some of my more minor wrongdoings, perhaps even share my plans for a few future indiscretions—small ones, of course—but Lodema beat me to the punch.

"This," she said, pointing to me, "is your perfect example of a fallen woman."

I gasped. That was going too far, even for Lodema.

The gang, however, was nodding eagerly. Too eagerly. It was time to set them straight on something.

" 'For *all* have sinned,' " I said, quoting the third chapter of Romans, verse three, " 'and fallen short of the glory of God.' "

"True," Lodema conceded, "but we don't all flaunt our sins like you do."

"Just what am I flaunting now?"

"As if you don't know."

"I don't. So either enlighten me, or skeedaddle."

🍃 It was Lodema's turn to gasp. "Well!"

"A well is a deep hole in the ground. Watch that you don't fall into it on your way out."

Somebody—one of the carnivores, I think—chuckled. Lodema was not amused.

"This woman needs no encouragement," she said, wagging her right index finger at the table. With her left index finger she pushed her specs back into place. "The next thing we know she'll be dating a certain Dr. Gabriel Rosen."

"I will not!"

She turned her narrow face to me. "But it's only a matter of time, isn't it?"

I shrugged. "Maybe, maybe not. Anyway, he's single, and so am I."

"He's Jewish."

"So what?"

"He's not of our faith."

"Well, maybe not yet. Besides, Jesus was Jewish."

"He most certainly was not!"

"Of course he was. Read your Bible sometime and see."

"Jesus was a Christian," Lodema said with all the authority of a pastor's wife.

"I suppose you think he was a Mennonite too."

That gave her pause. "Well, maybe not a Mennonite, but a Baptist, like his cousin John."

"Perhaps. Or maybe he was a Catholic," I said, just to bait the bear.

"He definitely wasn't a Catholic! You won't find *that* word in the Bible."

I smiled. "You might want to go straight home, dear, and mend your sleeves."

"My sleeves?"

"You wear your prejudices on your elbows, don't you? They've worn right through your sleeves."

"You're one to talk! Everyone knows you can't stand Presbyterians."

"That's not so," I wailed. "I just don't like them married to my sister."

"We're Presbyterians," the Doctors Hanson said in unison.

I nodded. "You see? I have nothing against Presbyterians in general. I'm sure a few of them will even make it into Heaven."

"And the Amish?" Freni asked anxiously.

"Definitely."

"I'm an Episcopalian," Darlene Townsend volunteered.

"You stand a chance."

"I'm a Buddhist," Gingko said.

"One can always hope," I said kindly, "although it's never too late to convert." I turned to Lodema. "Now if you'll excuse us, the door is that way."

Lodema must have suction cups on the bottom of her shoes. Even after I got out of my chair and gave her a gentle push, she didn't budge.

"You seem awfully anxious to get rid of me, Magdalena. What is it you're trying to hide?"

"Nothing—not that it's any of your business. It just so happens I have a busy morning planned."

"Doing what?"

"Well, uh—I—"

"She's having a therapy session with me." Dr. Margaret Hanson winked.

Lodema's eyes widened to the size of poor dead Lizzie's crepes. "Therapy? What kind of therapy?"

"Psychotherapy. I'm a psychiatrist."

"Is that so?"

"It's not what you think!" I wailed. "It wasn't even my idea."

The suction cups on Lodema's shoes were replaced by wings. "Just wait until the Reverend hears about this!"

"Just *please* don't tell the Mennonite Women's Sewing Circle," I begged Lodema's retreating back.

"Yah," Freni said helpfully, "and don't tell Elspeth Miller down at the feed store. That woman has lips that could sink a boat. And Sam Yoder at the Corner Market—ach, now that man can talk! Just as much as a woman, if you ask me. Only not as much as Zelda Root down at the Police Station—"

I moaned miserably. Every woman in Hernia was going to find out about my session with Dr. Hanson. Not only was my ship going to be sunk, but my goose was going to be cooked as well. The only possible good to come of it now was if some sailor—preferably a carnivore—found my remains washed up on a desert isle and had himself a feast.

14

The idea came to me while I was brushing my teeth. I thought about it while I wrestled with my sturdy Christian underwear and put on my dress. By the time I had finished tying my sensible shoes, I knew I didn't have anything to lose, so I tucked Little Freni in her favorite cup and set about my mission.

I found Dr. Margaret Hanson waiting alone for me in the parlor. I closed the door quickly behind me.

"How badly do you want to shrink me?"

Her look of surprise quickly changed to one of amusement. "I've been looking forward to it very much. Why, have you changed your mind?"

"Not at all. But here's the deal. You do the shrinking while I drive. I thought I'd take advantage of this nice weather to show you around Hernia."

She smiled broadly. "Sounds wonderful. What's the catch?"

"The catch is we use your car."

"That's a deal."

"Really?"

"Miss Yoder, I wouldn't miss an opportunity like this for the world; a guided tour, *and* the opportunity to shrink—as you so charmingly put it—a very interesting subject."

"You think I'm interesting?"

"Exceptionally so."

I beamed. "Then let's hit the road, Doc!"

When we told Freni we were going out for a spin, she seemed both relieved and disappointed. On the one hand, the strange world of "English" psychiatry was not going to invade her beloved workplace, but on the other hand, she was missing a golden opportunity for eavesdropping.

"We will speak when you get back, yah?"

I looked at Dr. Hanson, who shook her head. "Freni, you know I can't do that," I said, but as I passed her on the way to the kitchen door, I gave her arm a meaningful squeeze.

"Tell me about yourself," Dr. Margaret Hanson said, her voice suddenly assuming a professional tone. We had just turned out of the driveway, me behind the wheel of her luxury car, she beside me with a cassette recorder in her right hand.

"It's only two miles into town, dear, so I'm going to have to speak fast." I took a deep breath. "My name is Magdalena Portulacca Yoder. I was a difficult birth. Thirty-six hours of excruciating labor, Mama said. And I was a colicky baby—never slept more than an hour at a time. And stubborn too. Mama would let me lie in my crib and cry for hours. She used to say that if there ever was a crying marathon, I would win it lungs down. Anyway, for my first birthday Mama baked me a chocolate cake with chocolate icing, and I, being the little scamp that I was, slapped the top of the cake with my hands—after the candle was removed, of course—and got icing all over Mama's new Sunday dress. I'm sure it was a Kodak moment—I was such a cute little thing—except that Mama never could get all that icing out of her dress. It was her first store-bought dress, you see, and she'd paid seventeen ninety-five for it at the Sears over in Bedford. Then just a few months later I threw up on the quilt Mama was going to donate to—"

"Any sexual issues, Miss Yoder?"

"I beg your pardon!"

"Well, in the interest of time, I thought we'd skip some of the more mundane details of your life, and get at what seems to be the core of your problem."

"It isn't sex!" I wailed.

Dr. Margaret Hanson raised a well-plucked brow. "Oh?"

"Well, it isn't! I don't even have sex, because I'm not married."

"Really?"

"You can't count the washing machine."

The other brow went up. "Indeed."

"Only during the spin cycle!" I wailed.

Dr. Hanson mumbled something into her recorder. "All right. How about religious issues? Anything particular troubling in that arena?"

"Of course not. And I hope you didn't take Lodema Schrock seriously. The woman needs a hobby—besides me."

"I see. Miss Yoder, do you feel repressed?"

"How do you mean?"

"Well, for instance, do you think your religion keeps you from doing some things you might really want to do?"

"Of course not! If I wanted to do them, I would—well, except I wouldn't drink, of course, because the Bible says that strong drink is a mocker, and I wouldn't smoke, because our bodies are temples of the Lord, and I wouldn't swear because our lips are meant to stay pure, and I wouldn't clutter up my mind with movies, and I wouldn't wear a sleeveless dress—but then again, no woman over forty should do that."

"How do you feel about women's issues?"

"Such as?"

"Women's ordination, for instance."

I sighed. Some branches of the Mennonite church do ordain women, but mine doesn't.

"I'm all for it."

"How about a woman for President?"

"Lead the way!"

"How do you feel about sex?"

"Not again," I whined. "Is that all you therapists ever think of?"

I have great peripheral vision and I could see Dr. Hanson stiffen. "Sometimes the way we feel about sex is the key to unlocking our neurosis."

"I am not neurotic, and just for the record, I have nothing

against sex—well, not if the participants are married. *Legally* married."

"I see. And if they are married, does anything go?"

"I beg your pardon?"

"Are all forms of consensual sex okay?"

"Of course not!"

"Oh? Can you give me an example of a forbidden act?"

I blushed, from my prayer cap to the tips of my stocking-covered toes. "Well, one shouldn't have sex standing up."

"Why not?"

"Because it might lead to dancing."

I'm positive I heard a stifled chortle. At any rate, the good doctor pulled out a folder—she must have been sitting on it—and held up a picture of some kind.

"What do you see in this, Miss Yoder? I'd like your initial reaction, please."

I glanced at it, my hands gripping the wheel tightly. "Buns."

She scribbled something on her pad. "And in this picture?"

"More buns."

"Male or female?"

"What?"

"Do the buns you see belong to a man or a woman?"

"They're Freni's."

"And how long have you been fixated on your cook's buttocks?"

I pounded the steering wheel, giving Little Freni a fright. She mewed pitifully.

"Cinnamon buns!" I yelled. "I see Big Freni's cinnamon buns."

Dr. Hanson looked deeply disappointed. "There is no right answer, Miss Yoder. You are free to see anything you wish in these pictures." She held up a third picture. It looked for all the world like a pair of pecan twirls. "Now what do you see in this?"

"I see the end of this session. If you'll excuse me, dear, I have more important things to do than to look at pictures of food."

Her mouth pressed into a straight line for a few seconds. When she spoke, each word was enunciated with exaggerated care.

"And what would these more important things happen to be?"

"Well, I have to solve a murder, for one thing."

"I see," she said in a tone that indicated she didn't.

I turned in my seat and flashed her a magnanimous smile. "So, Doc, what is it? What's your verdict? Am I sane?"

"Nuts."

"Why, I never!"

"They're walnuts," she said, easing up on the diction. "These are pictures of walnut shells, side by side."

"Hah! And walnuts are food, right? Besides, Freni sometimes puts walnuts in her cinnamon buns. So I *am* sane!"

Dr. Hanson nodded. "As much as the rest of use, I'm afraid. Perhaps"—she paused, and then shook her head from side to side—"even more so than some."

I tried not to gloat as we drove the rest of the way into Hernia.

North Elm is Hernia's most prestigious residential street, but it has only one stop sign. I should have remembered that. I also should have remembered just who it was who lived on one of the corners. Lord only knows how many times I've parked there.

"Good morning, Reverend Schrock," I said to the man raking grass clippings on the corner nearest the sign.

The Reverend, whom I have no quarrel with by the way, looked like he wanted to bolt. Since I am Beechy Grove Mennonite Church's single largest supporter, and since the Reverend's wife is my single most vociferous detractor, I understood his dilemma. Nonetheless I had a job to do, and if the good man did make a run for it, I'd tackle him.

"Good morning, Magdalena." He nodded at Dr. Hanson.

I made the introduction and then got down to business. "I heard about the accident here yesterday. Did you see it?"

He nodded. Now how easy was that?

"It must have been horrible," I said. I was, of course, sincere. Never mind that sympathy is a sure way to gain allies.

"It was the worst experience I've ever had," he said.

"How does this make you feel?" Dr. Hanson said.

I gave her a warning. "Reverend, would you mind describing what you saw?"

"Well, I was out here mowing when suddenly this car comes barreling down the street. Thelma Hershberger was halfway across and she started to run, but the car swerved and threw her right into the sign. There was this sickening thud—kind of like if you threw a bag of potatoes at the sign, if you know what I mean."

Not having tossed many potato bags at stop signs, I didn't know. I nodded anyway.

"And then?"

"And then I ran inside and called the emergency squad up at the hospital." Hernia is too small for a 911 dispatcher, but the squad boys are usually on top of things.

"Then you called Melvin?"

He nodded again. By the glazed look on his face, he was obviously reliving the gruesome scene.

"But you didn't identify yourself, right?"

"It was *Melvin*. He didn't ask, and then he hung up before I could tell him."

"But he did ask about the make of car, etc., right?"

"Right. But like I told Melvin, I'm not good at cars. It was big, that's all I know."

"But you didn't even remember the color?"

Reverend Schrock blushed. "I'm color blind, Magdalena."

"Get out of town!"

"I beg your pardon?"

"That's just an expression, dear. I picked it up from some English. Wow, color blind! And all these years I thought it was some secret religious code when you wore two different-color socks to church. And those ties! Doesn't Lodema help you with your clothes?"

He shook his head. "Her interests lie elsewhere."

I wanted to throw my arms around the man, to tell him that if his wife ever left him, or died, God forbid, and if I was unattached at the time, I would be more than happy to lay out his clothes. Not wanting to throw temptation in his way, I refrained.

"Speaking of Lodema, dear, where was she at the time?"

"Uh—inside."

"Are you sure?"

"Quite sure." He seemed as nervous as a hen in a den of foxes.

"You sure she wasn't tooling around in that big boat of hers?"

"Magdalena!" Dr. Hanson said sharply. "Please, the man is still in shock."

"I have a job to do," I snapped. The truth be told, I didn't really think Lodema capable of murder. Not directly. She might have caused Thelma to fling herself at the sign, but she wouldn't have hit her. Just to be on the safe side, however, I would check the front of the car the next time I saw her.

"Yes, you have your job," the Reverend said quietly.

"Look, Reverend, it's just that Lodema was out to see me this morning and she didn't even mention the hit-and-run."

"She didn't?" He looked as happy as I must have the day I walked up the aisle. Bear in mind, however, I hadn't an inkling I was about to become a bigamist.

"She harangued me about just about everything else."

"I told her not to say a word to you," he said, practically giddy. "I forbade her, in fact. Praise the Lord, she listened!"

"But she got on my case for dating a Jewish doctor—hey, what's going on? Why did you forbid her from mentioning the accident? If indeed, that's what it was."

My spiritual director shrugged silently. Believe me, on a Sunday morning he is never at a loss for words.

"Come on, Reverend Schrock, out with it!"

"B-because," he stammered, "she thought the driver was you."

"She *what*?" My blood pressure soared, and if it hadn't been for the restraining hand of Dr. Hanson, I might have shot off across the lawn in a zig-zag fashion like an untied helium-filled balloon.

"Magdalena," the Reverend said quickly, "I'm sure you know that Lodema has her issues with you and—"

"Issues!" I roared.

"Come," Dr. Hanson said in a firm voice and pulled me toward the car. She was remarkably strong for a woman her age.

"Magdalena, please don't be upset," the Reverend said. He was too embarrassed to look at me now.

"We'll see how many issues I put into the offering plate," I yelled over my shoulder.

I know. It was unfair of me to take my rage out on the messenger. But if you can't yell at your pastor with impunity, then who can you holler at? Besides, there are some days when a gal just has to let it blow.

To her credit, Dr. Hanson refrained from chiding me. In fact, when I told her the first thing I wanted to do was to find a phone, she reached into a pocket and pulled out a doohickey barely the size of one of her cherished walnuts.

"Here, use this," she said.

I gazed at the gizmo, while grazing three mailboxes and a gazebo. "It's one of those cell phones, isn't it?"

"Yes. You mean you've never used one before?"

"They're the work of the devil," I said with conviction. I've been seeing them around Hernia and Bedford for years, but had never been within touching distance. They were an evil invention, after all. In Hernia, at least, there have been more car accidents caused by chatty drivers than drunken ones.

Dr. Hanson laughed pleasantly. "Magdalena, it's only a small telephone—without wires. If you want, I'll even dial the number for you, so you don't have to take your eyes off the road."

I clipped a fourth mailbox while pondering the situation. Then because I was already feeling so much guilt that a little more wouldn't even be noticed, I told her to dial.

"Lead me not into temptation!" I wailed as she handed me the phone.

Joseph Mast picked up on the fifth ring. He sounded sleepy. "Hello?"

"Joe, this is Magdalena. Did I wake you?"

"Yeah, but it's all right. I had a bad night."

"Sorry. Look, I just have a quick question. Did Gertrude Troyer ever pay your wife a visit."

"Who?"

"She's Amish. Really mousy-looking herself, but married to a really hot—I mean, a good-looking man."

He took so long to answer, I was afraid he'd gone back to

sleep. I've been known to fall asleep in the bathroom, so I know how that goes.

"Joe, are you still there?"

"Yeah, I'm still here. I was just thinking. An Amish woman came to see her the morning she died. I was back in the shop when I saw her pull up in her buggy. I thought it was Catherine Keim at first—they were friends, you know, despite everything. Anyway, I got a closer look and it definitely wasn't Catherine. She's a real knockout, and this one, like you said, was kind of plain."

"Catherine may be exotic," I said as I swerved to miss a bantam rooster crossing the road, "but she isn't a beauty. At any rate, what did Gertrude Troyer want?"

"Beats me. My Elizabeth rarely got visitors and I wasn't going to intrude on this one."

"So you didn't speak to her at all?"

"That's right. Look, Magdalena, like I said, I had a rough night."

"Just one more thing! How long did Gertrude stay?"

"I didn't keep track. But long enough to eat craps with my Lizzie."

"I beg your pardon!"

"Craps. You know, French pancakes."

"Ah, you must mean crepes!"

"Yeah, that's what I said. They had craps and coffee together. The Amish woman brought the craps."

"Well, how nice of her." I was going to stop judging people by their looks. "Did they save any for you?"

"Yeah, one or two."

"Were they good?" Most Amish women are excellent cooks, and remarkably adventurous. It wouldn't surprise me a bit to learn that Gertrude had a stack of cookbooks. If only Lizzie had.

"I didn't taste them," Joseph said.

"Why not?"

"Because I'm diabetic. Those things were covered with powdered sugar."

"Oh. I thought maybe you couldn't resist on account of—"

"No one can cook like my Lizzie," he said defensively.

"No one," I agreed.

He hung up.

My feelings weren't hurt. Nothing was going to get me down that day. I'd been shrunk and proclaimed sane. What more could one possibly want out of life?

15

Scallop Mushroom Crepes

1 cup white wine
2 cups chicken broth
2 celery stalks, cut into chunks
3 green onions, sliced
2 bay leaves
10 peppercorns
½ pound mushrooms, sliced
2 pounds scallops, cut in half
4 tablespoons butter

5 tablespoons flour
¾ cup milk
2 egg yolks, slightly beaten
½ cup cream
1 teaspoon lemon juice
dash salt
1½ cup grated Swiss
    cheese, divided

Combine wine, broth, celery chunks, green onions, bay leaves, and peppercorns. Bring to a boil and simmer for 15 minutes. Then pour through a strainer into a 12-inch skillet. Discard vegetables. Return broth to a simmer and add mushrooms and scallops; simmer for about 7 minutes. Remove mushrooms and scallops and boil until only 1 cup remains.

In a saucepan, melt the butter and stir in the flour. Cook over medium heat for a few minutes, stirring constantly. Stir in the milk and 1 cup of broth; continue stirring until sauce boils and thickens.

In a bowl, beat the egg yolks and add mixture to the saucepan with the hot broth. Bring to a boil and then remove from heat; stir in the lemon juice and salt. Drain the scallops and mushrooms; discard the liquid. Add about half of the sauce and ¾ cup of cheese to the mushrooms and scallops to make the filling.

Fill 12 crepes with the filling; fold into desired shape and place seam side down in a large, greased baking dish. Pour remaining sauce over the crepes and sprinkle with remaining cheese. Bake at 400 degrees for about 10 minutes.

16

Dr. Hanson went in the front door, but I chose the back. Freni saw me float smugly into the kitchen. She was peeling carrots and potatoes, no doubt the beginnings of one of her world-famous stews.

"Ach, such an attitude. Are you shrunk?"

"As much as I'll ever be."

"And?"

"I'm normal!" I cried jubilantly.

"Yah? What exactly did the head doctor do?"

"She asked me a few questions about sex and religion, showed me a couple of pictures of walnuts, and that was it. I'm as sane as you and the next person—well, possibly saner than you."

"Ach! Walnuts? From this she knows you are not crazy?"

"Go figure."

"Yah, go figure. The English are a mystery." She scraped the last strip of peel from a long slender carrot and ran the root under the faucet.

"Speaking of mysteries, Freni, yesterday you intimated that those newcomers, the Hamptons, might be a good place to start if I was looking for a source for the drugs that killed Lizzie Mast. Were you basing that on hearsay, intuition, or what?"

Freni tapped her head with the vegetable peeler. "Such fancy words, Magdalena. Maybe you should ask the doctor to shrink your tongue."

"Freni!" I said sharply.

She stared for a moment behind smudged lenses and then shrugged. "Yah, I spoke too strong. Maybe my tongue should shrink too."

"Is something wrong, dear?"

She looked desperately away, found a potato, and flailed at it with the peeler. The spud had already been peeled, however, and Freni's deep strokes produced thick strips of white potato flesh, leading me to conclude that it had been an angry Amish woman in Paris who invented the French fry.

"Freni, out with it!"

She set the spud and peeler down, removed her glasses, and rubbed her eyes with her left sleeve. Then she saw me watching and turned away.

"It's Barbara," she said.

"Your daughter-in-law?"

"Ach, what other Barbara is there?"

"Well, there's Barbara Stucky, Barbara Augsberger, Barbara Stutzman, Barbara Miller, Barbara—"

"Yah, my Barbara! Ach, I mean Jonathan's Barbara!"

"Your son's wife. Who just so happens to be the mother of your grandchildren."

"Yah, but not anymore."

"What do you mean by *that*? You can't take the babies away from their mother, Freni, no matter how much you may want to."

Freni clamped a pudgy hand over her forehead, to further prevent me from reading her mind. "I would never do such a thing! It is she who takes them from me."

"How so?"

"She takes them to Iowa." Freni pronounced the four-letter word bitterly. "To their other grandmother."

I gasped. "For how long?"

Freni shrugged.

"You didn't ask?"

"Ach, maybe for three weeks. Something like that."

"That's *all*? Three measly weeks? And this has your knickers in a knot?"

"So maybe she won't bring them back."

"Is Jonathan going?"

Freni shook her head no. "Thank God, yah?"

"Yah. If Jonathan is staying here, you have absolutely nothing to worry about. He loves those kids more than I love——uh——well——"

"Money?"

I shrugged. "Whatever. How is Barbara getting to Iowa and back?"

She stabbed the air with her peeler. "Those English."

"Which English?"

"You know, the ones you just asked about, the ones who bought the Berkey farm."

"You mean the Hamptons? The man with the perfume and the old woman with the young face?"

Freni smiled. "Yah."

"How did Barbara meet them?"

"Miller's Feed Store, how else? She heard them talking about this trip they are going to take. Some place called the Big Canyon. A hole in the ground, that's all it is. And tourists drive all the way past Iowa to see it."

"*Way* past," I said. "And it's called the Grand Canyon."

"Yah, that's what I said. So, anyway, these English will take Barbara and my three little ones to Iowa on their way to see the big hole, and pick her up on the way back. You think I should trust these people, Magdalena?"

"Do you have a choice? And who knows," I said wickedly, "maybe Barbara will decide to leave the little ones with her parents and go see the big hole herself. You know how clumsy she is. With any luck she'll fall in."

"Yah? You think so?"

"Freni!"

"Ach, you lead me into temptation."

"Yes, but you come along so willingly."

Freni grabbed another carrot, and shredded it before my eyes. The guests were going to have to settle for soup instead of stew.

"But, Freni, didn't you say they might be drug dealers?"

"Ach, they're English, aren't they?"

"You can't just stereotype people like that, Freni," I sighed.

"Tell you what," I said, "I've been meaning to speak to the Hamptons anyway. Why don't I pop on over there now? I'll ask them to take really good care of your grandbabies and to make sure they bring them home on schedule."

"You would do that for me?"

"Of course, dear. And if Barbara does go with them to the Big—I mean the Grand Canyon—and stands near the edge, I'll tell them to give her a little shove."

Freni stifled a laugh with her apron. "But how will you pop, Magdalena, when you don't have a car?"

"Of course I do. It's right—oh my gracious, I completely forgot! It's still at the Keims' house."

"Yah, but maybe you can borrow one of the guests' cars."

"You can borrow mine," a male voice said just off my left shoulder.

I whirled. Archibald Murray was standing behind me, not an arm's length away. How he had managed to sneak up on me, what with my creaky kitchen floor, was beyond me.

"Goodness!" I said and clapped both hands to my bony chest, narrowly missing Little Freni. The poor mite screeched in terror, turned this way and that in her confusion, and even changed cups twice. In fact, it took her several minutes to settle down.

Archibald watched, utterly fascinated, as the contours of my meager bosom rose and fell. "Man," he finally said, "that's really something. I've heard of hearts pounding in chests before, but I've never seen anything like that. Maybe you should go see a doctor, Miss Yoder."

Freni twittered at the sink.

"That wasn't my heart, dear," I said patiently. "That's my kitten. Now, about this car you offered. . . ."

"Yeah, no problem." He tossed me the keys to his rental car. "It isn't anywhere as nice as your BMW, but it will get you where you're going." There was maybe just a hint of question to his statement.

"I'm off on an errand of mercy," I said, and winked at Freni.

She actually giggled, perhaps a first. "Tell them just a little shove."

Archibald grinned and ran tanned fingers through bleached hair. His eyes were, of course, hidden behind the ubiquitous shades, but I knew he was dying to get in on our private joke.

"You had to be there," I said, and then excused myself to call the garage.

The Berkey farm hasn't seen a plow for over a generation. Mama played there as a little girl, and often told me of the wildflower garlands she and the Berkey girls made. Then a botanist from the University of Pittsburgh "discovered" that these asters were the remnants of a species once thought to be extinct, and the farm was bought by the state. No good came from that sale. The "fair price" the Berkeys were offered (there was no option to refuse) wasn't enough to buy comparable acreage anywhere else in Bedford or Somerset Counties and the family emigrated north and west, to the area around New Wilmington. A year after their eviction the entire family was killed when a bus full of musicians skidded on a snowy road and crashed into the Berkey buggy. The very next year another botanist discovered that the Hernia asters (*dis*asters we now called them) were not a distinct species after all, but a stunted form of the common aster (*Chrysopsis mariana*). The Berkeys, it seemed, had farmed the most infertile piece of land in the county. It was a wonder they'd been able to live on it for six generations.

At any rate, the land remained fallow until last year when the state dumped it on a developer out of Pittsburgh. Create-A-Dream subdivided the hilly property into eight five-acre plots and offered the concept of "estate living." So far only one couple had coughed up the requisite dough to live the life of a country squire. Although the Hamptons, who hail originally from New York, had immediately dubbed their place Hampton Hill, and set out an attractive and expensive sign advertising the name, we locals still referred to it as the Berkey farm.

I drove Archibald's rental car up a long gravel driveway lined with newly planted maple saplings and marveled at what I saw. Ahead of me loomed a house, the likes of which Hernia had never before seen. To call the columned three-story brick structure pretentious was like calling my sister Susannah a floozy. At least in the years before she married Melvin. Susannah once dated an entire team of amateur baseball players, at the *same* time, and—well, perhaps I shouldn't be telling tales out of school. My point is that the Hamptons did not subscribe to understatement.

We Mennonites and Amish could not understand what just two people did with all that room. The English among us—Hernia has its share of Lutherans, Baptists, and even Presbyterians—were just plain jealous. If pressed, I may admit that there have been times when I have lusted in my heart, and maybe even drooled over my steering wheel while driving past the mansion.

Unfortunately for the Hamptons, bewilderment and envy are not emotions conducive to making friends. No doubt it was loneliness that drove them to seek human company among the aisles of Miller's Feed Store. For all I knew, their trip to the Grand Canyon was bogus, thought up just as an excuse to take Barbara and her babies out to Iowa.

My poised finger had yet to touch the bell button, when the massive door flew open. The suction created by this sudden action pulled me into the foyer, and I found myself sliding along a polished hardwood floor. I dug in my heels and came to a stop just inches from an authentic Roman bust atop a marble pedestal.

"Hail, Caesar," I said.

"Actually that's Nero."

I turned. Mr. Hampton was standing there, all dressed up as if he were going to church.

"Did I come at a bad time?" I asked.

"Absolutely not." He extended a manicured hand. "Cleveland Hampton here. You must be Magdalena Yoder."

"What? I am, but how did you know?"

"Everyone in Hernia knows who you are. You've been pointed out to us a number of times."

"You mean," I wailed, "my reputation precedes me?"

"We've heard only good things, I assure you."

I beamed. It was hard not to like the man. He was good-looking—he would have been downright handsome even, except for that softness that often overtakes men in their fifties as testosterone levels drop and appetites are allowed to go unchecked.

"And I've heard things about you."

"Good too, I hope?" This now was the wife who appeared in the doorway of the largest parlor I've ever seen.

"Positively," I said, and tried to cross my toes. Alas, I only succeed in giving myself a foot cramp, and had to stamp that tootsie like the counting pony at the state fair.

"Dorothy Hampton," she said, extending her hand. "Please call me Dottie."

"Please call me Magdalena." Only one person dares to call me Mags and that's my incorrigible sister.

"Of course. Won't you come in?"

I took a moment to stare before answering. Freni was right. Dottie Hampton had the face of a twenty-year-old on the body of a woman my age. No, make that a woman much older than I. But I've met enough celebrities to recognize a knife job when I see one. The woman before me had been under a blade more times than last week's Sunday roast. I daresay Dottie was familiar with lasers and chemical peels as well. Skin that smooth is commonly found on cheeks—but only on that certain pair of cheeks upon which the sun never shines (well, it ought not to, at any rate).

"Is something wrong?" Dottie asked. She nervously fingered an upswept hairdo. It was an attractive style on her, and a warm fresh brown. I'd seen that same shade on the shelves of Yoder's Corner Market.

"Nothing's wrong," I said. I peered behind her. "My, what a beautiful room."

"Thank you. I coaxed Oliver down from the city. He's such a thoughtful man. He wanted to use distressed pieces, but I said I didn't see the point, when real antiques could be so easily had in these parts. Why pretend something is old, when it's not?"

"Why, indeed."

She led me into the parlor, which she referred to as the sitting room. Cleveland followed a step behind, as if he were my equerry.

I couldn't help but admire Oliver's handiwork. It had taken a good eye to mix the dark wood furniture so common in this area with more luxurious, upholstered pieces. Some were covered in fabrics, the likes of which I had seen only in magazines.

"My grandmother had a love seat just like that," I said. "But it was covered with horse hair, and of course she didn't call it a *love* seat."

"What did she call it?" Dottie asked pleasantly.

"She called it a bench, and we were never allowed to sit on it. Granny Yoder believed the only time a person should sit was if they were too old or too sick to stand."

"How charming."

I rolled my eyes. Granny Yoder didn't sit until her ninety-third birthday. She never stood again, and in fact, died less than a month later.

"I much prefer something like that," I said and pointed to an overstuffed chair upholstered in pale yellow silk. There was a matching ottoman.

"Then please, be my guest."

I plopped my bag of bones on the cool soft chair and propped my size elevens on the cushiony stool. I'm afraid a moan of contentment may have escaped these lips. Few things have ever brought me so much pleasure, and so quickly. A warm bath, homemade fudge, lilac bouquets—not even my Kenmore— could compare to the Hamptons' armchair.

The Hamptons perched on the love seat, their faces wreathed in anxiously gracious smiles. It was clear that I was their very first visitor.

"May we offer you a drink?" Dottie asked.

"That would be nice. Thank you."

Cleveland stood. "What can I get you?"

"Oh anything. I'm not particular. Juice would be nice if you have it."

"Dottie squeezes fresh orange juice every morning. In fact, we just made a pitcher of mimosas. How does one of those sound?"

"That would be lovely." I certainly hoped the mimosa oranges were better than the Valencias I bought at Yoder's Corner Market. No doubt sophisticated folks like the Hamptons bought their oranges at Pat's IGA over in Bedford.

"Be back in a flash," Cleveland said and practically ran from the room.

"My, what a helpful husband," I couldn't help but say.

"Cleve loves to entertain. Back in the city we did a lot of that." Dottie sighed as she slumped, like a balloon losing air. "Well, there's no use looking back, is there?"

I shook my head. "Not unless going back is an option. Is it?"

"Well—uh, I suppose we could. *If* we could find a buyer for this place."

"I'm sure you'd have no trouble at all," I said, just to be kind.

She glanced around at a parlor big enough to host a Hernia High football game. "You really think so?"

"Every house is salable—at the right price. Who knows, some other city couple might come along and decide to turn it into a bed-and-breakfast."

"Really?" Dottie straightened, her voice edged with excitement. "I hadn't thought of a bed-and-breakfast. What a wonderful idea! I bet you could give us a lot of pointers. From what I understand, your business has done quite well for you."

"It's not an easy business," I wailed. "Guests are always ruining things, and you never have a moment of privacy."

"Oh, but we love company and these"—she waved at the room—"are only things. Things that can easily be replaced."

"Not this chair and ottoman. A guest might spill food on them."

She laughed gaily. "Oh, I wouldn't care. This is a wonderful idea, Magdalena."

"What's a wonderful idea?" Cleveland had returned bearing a silver tray, upon which stood three tall tumblers filled with liquid gold.

"Magdalena thinks we should turn our house into a bed-and-breakfast."

"Hey, that's a great idea!" Cleveland handed me a cold glass, gave his wife one, and held up the third. "This calls for a toast."

"To brilliant ideas," Dottie cried and took a swig of her drink. Cleveland did likewise, so I had no choice but to follow. But when that home-squeezed juice passed my lips, I nearly gagged.

17

It was all I could do to swallow. Clearly the Hamptons were used to inferior produce back in the Big Apple. Even the frozen concentrate Sam Yoder sold at the Corner Market tasted better than the orange swill in my glass.

"To generous neighbors!" Cleveland said. The poor, ignorant man seemed quite pleased with his beverage.

I was forced to take another slug of the awful stuff. It was exceedingly bitter. Either the oranges had been picked too green, or else the opposite was true, the fruit had been allowed to ripen too long and had turned. Yes, that almost certainly was it. The Hamptons, sophisticates that they were, had served me the juice of rotten oranges.

"To Magdalena!" Dottie held her glass up again.

Well, I simply had no choice but to quaff the horrible-tasting orange juice. Experience has taught me that the best way to consume a foul substance is to do it quickly. Why, even as young as age ten I could down one of Mama's cod liver oil milkshakes—given whenever I was constipated—without pausing to breathe.

I slurped the last drops loudly. I read somewhere that this is considered good manners in some island societies. Perhaps Manhattan was one of these.

"My, that was good," I said. The lie came surprisingly easy.

"Then have some more."

Before I could protest, Cleveland was back in the room with a half-filled pitcher. He filled my tumbler almost to the brim.

"Now you make a toast, Magdalena."

I felt surprisingly relaxed. "Okay, to—uh—to new neighbors and friends."

"Yes, friends," Dottie said. Although she and Cleveland took healthy sips of their drinks, they came nowhere near to draining their glasses. Never mind, I would set them a good example.

"More?" Cleveland asked.

I nodded. "Frankly, Frank, I mean Cleveland—what kind of name is that for a man from New York?"

"It was my mother's maiden name. She was related to the President."

"Bush?"

"Grover Cleveland."

"Oh. Well, at any rate, I didn't think so much of this juice of yours at first, but now it's kind of growing on me." I giggled. "Am I turning orange?"

"Cleve, I think she's had enough," Dottie said.

"Nonsense. Orange juice is full of vitamin C. You can never have too much."

"Yes, but—"

"Pour away, Cleveland!"

Cleveland poured and then set the pitcher down on a glass-covered slab of granite that passed for a coffee table.

I drank. The amazing thing about those mimosa oranges, the juice gets sweeter the more you drink.

"Mmm," I said, licking my lips, "now that really hits the pot."

"Cleve, I think she's getting tipsy."

"Topsy-turvy!" I cried.

"People will think we're a bad influence on the Mennonites and Amish."

"Ah, exactly," I said, and poked at the air with my index finger. "That's why I'm here."

"To drink mimosas?"

"To influence your badness. Do you, or do you not, sell drugs to the Amish?"

They gasped in unison. "We most certainly do *not*," one of them said.

"Yes, but do *they* sell *you* drugs?"

"Of course not!" Cleveland snatched the pitcher off the coffee table and cradled it protectively in his arms.

"I see." I waved my empty glass aloft. "To the Amish. May they all be as cute as what's his name. And speaking of cute"— I smiled at Cleveland—"you're not so bad yourself."

"Cleve, we should do something."

"Cleve—now that's from the Bible, isn't it? 'For this reason,' " I said, quoting the book of Mark, " 'a man will leave his father and mother and cleave unto this wife.' I bet you've been doing a lot of that."

"I beg your pardon?"

"Cleaving." I giggled.

"Cleveland, *do* something!"

Still holding the pitcher, Cleveland turned to me. "Coffee. I can get you coffee."

"Never touch the stuff so early in the day." I laughed at my little joke. "But you know what? You can tell me about yourselves."

"Maybe some other time," Dottie said.

"No time like the present," I said.

Dottie stood. That was definitely the body of a sixty-year-old. I told her so.

"She doesn't know what she's saying," Cleveland said.

"I do so. And I have nothing against plastic surgeons. It's the rubber ones I can't stand."

"Magdalena, we will be happy to give you a ride home."

"But I'm not through with my interrogatives."

"Your what?" Dottie asked, her voice rising.

"You know, my questions. Like have you ever taken drugs? Maybe smoked a little reed?"

"I think she means 'weed,' " Dottie said. "Cleve, we have to do *something*."

"Confess!" I cried.

"Confess to what?"

"That you sold fairy dust to the Keims, of course. It killed

Lizzie Mast, you know. That would make you murderers. Actually that would make you a murderess and Cleveland here just a plain murderer. But you're both killers!"

I stood up to make my point, but my legs were as fluid as a rubber surgeon's and I slumped to the floor in slow motion. I pretended to be a melting snowman.

"I'll grab her arms," Cleveland said, "you get her legs."

"Rock-a-bye baby in the tree tops," I sang, as they carried me out to their car.

From the depths of my meager bosom Little Freni mewed an accompaniment. I hate to say it, but I think she was the only one on key. At any rate, that was the last thing I remembered for a while.

Somebody put me to bed, and in the middle of the day! When I awoke from my nap, I was surrounded by loved, and not-so-loved, ones. I wanted to puke.

"Yoder, you are a disgrace."

I stared up at the moving mandibles of my brother-in-law Melvin. Fortunately for me, praying mantises don't eat ailing innkeepers. Or do they?

"Give me a little space, dear. I don't feel so hot."

Freni touched my forehead quickly with a pudgy little hand. "Yah, she feels cold to me."

"I'm not cold," I wailed, "I'm about to throw up."

"Way to go, sis!" Susannah said. Her eyes were shining with pride.

Melvin rudely pushed his wife aside. "Yoder, what the hell am I going to do now?"

"You'll stop swearing in my inn," I said. I tried to sit, but was hit by a wave of nausea, which mercifully subsided somewhat when my head reconnected with the pillow. Still, it was touch-and-go. I felt like I could blow anytime.

"You still don't get it, Yoder, do you? You have really screwed up big time on this one. It's bad enough that you shamed your family, but what you did just might be illegal. I have Zelda checking on that now."

"Drinking orange juice is not against the law."

"But drinking alcohol while on duty might be."

I started to roll my eyes, but even that made me dizzy. "You're crazy, Melvin. I've never had a drink in my entire life—okay, so there was that one time I tasted beer in college. But I didn't swallow!"

"Oh yeah? According to the Hamptons you drank almost half a pitcher of mimosas."

"So what's your problem?"

"Mimosas contain champagne!" Susannah chortled with glee. "Oh, Mags, I'm so proud of you. Your first drunk! Of course, it's a little late for you—I was fifteen when I first blacked out—but better late than never, right? Maybe next time we'll tie one on together."

"Ach!" Freni clapped her hands tightly over her ears. As our surrogate mother, she is genuinely concerned about our welfare and strives to keep herself informed, but because she is *only* our surrogate mother, and unofficially at that, she reserves the right to tune out whenever she is confronted with more information than she wants to know.

I struggled to a sitting position. I was now too shocked to be sick. Besides, if I did blow, I'd make sure to aim at Melvin.

"*Champagne?* There was alcoholic champagne in with the mimosa juice?"

Susannah twittered. "Don't be silly, Mags. Champagne and orange juice *is* mimosa. But they don't usually make people drunk. I guess it's because you never had anything to drink before. Next time try the orange juice with vodka. They call that a screwdriver. Half a pitcher of those and you'll really be sailing."

"But I'm innocent!" I wailed.

"Like a weasel in a hen house," Melvin growled. "Now the Hamptons know you suspect them in Lizzie's death."

"But I don't. I just wanted to sound them out. After all, they're from the city, and everyone knows that's where drugs come from. Besides, talking to them was Freni's idea."

"Ach!" Freni squawked. Covering her ears was just an excuse for selective hearing. She removed her right hand from that ear. "Did you talk to them about you-know-what, Magdalena?"

"I didn't get a chance, dear." There was nothing to be served by telling her I plum forgot.

"What did Freni mean by you-know-what?" Susannah asked. She knew from experience that there was no point in asking the woman directly.

It was a reasonable question under the circumstances, but the answer would have needlessly embarrassed Freni. A small detour from the truth was in order.

"Freni has extra eggs to sell. You want to buy some?"

"Nah. The ones I get from the grocery store have the chicken poop already washed off them."

"Well," I said, "it has been nice of everyone to be so concerned about my welfare. But now"—I yawned—"if you'll excuse me, the sandman is calling."

Freni dropped her left hand as well. "Ach, in the middle of the day? You have already missed lunch, Magdalena."

"I always sleep after a bender," Susannah said sagely. "It restores damaged brain cells."

"I wasn't on a bender! I was doing police work for your husband. Remind me next time to just let him flounder on his own."

The mantis loomed menacingly over me. "I wasn't floundering, Yoder. And if it's the big-city connection you're after, why didn't you talk to your boyfriend? Rich doctor like him packing it in to take up life in the country—sounds mighty suspicious to me."

That hiked my hackles. That made me so mad I was no longer nauseated. That in turn made me even madder, since now I couldn't hurl on my tormentor.

"Aaron—I mean Gabriel—is not a drug dealer!"

"Yeah? From what I hear, doctors get hooked on drugs all the time. From using to dealing, that's just a matter of time."

"That may be, but it has nothing to do with Gabe."

"Maybe it does, and maybe it doesn't. Maybe you're covering for him."

"Get out!" I ordered.

No one moved.

"Out!" I shrieked.

Big Freni scowled, Little Freni yowled, and Shnookums, Susannah's dinky dog, howled, but no one budged.

"Hey, Yoder, take it easy. I was just yanking your chain."

"Well, you've yanked it too far this time. If I was feeling any better—and if I wasn't a pacifist—I'd wrap that chain around your scrawny neck."

"Sweetie Pie," Susannah said meekly to her spouse, "maybe you should apologize to sis."

"In a pig's ear."

"But Sugar Lump, if you don't apologize to Mags, she might drop out of this case, and then you won't have time to work on your campaign."

"Forget it, Susannah," I said. "Too much damage has been done. You're right, I'm off the case. In fact, not only am I off the case, but I have just decided to devote all my spare time to running *against* Melvin in the election."

Susannah wears too much makeup to ever visibly pale, but Melvin turned baking soda white. For the first time that morning both eyes focused on me.

"You're kidding, Yoder, right?"

"I never kid when I'm drunk. Face it, Mel, you don't stand a chance now. I've got plenty of money for a campaign, everyone knows who I am, and unlike you, I've never had to arrest somebody's son, or brother, or cousin. You get the picture. Besides, it's the year of the woman."

Melvin's enormous noggin teetered on his knotty neck as one eye focused on Freni, the other on Susannah. "She's just kidding, right?"

Freni shook her head. "That Magdalena is a stubborn one. She would do this thing just to spike you."

Susannah nodded. "That's 'spite,' Freni, but Stud Muffins"— my sister put a long slender hand on her husband's shoulder— "I'm afraid she's right. And if she does run, Mags could win the election."

Both oversized orbs attempted contact with me, but only one eye made it. Melvin's left eye focused on my ceiling, which quite frankly was in need of a good dusting.

"Okay, so I apologize. Is that good enough for you?"

"Not hardly."

"Well, what the"—he caught himself just in time—"what is it you want, Yoder?"

"Say 'I'm sorry.' "

"I'm sorry."

"Now say it with feeling."

"I'm sorry!"

"And you'll have my car towed from the Keims' farm and re-place the three ruined tires?"

"Don't you have insurance?"

"Sure, but I don't want my premium to rise."

"Do it," Susannah urged. *"Please,* Snickerdoodle."

"My sister wants to be the First Lady someday," I said. "Don't you want to see your carapace in the Oval Office?"

"Okay, damn it, I'll do it."

"Don't swear," I said sternly, and then dismissed the motley crew again.

This time they couldn't wait to leave.

18

The first thing I did when I was alone was to get down on my knees and beg the Good Lord to forgive me for my intemperance. "But you turned the water into wine at Cana," I reminded Him. "So a little bit of champagne—which is really just a fancy kind of wine—is not so bad, is it? No, of course not, because as I recall, your mama got in on the act too. And so did your brothers. Why, that whole wedding party was just sipping away, and none of it mixed with orange juice either."

When the Good Lord didn't contradict me, I got up, brushed my teeth, and took a long shower. To be perfectly frank, I was feeling pretty darn good. I, Magdalena Portulacca Yoder, was a woman of the world. Okay, maybe not *of* the world, because that surely was a sin, but I had dipped my toe in the waters of sophistication and lived to tell about it. No lightning bolt from Heaven, no earthquake from Mama rolling over in her grave. Of course, I would never again let alcohol pass these lips—in case Reverend Schrock was right when he said Biblical wine was really just grape juice—but still, I was glad I'd had the experience.

Then, because I no longer felt guilty, I felt guilty—if you know what I mean. And forget what you may know about Catholic or even Jewish guilt—we Mennonites do it best, and I am particularly skilled in that emotion if I must say so myself.

In fact, I would venture to say that I feel more guilty during an average day than any three people in Bedford County. But just thinking about all that guilt made me guilty of the sin of pride, so I got down on my knees again and prayed for deliverance from that sin.

Finally, feeling both spiritually and physically refreshed, I decided to take a walk. That's the first thing I should have done when Melvin asked me to help solve—rather, to *solve*—the murder of Lizzie Mast, because walking clears my head. It can, however, do terrible things to the sinuses, so before stopping outside, I sprayed the inside of my generous proboscis with that green thumb thing so frequently prescribed now by allergists.

There are a number of pleasant destinations one can easily reach from the PennDutch Inn. The woods behind my place are lovely, dark, and deep, and not particularly dangerous if one stays away from the Mishler property during hunting season; the pair of elderly brothers are blind as bats and trigger happy. And if one is easily offended, one might do well to stay clear of Dinky and Flora Williams's place. This couple, transplants from Philadelphia, are Hernia's first official nudists, and believe you me, Dinky is not aptly named. In fact, I'm almost positive I saw *two* of them the last time I peeked, and I've been meaning to check a medical encyclopedia at Bedford County Library to see if that is indeed possible. At any rate, there is Slave Creek just down the road, and the town of Hernia itself. And then there is the Miller farm.

Don't ask me why, but the Miller farm has always drawn me like a magnet. I'm sure a lot of it has to do with Aaron Miller, whom I fell in love with, first as a young girl, and then as an older, but still innocent, woman. And perhaps the fact that it is now owned by Gabriel Rosen has something to do with my current obsession with the place. But I daresay, even if the place had always been owned by ugly strangers, I would still find it exceptionally beautiful.

The house, which is backed by wooded hills, is set a long way in from the road. Flanking the driveway are broad sweeps of verdant cow pasture, and the one on the right, as you face the house, is punctuated by a large pond. On the near bank of the pond is a magnificent weeping willow. In short, it would make a perfect painting.

And a perfect painting was exactly what Dr. George Hanson was creating.

"Wow, you're really good!"

He looked up grudgingly from his work. "My last six won Best of Show. I expect this one to take a blue ribbon as well."

"I'm sure it will. That pond looks so real I could jump in it right now, if it weren't for the snapping turtle you painted on that log."

No comment.

"I love the realism. So much of what you see these days looks like"—I remembered my bout of nausea—"like someone threw up a pizza and decided to call that art."

"Abstract expressionist paintings have their merit," he said crisply.

"Yes, but do the artists have talent? *You* certainly do."

He said nothing.

"You needn't be afraid of talking to me, dear. I'm not crazy. Your wife gave me the walnut shell test this morning and I passed with flying colors."

"She told me. And incidentally, we don't use the word 'crazy' in our profession."

"Well, do you believe her?"

"I believe her."

"So why are you being so aloof?"

He sighed and put his brush in a little jar of water. "Because I don't like you."

"*What?*" I was so shocked I had to sit down, and since this pasture has at times been used to actually graze cows, I chose my spot carefully.

"There's no law that says I have to like everyone I meet," he said. "I'm sure you don't like me either."

"That may be true now, but it wasn't just a few minutes ago. *Why* don't you like me?"

"Look, coming here for vacation was my wife's idea. I made it quite clear to her that I wasn't interested in visiting a culture that's so segregated."

"Segregated? What do you mean by that?"

He laughed. "Surely you're joking. Come on, Miss Yoder, how many black Amish do you know?"

I swallowed. "Well, none, but that doesn't prove anything. I mean, it's a culture as well as a religion. But anyone is welcome to join."

"I bet."

That was true, although very few outsiders have joined the faith in this century. Although believers would be welcomed in theory, they would find it very hard to live in a society where virtually everyone else is related by blood. And—this pains me to even think about it—a family of white converts would find it easier to blend in than would a family of color.

"There are lots of black Mennonites," I said defensively.

He looked around the pasture in a mocking gesture. "Where?"

"Maybe not here, but in other towns—Philadelphia, for instance—and in other states. And there are hundreds of thousands of them in Africa."

"You don't say."

"Is that a taste of my own medicine, Doctor?"

"I beg your pardon?"

"Sarcasm. Purportedly I'm quite an expert on that myself."

His smile was genuine. "I may change my mind after all."

"About?"

"Liking you."

"Don't do me any favors, Doc. The feeling may not be mutual."

"Are you always so straightforward?"

I didn't have to think about that. The answer was no. I was, in fact, rather quiet the first three decades of my life. It's not that I didn't have anything to say, it's just Mama usually said it for me, or corrected, often publicly, what I did say.

Susannah, on the other hand, was given free rein. When she told Mrs. Lehman that her coffee cake was "as dry as straw," Mama had nodded in agreement and suggested the woman add more water the next time, or use a little less flour. And when Susannah told Mr. Kreider he sang like a frog, Mama had merely smiled behind her hymnal. When, at a church picnic, my little sister informed Reverend Lantz, our then pastor, that she smelled something bad whenever he raised his arms, Mama had practically beamed with pride. Of course, the good Reverend's body odor was a major concern for the members of Beechy Grove Mennonite Church, many of whom had stopped attending just on that account. There had even been a meeting of the elders to discuss what to do about the situation. One suggestion had been to send the pastor an anonymous letter, along with a bar of soap and a tube of roll-on deodorant, suggesting he use the toiletries from time to time, perhaps on Sunday mornings. The problem was no one wanted to offend the Reverend, who was really a very kind and gentle man. Then along came my little sister and her mouth, and the next Sunday I could actually breathe in church without holding a handkerchief over my face. But you can be sure if *I* had told Reverend Lantz the very same thing, I would have had to eat the bar of soap. Maybe even the deodorant.

At any rate, in my thirty-third year two things happened to loosen my tongue. First was the death of Mama; without her to shush me, my tongue gradually began to do more than just taste. The second incident—and this is undoubtedly an outgrowth of the first—was my realization that my own life was one third over (we Yoders tend to be long-lived, tunnel accidents excepted) and I had millions of things yet to say.

"Life's too short to beat around the bush," I said to Dr. Hanson. "An old man like you should know that."

He laughed. "I'd offer you my chair, Miss Yoder, but an 'old man' like me needs to sit."

"I've already got the grass stains," I said cheerfully. "It's really not necessary."

"Tell me about yourself, Miss Yoder."

"That's Magdalena. And you're not trying to shrink me, are you?"

He laughed again. "Call me George. And no, I'm not doing my doctor thing. I have a feeling you wouldn't cooperate if I did."

"You've got that right. So, what do you want to know?"

"Are you from here? I mean, born and raised."

"You might say that. My family founded Hernia two hundred and twenty-three years ago."

He whistled. "That's a long time. I have no idea where my family was then. Maybe on a slave ship headed toward the Carolinas."

"Amish didn't own slaves," I said quickly. "That stream you may have crossed on your way here—just outside of town—is called Slave Creek. No one knows why for sure, but several historians have speculated it was named that because runaway slaves from Maryland followed it up to freedom. I'd like to think that my ancestors fed and clothed them."

"Easier on your conscience that way, huh?"

"I don't have a guilty conscience," I snapped. And then, remembering our truce, arranged my mouth in facsimile of a smile. "How about you, George? Where are you from originally?"

"Orangeburg, South Carolina."

I tried to whistle, but sounded like a teakettle with the lid half off. "You're a long way from home."

"Came up north to go to school. Harvard. Got all my degrees there. Met Dr. Hanson—I mean, Margaret, as a freshman med student. We shared a cadaver."

"How exciting."

"Actually, it was. I proposed to her over the spleen."

"You're kidding, right?"

"I'm dead serious."

"And you thought I was nuts."

"Ah, ah, ah, we don't use that word, remember?"

"I thought it was 'crazy.' "

"Same thing." George removed his brush from the water jar, and pressed the bristles carefully between two folded paper towels. "You paint, Magdalena?"

"I don't have any talent—except for making money. I do all right at that."

"I'm not surprised. You have any hobbies?"

I shrugged. "I quilt."

"Yes, yes. That big quilt I see on the frame in the dining room—did you do that?"

"Didn't you read your brochure? That quilt is there for the

benefit of customers who want to try their hand at Amish crafts. You're welcome to add a few stitches if you wish."

"But you started it, right?"

"Right." The truth be known, the quilt is there for my benefit as well. Each time one is completed, I haul it over to Lancaster County, where Amish goods sell at a premium. Selling it as authentically Amish is not dishonest, mind you, since Freni adds a stitch or two whenever she has time.

"Ever create your own designs?"

"I'm not creative," I mourned.

"I bet you are. You just haven't given yourself a chance."

"You'd lose."

We sat in companionable silence for a few minutes. While George added a second, smaller turtle to the log, and a couple of cattails to the bottom-right-hand corner, I pondered my pitiful contribution to life. No children, no works of art, no important discoveries, no cures for anything, just a silly bed-and-breakfast and enough money in my checking account to choke a goat named Amanda.

Okay, so maybe that wasn't the entire sum of my accomplishments. I did teach Sunday School, I looked after Susannah whenever she was truly in trouble—which is to say, at least once a week—and I helped Melvin solve Hernia's most difficult crime cases. In other words, nearly all of them. If I had one talent, besides the ability to make money, it was to ferret out the truth. "It takes a liar to know one," Mama used to say. Well, I most certainly am not a liar, but I have shaded the truth a few times, and from my vantage point in the dappled shade, I can usually spot a liar.

"I don't mean to brag," I said, "but I *am* a damn good private detective—pardon my language."

George's brush paused in midstroke. "Really?"

"Oh yes. Our Chief of Police Melvin Stoltzfus is a total nincompoop. He once gave his favorite aunt a gallon of ice cream."

"What's wrong with that?"

"He sent it by UPS. Anyway, Melvin needs my help more than a duck needs water."

"Doesn't he have a department?"

"This is a very small town, George. His department consists of Zelda Root, Assistant Chief of Police. Zelda is great at mediating domestic disputes, picking up dead animals and disposing of them—oh, and she hangs out at the high school whenever there's a game. But just between you and me, Zelda couldn't find her bosoms if it weren't for her bra." I giggled nervously, thinking maybe I'd overstepped the boundary of intimacy in a friendship as new as ours.

But George smiled and nodded. "I see. Well, what is it the Chief himself does?"

"Traffic tickets."

"In a little town like this?"

"We get lots of tourists, and Melvin isn't above ticketing Amish."

"Whatever for?"

"Road apples."

"I beg your pardon?"

"The product of equine elimination," I said, "if you prefer a more delicate phrase. There is a town ordinance requiring horses to wear a sort of diaper, but most of the Amish don't comply—it's just too much trouble."

"Hmm. I always thought of them as being law abiding."

"Well, they are. For the most part. One family actually upped and moved to Ontario, rather than break a law they felt was silly."

"Road apples and lovers' quarrels. It doesn't sound like you get to exercise your detecting skills very often."

"Oh, but I do. There have been more murders here than you might think. Kidnapping too. And now I'm working on a drug case."

George put the brush back in water and folded his hands over the barest suggestion of a paunch. "You don't say."

"Actually it's a murder slash drug case."

"You're kidding, aren't you?"

"I wish I was. The victim was a middle-aged Mennonite housewife. The coroner says she died of—"

He held up a hand. "Magdalena, should you be telling me all this?"

"Actually, I was hoping maybe you could help."

"*Me?*"

I could tell that he was offended. "It has nothing to do with your race, or the fact that you come from a big city. I was hoping for your professional opinion."

"As a psychiatrist?"

"Yes."

He sighed. "But I'm retired. You should be talking to my wife. For a fee."

"Well!" It was my turn to be offended.

"Sorry. I couldn't resist it. So, what is it you want to know?"

"How can you tell if someone is crazy—I mean, has parted company with reality."

He chuckled. "Now that's a good way of putting it. But you're right, it is sometimes difficult to tell."

"You and your wife seemed pretty certain that I was cra—uh, had parted, so to speak."

George grimaced. "Touché. You did seem a bit stressed. At first. But it has since become quite clear that you function well within the parameters of what appears to be normal in this community. Although I still say a cat in one's cleavage is pushing the envelope."

I grinned. Little Freni had chosen that very moment to stretch, turn, and resettle herself in my right cup. I'm sure all that movement appeared odd when viewed from outside my dress.

"She's only a little kitten. When she gets over two pounds, then out she goes. So anyway, how *can* you be sure someone has genuinely slipped over the line, or if they're just faking it?"

He nodded. "Ah, your cook. Trust me on this one. Both Margaret and I—"

"I'm not talking about Freni," I wailed. "I'm talking about him!"

"Who?"

"*Him!*" I pointed to the man approaching us from the direction of Hertzler Road.

19

George removed his glasses, rubbed his eyes, and put his glasses back on. "I still don't see anyone."

"That's because he's wearing a camouflage suit and is crawling along on his belly."

George repeated the ritual just to be polite. This time, however, he did see something. He stood for a better look.

"A fat little man with red hair?"

"Joseph Mast. And he's not so much fat, as husky. He's a carpenter by trade."

"*Why* is he doing that?" Hernia was turning out to be a rich source of material, should George ever decide to publish a textbook on nut—I mean, parted-from-reality cases.

"He thinks he's in Vietnam. No doubt he's trying to avoid detection from the Viet Cong."

"Is he a friend of yours?"

"He's my prime suspect in the drug/murder case. My only suspect, in fact. Say, you don't see a goat with him, do you?"

"You mean the one in the pink dress and high heels?"

"Very funny. But I'm warning you, if one does show up, just butt it on the head."

"With what?"

"Your head, of course."

George groaned, but mercifully kept any other comments to

himself. We watched in silence as Joseph wiggled his way across the pasture toward us. He didn't come in a straight line, but following the logic of his damaged—or supposedly damaged—mind, took advantage of grass clumps, almost infinitesimal changes in elevation, even old dried clumps of cow manure.

Finally Joseph got close enough to risk speaking in a loud whisper. "Magdalena, you all right?"

"I'm fine, dear."

"Who is that with you?"

"Colonel Sanders."

"V.C.?" His eyes behind the round rimless lenses were dull, and he seemed to be looking right past me. Or maybe just inside his head.

"AC/DC," I said and winked at George.

"It isn't funny," George said sternly, albeit in a whisper. "Mental illness is not a laughing matter."

I blushed with shame. "Sorry. Joe," I said in a normal speaking voice, "this is one of the guests at my inn. He's a—"

"My name is George Hanson." George stuck his hand out, but poor Joseph remained prone.

"How are Amanda and Benedict?" I asked. I wasn't mocking him, just trying to be friendly.

That triggered something. The lights came on in Joe's head and he stood. Bits of grass and cow dung clung to his clothing, perfecting the camouflage.

"They're fine. Benedict can't stop saying your name."

"Is he still being rude?"

"He's only a parrot, Magdalena. He doesn't know what he's saying."

"Yeah, right." I reintroduced George, but taking a cue from him, did not divulge his profession. "So what brings you out to see me?" I asked when the pleasantries were done.

Joe rolled his eyes a quarter turn, indicating George.

"A walk?" I said brightly. "You want to take a walk?"

Joe looked around desperately. "Where?"

George touched me lightly on the shoulder. "I could use a walk," he said. "Been painting too long."

"You sure?"

"Call of nature. You think it would be all right to leave my stuff here?"

"We don't lock our doors in Hernia, dear."

Joe waited until George was presumably out of earshot. "My Lizzie died from an overdose of Angel Dust."

"Yes, I know that. Melvin told me."

"There's your connection."

"I beg your pardon?"

"The Keim boys."

"Oh Joe, please not that again."

"They use drugs."

"Really?" I could only hope that the sarcasm dripping from that word wouldn't stain my shoes.

He nodded. "I followed them last night. They met up with a bunch of other kids—maybe twenty in all. They were smoking and drinking pretty heavily, and then about an hour after that someone brought out a little brown bag, and they got into the really hard stuff."

"Angel Dust?"

He shrugged. "I only smoked weed in Nam. I don't know what all they were doing, but it wasted a couple of them."

"Killed them?" I asked in alarm. He was remarkably convincing.

"No, not that kind of wasted. I mean really strung-out. You know, *high*."

"Oh. How could you tell?" I have often suspected that guests at my inn—particularly the Hollywood crowd—were on something besides aspirin, but had no way of confirming my suspicions. Susannah only drinks, and usually has the good sense to stay well away when she does.

"Well, they started acting crazy." He didn't seem at all embarrassed by the word.

"Please elaborate, dear."

"One of them thought he was the devil. He was jumping around trying to catch the others. Then one girl said she was you and—"

"She most certainly did not!"

"But she did. Magdalena Yoder is what she said. Of course

there are other Magdalena Yoders in the county, so maybe she meant someone else."

"You bet your bippy."

"Anyway, this really scared some of the other kids and they left. But the girl who said she was—uh, Magdalena, and the boy who said he was Satan, they hung around. So did the oldest Keim boy. You know, the dark one. Then the other boy and girl got all quiet, like they were asleep or something, and the Keim boy tried to wake them up, but had a real hard time of it. Finally, he got them on their feet and they all left. That's when I left too. Well, a few minutes later, of course, so they wouldn't see me."

"Of course." I prayed for a charitable tongue, but feeling no difference in my mouth, decided to take my chances. "And where did this all happen, Joe? Out among the haystacks?"

He gave me a pitying look. "Of course not. It happened in a barn."

I sighed. "Benjamin and Catherine might turn a blind eye now and then, but they're not ostriches."

"Actually, Magdalena, ostriches don't bury their heads in the sand. You see, their heads are very small in proportion to their bodies, and when they peck at the ground to eat, or turn their eggs, it only appears as if their heads are buried."

"Thanks for the nature lesson, dear. But you know what I mean. It is preposterous to think the elder Keims wouldn't stop such a thing from going on in their barn."

"Oh, it wasn't their barn."

"Then whose was it?"

"Nobody's."

"Figures."

"But it used to be the Berkey barn. You know, out there where Create-A-Dream is selling those estates?"

I gasped. "Not a half mile away from where that English couple, the Hamptons, have carved out their little kingdom?"

"You know them?"

"We've met. Joe, do you think the Hamptons are involved?"

His thick shoulders twitched. "Who knows? They weren't there, of course, or I would have mentioned it."

It was amazing, but I totally believed Joe now. Which is not to say that I didn't still think he had problems. But then again, don't we all?

"Okay, Joe, so Elam Keim and some of his cronies are doing drugs in an old abandoned barn." I smiled kindly. "How does this relate to Lizzie?"

It was a definite shrug this time. "I don't know. But it's got to somehow. Next-door neighbor kids taking drugs, and that's how Lizzie dies. You now, she never even had as much as a sip of wine her entire life."

"Temperance is not all it's cracked up to be," I wailed.

"What?"

"Never mind, dear. Do you think those kids will be back there tonight?"

"Don't know. That would be your job to find out, right?"

"Right."

He looked around, suddenly nervous. "Well, got to go."

"So soon? And we were just getting along. Can't you stay long enough to get better acquainted with George when he gets back from his potty break?"

Joe's response was to drop to his belly and begin the long, slow process of scuttling back across the cow pasture. He never looked back.

George was obviously not in any hurry to get back. I sat in his chair, in the shade of the willow, waiting patiently to talk to him about Joe. Then I waited impatiently. Finally boredom forced me to pick up one of his brushes, squeeze a bit of brown pigment from a half-rolled tube, and paint the outline of a third turtle on the log. Then, still bored, I took another brush and hid my name in green among the cattails.

By then it was time to boogie on out of there, so I skipped across the remaining pasture to Gabe's. While skipping may sound like an odd choice of locomotion for a woman in her middle years, it is nonetheless a very good form of aerobic exercise. When I knocked on Gabriel Rosen's front door, I was breathing rather hard.

"Calm yourself," he said with a grin. "I know I have that effect on women, but I thought it was lost on you."

I choked back my gut response. What wasn't lost on me was the fact that Gabe was wearing only cutoff denim shorts. *Short shorts* that displayed strong, well-toned thighs. I had never seen his naked torso before—well, not during waking moments—and was, to put it frankly, pleased at what I saw. He was muscular, without being bulky, and he had a patch of dark hair in the middle of his golden chest that ran like a funnel down to his waistband. As far as I could see, he had no more hair on his back than did I.

"Anything wrong, Magdalena?"

"Nothing," I squeaked.

"Come in." He ushered me in, and as I squeezed past him, his smell made me every bit as heady as the Hamptons' champagne. It was times like that when I wished I were a Roman Catholic. Without someone to confess my lust to, guilt was going to stay with me a long, long time.

"Have a seat," he said. He didn't seem at all upset with me for standing him up the previous evening. Maybe he had a very generous, forgiving spirit, or maybe he just didn't care.

I sat on one end of a buttery soft, black leather couch. Gabe sat on the other.

"So what have you been up to?" I asked.

He picked up a book, which had been lying facedown, spine bent, on the heavy wood coffee table in front of us. "I've been reading this most fascinating memoir by a woman named Ramat Sreym, which I bought, by the way, at Yoder's Corner Market. Anyway, Ramat's parents were missionaries to the Belgian Congo, one of the most remote places on the face of the earth. She was also a well-known mystery writer, but it took her years to find a publisher willing to publish this book."

"Why?"

He shrugged and his chest muscles rippled. "Who knows? The publishing industry doesn't make a whole lot of sense to me. Ramat's memoirs are every bit as riveting as *Angela's Ashes*. In the end she had to resort to asking her fans to write her mystery publisher and request the memoirs. Of course she couldn't do this directly, so she made a veiled reference to it in one of her books." He put the book back on the table. "So, what have you been up to?"

"Me? Well, you know, business as usual."

He nodded. "So how did your errand go last night?"

"What?" I prayed that he had selective amnesia. If my prayer was answered, he wouldn't remember the hours spent awaiting for me atop Stucky Ridge.

"You were in a hurry to get someplace yesterday afternoon. Everything go all right?"

"I'm sorry," I wailed. "I tried to get there, I really did. But who knew I would have three flat tires in an Amish driveway?"

He put up a quieting hand. "Look, I'm not blaming you. In fact, I should be blaming myself. *You* should be blaming me."

"Whatever for?"

His warm brown eyes left my face and focused on Miss Sreym's book jacket. "Well, because I was a no-show myself."

"*What?*"

He grinned and ran long fingers through thick black hair. "I got kind of caught up in the book *I'm* writing. It was the final scene, you know, where everything gets tied up neatly in a little package. Anyway, when I looked at the clock, it was already a quarter past eight. I know I should have called, Magdalena, but I was just too chicken."

"Well!" I said with righteous indignation.

He looked back at me, his eyes now dancing with merriment. "Well, indeed. So why didn't you call?"

"Because—well, because—" I grabbed the book off the coffee table. "*Where Jackals Sing.* That's certainly an intriguing title. So it's a good one, eh?"

"The best. But don't try and change the subject."

"Okay," I wailed, "I was chicken too. And mad. I thought you didn't care."

He laughed. "So we're a pair of chickens."

"I guess so."

"You want to try again?"

I blinked. "Try what?"

"This date thing. Our picnic."

My heart pounded. It hadn't beat that hard since the day I

found Sarah Weaver in a barrel of sauerkraut—and she'd been dead twenty years.

"Sure," I said through lips as dry as Mrs. Lehman's coffee cakes. "Tonight?"

"I can't," I said miserably. "I already have plans."

Gabe's beautiful brow creased with the merest suggestion of a frown. "My, aren't we fickle."

"It's not a date," I wailed. "I have to spy on a barn full of Amish teenagers."

"Always ready with a joke, Magdalena. I don't know how you do it."

"I'm not joking!"

"What is this? Some sort of chaperone thing?"

I sighed. "Okay, if you must know, I'm investigating the death of Lizzie Mast."

"Amish teenagers killed her? Rumor has it she died of an overdose of phencyclidine."

"Rumor?" I said, startled.

"This is a small town, Magdalena. A *very* small town. Fewer people live here than on my block in Manhattan. Maybe even fewer than in my apartment building. Five minutes down at Yoder's Corner Market or Miller's Feed Store and you get enough information to fill the *Times*."

I swallowed hard, praying that it wouldn't be my lips to sink the ship, in the event that it sank. "But nothing about Amish teenagers, right?"

"Nothing about Amish teenagers and drugs. But this rumschpringe thing. That seems to be the main subject of conversation. It seems to be getting out of hand."

"You know what that means?"

He nodded. "I have a good idea from the context in which it was used. My grandparents lived with us when I was a little boy, and they spoke only Yiddish. It's remarkably similar to Pennsylvania Dutch. I can understand about three words out of four."

That made me just a mite envious. My grandparents, with whom we lived, had spoken only Pennsylvania Dutch at home, but I had studiously ignored them—well, as much as I could. Granny Yoder had been impossible to ignore. Even after death she's made a couple of appearances back at the PennDutch Inn, which wasn't an inn in her time, but *her* domain. Anyway, after Granny died, our conversations were always in English, for my sake as well as Susannah's. But I can't tell you how many times I've regretted losing that integral part of my heritage. I can still understand some "Dutch," but apparently not as much as my Jewish doctor friend from New York City. Go figure, as he would say.

I sighed. "If my source can be trusted, rumschpringe has definitely got out of hand. The kids are supposedly using drugs."

"Moonshine? That kind of thing?"

I shook my head.

"Not phencyclidine!"

"*That* I don't know. But apparently they were aphrodisiacs."

He grinned broadly. "You don't say? One doesn't normally think of a bunch of teenagers needing sexual stimulants."

"*What?*"

"You did say aphrodisiacs, didn't you?"

"Psychedelics!" I wailed. "They were imagining themselves to be devils and such."

"Ah, well, now that makes sense. So just what are you going to do, Magdalena? Peek through the barn slats and watch them freak out?"

"Something like that."

"Then what? Are you going to arrest them?"

"I don't have the authority," I said. "But I will eventually report it to Melvin. In the meantime I'm going to try and find the connection between Lizzie's death and these kids. Assuming what I've heard about these kids is true."

"Who is your source, Magdalena?"

I hesitated for a few seconds. Why did I feel more comfortable confiding in George Hanson, a complete stranger, than in Gabe? It didn't make a lick of sense.

"Joseph Mast," I said reluctantly. "Lizzie's widower."

One of Gabe's dark brows lifted. "You think 'Mr. Noah' could be telling the truth?"

"Mr. Noah?"

"That's what they call him down at the feed store."

That angered me. I'm a lifelong resident of Hernia, and I keep an ear to the ground, and sometimes to a glass pressed against a wall, and I hadn't, until yesterday, known just how disturbed Joe Mast really was. How was it that some big-city outsider, who had only been in town a few months, knew more about my town and my people than did I? It couldn't have been just the language bit either. Gabe the Babe had to be the most inquisitive man this side of the Delaware.

"Joseph Mast," I said emphatically, "is at times very coherent. In my professional opinion this lead needs following."

"Then I'm coming with you."

"No, you're not."

"The hell you say. I'm not going to let something potentially horrible happen to you. Kids on drugs can be extremely dangerous."

I stood. "First of all, I'll thank you not to swear in front of me. And second, I may be just a simple Mennonite woman from a nowhere town with a somewhat bizarre, if not appropriate, name, but I have had a lot more experience dealing with criminal types than you."

His grin looked mocking to me. "I bet you have. Look, I'm just trying to protect you."

"Bet all you want, buster, but I don't need your protection. And I'll thank you to forget we ever had this conversation."

"But Magdalena—"

I ignored him and walked resolutely toward the door. He jumped to his feet and followed me.

"What about the book? Don't you want to borrow Ramat Sreym's memoirs?"

"I have work to do."

"Okay, so what about our picnic? I know tonight won't do, but what about tomorrow evening?"

"Maybe," I said over my shoulder, "or maybe not. I'll tell Freni my answer, and then you run down to Miller's Feed Store, or Yoder's Corner Market, and see how long it takes you to get the scoop."

"Magdalena, don't be childish."

I sailed out of there on the wings of pride. Unfortunately pride has rather flimsy wings, and, as the Bible warns us, is often accompanied by a nasty fall.

20

Italian Crepes

Filling

1 cup ricotta cheese
2 tablespoons grated Parmesan cheese
⅛ teaspoon salt
⅛ teaspoon pepper
¾ teaspoon crushed oregano

Sauce

2 tablespoons butter
2 teaspoons flour
1 cup tomato sauce

Filling: Combine all ingredients and mix well. Spoon mixture onto crepes and fold into triangles. Place in a baking dish and top with the sauce. Fills 8 crepes.

Sauce: Combine butter and flour in a small saucepan, cooking and stirring until smooth, about 30 seconds. Add the tomato sauce and cook for 5 more minutes. Spoon over crepes, then broil until brown.

21

I didn't fall until I got home, and for some inexplicable reason I tripped on the sill of the kitchen door. I may be tall and skinny, but that's not the advantage you may think it is. I didn't fall straight down, but shot forward like an arrow, my Yoder nose leading the way.

"Ach!" Freni squawked as I plowed headfirst into her soft middle.

I scrambled to my feet. "Sorry, dear. Are you all right?"

"For shame, Magdalena. You said this drinking was a one-time thing."

"It was! I'm just clumsy."

Freni stood on tiptoes and sniffed my breath anxiously. "Magdalena!"

"I didn't drink anything," I wailed.

"Yah, maybe. But I smell a man's perfume."

"You *do*?" I grabbed my collar and tried to smell it, but alas I smelled only myself. There was not a trace of Gabe. And why should there be? The man hadn't even touched me.

But Freni was nodding. "You have been to see Dr. Rosen, yah?"

"Maybe. But so what if I have? You like him, and you know it."

"Yah, that is so. But what would your mama say?"

"*Mama?* What does she have to do with this? She's been dead for twelve years, for crying out loud."

Freni looked away, just as I thought I saw a tear glistening behind one lens. "She would remind you about the horse and the donkey, and not to tie them together."

"I haven't tied a horse and a donkey together in all my born days, and I'm not about to start now. But just for the record, did Mama tie animals together on a regular basis?"

"Ach, you make fun!"

"And you're not making any sense, dear."

"The Bible," Freni said, and thumped the kitchen table like a preacher with tiny fists. "It's in there."

"What is?" I asked with the patience of Job.

Freni recited a passage of scripture in High German, the language in which she reads her Bible.

"That's Greek to me," I said facetiously.

"But this tying of the animals—to pull the plow—they must be the same."

Then it dawned on me. She was referring, of course, to the passage in 2 Corinthians in which Paul exhorts his fellow Christians not to be yoked together with unbelievers. The verse says nothing about horses or donkeys, but Freni had been unable to translate "yoke" into English. Of course this hadn't stopped her from trying to interfere in my personal life.

"Not to worry, Freni dear. Gabe and I are nowhere near getting tied together like a horse and donkey. Neither of us has mentioned marriage. In fact, we haven't even been on a single real date. We're just friends."

Freni breathed a sigh of relief and wiped the corner of her eye with her apron. If you ask me, she didn't deserve to be let off the hook that easily.

"You sound just like Lodema Schrock," I said wickedly. "The two of you been putting your heads together lately?"

"Ach!"

"Now there's a matched set. The question is, are you both horses, or are you both asses?"

Before a shocked Freni could respond, the door to the dining room swung open and in flitted Gingko Murray. The waif was wearing a yellow sundress scalloped with white lace, and her long dark hair had been woven into a single braid that was studded with dandelions. Her tiny feet were clad in white plastic sandals and there were more dandelions tucked in the various slots. I suppose the picture the pixie created might be considered attractive by some, but I was annoyed.

"If you'll excuse me, dear, I'm having a private conversation."

"This is important, Miss Yoder."

"But so are good manners, dear. Now go back out and try knocking."

She flounced impatiently to the door, and the second it stopped swinging, she knocked.

"Who is it?" I called pleasantly.

"It's me."

"Me who?"

"You know. Gingko."

"I'm busy, Miss Biloba. You'll have to try me later."

"Later when? And the name's Murray, not Biloba. Gingko Murray."

"Right. Uh, I think I still have a few minutes available Thursday afternoon. How about between four and four-eleven? That suit you, Ginger?"

She pushed her way back in again. "Now who's being rude?" she demanded.

I slapped a hand to my breast in mock astonishment. "Well, certainly not me."

Freni nodded. "Yah, but you are, Magdalena. So maybe you won't listen to your mama, or to me, but what would your friend Gabe say if he knew you were rude to the English?"

"I am anything but rude." I grabbed one of Gingko's slender wrists. "You want to talk? We'll talk." I pulled her to the door. "And just to show you that I am a generous and considerate hostess"—I grabbed a wicker basket from the counter beside the door—"I'm going to let you help me gather eggs."

Gingko's eyes widened to the size of omelets. "Really?"

"Really."

She trotted eagerly behind me to the hen house.

"That one," I said, pointing to my favorite hen, "is Pertelote. No one touches her eggs but me. But that big one there"—I indicated a Rhode Island red—"is Mandy. You get to collect her egg."

Gingko grinned. "Awesome. How do I do it?"

"It's really quite simple. You lift her with one hand, and take the eggs with the other."

"Does Mandy bite?"

"Hens don't bite, dear, they peck. Now go on."

Gingko was stubborn girl. "Does Mandy peck?"

Alas. Lying then would have been every bit as much a sin as King David sending Uriah out to battle so he could sleep with Bathsheba. Not that I had designs on sleeping with Mandy, mind you, but you get my point. Despite her pretty looks, Mandy is as mean as a junkyard dog and would just as soon peck you as eat. For weeks I'd been threatening to send her to the stew pot. In fact, the last couple of days I hadn't even bothered to collect from her.

"All hens peck, dear," I said peevishly.

Perhaps Gingko didn't hear me. She glided over to the row of wooden nesting boxes and began cooing in her high-pitched childlike voice.

"They're not pigeons, dear."

"*Oooooo.* You're just the sweetest little thing."

Rhode Island reds are not little. If they got any larger, you could saddle them, and only a hungry fox would find them cute. But Mandy didn't seem to mind Gingko's silly observation. She sat there just as calmly as could be.

"Maybe she's dead," I said hopefully. While I certainly wouldn't eat a hen that had expired from natural causes, for the chubby carnivores, Keith and Honey Bunch, she might be just the ticket.

"Don't be rude, Miss Yoder, she can hear you."

"So?"

"You'll hurt her feelings."

"She's a chicken, for crying out loud! She doesn't have feelings."

Gingko gasped softly. "Every living creature has feelings."

"Some feelings! Chickens are cannibals, you know. We ate her mother, Elizabeth, Sunday before last, and when we threw the viscera into the chicken yard, Mandy ate more than her share."

"You *ate* Mandy's mother?"

"She was a mite tough, but we stewed her for dumplings."

Gingko had turned the color of chicken droppings and she was shaking like an aspen. "It just so happens that Mandy and I were friends in a past life."

"*You* were a chicken?"

"Of course not. I was Cleopatra and Mandy was Ahmontut, my wine taster."

"So how did she end up as chicken?"

"Ahmontut was a *he*, not a she. Miss Yoder, do you want to hear this story or not?"

"Do tell." My eyes were rolling like pinwheels in a stiff breeze.

I gathered while Gingko gabbed. "Well," she said and, to my utter amazement, actually picked up mean old Mandy and cradled her in alabaster arms, "Ahmontut sold me out to that horrible brother of mine, and was about to let me be poisoned, when there was a mix-up of wines, thanks to an addled old slave, and Ahmontut drank from the wrong cup." She sighed as she gently fingered Mandy's comb. "I've had five lives since then, but this is Ahmontut's first reincarnation. Anyway, he—I mean she—is very sorry about what happened."

"Certainly one of us is." I tried not to yawn. Hen houses are not the most hygienic of environments, and I didn't want a mite-infested feather floating into my gaping maw.

"You don't believe me, do you?"

"It is not my place to pass judgment, dear. Now grab those three eggs while you have a chance. I've already collected from ten hens, and you have yet to get a single egg in your basket."

"Miss Yoder, please reconsider. Mandy really wants to hatch some chicks. She's convinced that being a good mother is the only way she can work herself up to the next level."

"No offense, Miss Biloba, but that's utter nonsense."

"Please, Miss Yoder. Mandy promises to be good from now

on. She'll never peck at you again, if you let her raise this one batch."

"That's clutch, dear."

"Please."

I sighed. "Okay. I've been needing some new young layers anyway—although normally Pertelote gets the honors. But if she pecks at me even once after this, she's fricassee."

Gingko murmured something into Mandy's ear hole—chickens don't have external ears, by the way—and then turned her face to me and smiled. "You've got a deal, Miss Yoder."

I collected the last egg from Abigail, a hen with very little personality. Surely in her past life she had been nothing more than a mushroom.

"Okay, dear, we're all done here. Put the hen back, and let's get going."

"Don't you want to hear what it is I wanted to speak to you about?"

Frankly, I had quite forgotten what I was doing in a chicken coop in the middle of the day. Egg gathering is something I generally do in the evening.

"I'm all ears, dear," I said, and chuckled.

Gingko put Mandy gently back into the next box and straightened. She spoke to me as she brushed chicken poop from her cheerful yellow skirt.

"I had another vision involving you."

"Did it have to do with my next life? I want to come back as Prince William's oldest daughter. I want to be the Queen of England in my own right." I was, of course, just pulling her leg. I don't believe in reincarnation. We are born once, saved once, and that's all there is to it. If that were not the case, things could get mighty confusing for the Almighty. What would happen at the rapture, for instance, if I was a rooster? Then who would get my mansion in the sky?

"It had to do with this life, Miss Yoder. Actually it had to do with your death."

22

I sucked in enough feathers to stuff a pillow. "*My* death?"

She nodded vigorously. "I was washing my face, you see—water is a powerful transmitter—when I saw you, lying dead in a cave."

I laughed with relief. "Well, then it wasn't me! I don't do caves—not since a school picnic in the sixth grade. We went up to some state park and there was a little cave there, and Jimmy Blough convinced me to play Huck Finn and Indian Joe. I forget who was supposed to be who, but as soon as we got back far enough in the cave that it got dark, Jimmy Blough kissed me and tried to make me touch his—well, let's just say, when we visited the Bedford fire department the next week, he still wasn't able to slide down the pole."

Her large green eyes regarded me earnestly. "What I have to say is serious, Miss Yoder. In my vision you weren't playing post office, you were dead. I hate to have to tell you this, but I've had these death visions six times before, and every time but one, they've come true. In fact, I was having a vision that John Lennon died the very moment the announcer came on the radio to say he'd been shot."

"But that's impossible. You probably weren't even born then. At best, you would have been only a little girl."

"I was seven."

"Seven years old?" I asked in surprise. "As old as that?"

"Seven months."

I bit my tongue. It has been pierced so many times that I can no longer effectively lick an ice cream cone. Indeed, if I could stand the heat, my tongue would make an excellent pasta strainer.

"Miss Yoder, you *must* listen to me. You're in great danger."

I set my basket of eggs on the straw-strewn floor. "Okay, let's just pretend for a minute that your visions really mean something."

"They do!"

"Please, dear, I'm being very generous as it is. Now back to what I was about to say: *If* what you saw in your vision comes true, how will I die? Surely I won't be groped to death." I chuckled pleasantly.

She tossed her head and the dandelion-studded braid whipped across her back, knocking off a flower or two. Clearly we did not share the same sense of humor.

"I heard an explosion," she said. "The walls of the cave came tumbling in. Maybe you were crushed to death."

The sound of clucking chickens in the yard alerted me to the fact that we had visitors. Either that, or several of the hens needed to come in and lay. If the latter were true, the poor dears were just going to have to hold their eggs in, because I wasn't quite through with the psychic nymph.

"Maybe?" I asked. "That's all you can say?"

"I told you before, Miss Yoder, that my visions are more like impressions than photographs."

"So you did. But now—still pretending, of course—you said that one of your six death visions did not come true. Why was that?"

She shrugged, losing a few more blossoms. "I don't know. Maybe it's because it was my own death I saw. It could even be a past death I don't consciously remember."

"Good excuse," I mumbled just as the chubby carnivores, Keith and Honey Bunch, pushed their way through the narrow opening of the coop. Once inside they fluffed out to twice their doorway volume.

"Oh my," Honey gasped when she saw me standing next to

the basket. "You've already gathered the eggs." She sounded genuinely disappointed.

"Miss Yoder," Keith said, "we paid extra for the privilege, remember?"

"So you did. I'd quite forgotten. Tell you what, for just a one-time fee of fifty dollars, I'll let the two of you rake up this old straw and pile it behind the barn. There's already a pile there which you need to first spread around in the garden. Make sure to get between the rows of green beans. I've been having a lot of problems with weeds there this year."

"Wouldn't it be simpler to just take this straw straight to the garden?" Gingko asked. No doubt about it, she wanted to show me up in front of the Bunches.

I gave the clever little clairvoyant a smug smile. "Chicken manure is very strong, dear. If they put this stuff on the garden, it would burn those beans right to the ground."

"Oh," was all she could say.

I smiled graciously at Mr. and Mrs. Claus. "Well, just don't stand there, dears. The rakes are in the tool shed next to the barn, and so is the wheelbarrow. If you look around, you may find some old gloves as well."

The cuddly carnivores thanked me profusely, squeezed back through the narrow door, and out into the chicken yard. The chickens clucked louder than ever. That should have tipped me off, I guess, but it didn't. I will admit to jumping practically out of my brogans when the giantess from Philadelphia stepped into the hen house.

"Miss Townsend!" I gasped.

"There you are, Miss Yoder."

"As big as life and twice as ugly," I said and then immediately regretted my remark. Darlene Townsend *was* bigger than life, and had to stoop inside the coop. And while she may not have been ugly, a face that large needs a nose at least as big as mine to punctuate the landscape.

"Miss Yoder"—she frowned, apparently just noticing the Hollywood wisp—"what are *you* doing here?"

Gingko glared at the newcomer. "*Me?* I might ask the same thing of you."

"This woman is bizarre, Miss Yoder," Darlene said loudly.

I stopped myself in mid-nod. "Please tone it down, dear. Too much noise puts the hens off laying."

"Miss Yoder," Gingko said, tugging on my sleeve like a schoolgirl trying to get my attention, "I had a vision about Miss Townsend too. She's not who she says she is."

"You little runt," Darlene snarled, "you repeat one word of what you told me, and I'll sue you for slander."

Frankly, I was shocked by Miss Townsend's viciousness. She seemed like a nice enough, if overly big, gal. And wasn't she supposed to be a teacher at an exclusive girls' school? Betty Quiring, Hernia's gym teacher, might pull ears now and then, but she never called anyone names.

Gingko's green eyes regarded the giantess calmly. "You're a lying, cheating fraud."

"*Me?* You're the one who goes around telling people you've had prophetic visions, like you're some kind of New Age seer. I bet anything you're on drugs." Darlene was shouting again, and even the normally laconic Abigail was running around like a chicken with her head cut off. Abby, however, was clucking, something headless chickens rarely do.

"Ladies, that does it! Out you both go!"

But they didn't budge. They just stood there glaring at each other, one staring almost straight up, the other down. It would have been almost funny, except that in a misguided attempt to give one or both of them a gentle shove, I set one of my size elevens carelessly down in the egg basket.

"Now see what you've done!" I wailed.

So intent was their hatred of each other, they couldn't be bothered to notice I was standing in an omelet.

"That does it!" I shouted, adding to Abigail's agitation, and stomped from the coop, still wearing a basket on my foot. Outside the narrow door I paused and, after just a second's hesitation, flipped the hook into the eye.

Perhaps you think it wrong of me to lock the two hotheads in with my hens, but birds forgive rather easily. Besides, Keith and

Honey Bunch would soon be back, rakes in hand, wheelbarrow in tow, to liberate my fine, feathered friends.

Needless to say, I was in a foul mood when I stormed into the kitchen, sans one shoe, and found Freni and my sister Susannah about to engage in fisticuffs. Okay, so perhaps that's putting it a bit strongly for two women who, between them, claimed almost a thousand years of pacifist inbreeding, but I'm not far off the mark. Freni was wringing her stubby little hands, and Susannah was wringing what appeared to be a dishtowel. They looked like they wanted to wring each other's necks.

"Tell her!" Freni ordered me.

"Tell her what?"

"She cannot wear such a thing on the TV."

"A dishtowel?"

"Ah, Mags, it's not a dishtowel. It's a dress. See?" Susannah stopped ringing the thing, gave it a good flip, and suspended it in front of her. It hung from the middle of her chest to just below the beginnings of her legs.

"*That's* a dress?"

"It's a retro-micro-mini."

"Excuse me?"

"They're in this year."

"They are?"

Susannah nodded vigorously. "Poor sis, haven't you heard? The age of 'anything goes' is over. For the new millennium it's going to be short all the way. A thousand years of skin is what *Rage Magazine* is predicting."

I shuddered, but in a strange sort of way that was good news. I wear my skirts well below the knee. My bosom is always properly covered, as are my shoulders. But the recent trend of ankle-length skirts—particularly popular among Episcopalian women, I've noticed—has made feeling virtuous a difficult task. I've had to content myself with the knowledge that skirts that are *too* long are showy, and therefore worldly.

"Well?" Freni demanded. "Say something, Magdalena."

My private line rang and I picked up gratefully. "Yoder's House of Pandemonium."

"Sorry." There was just that one word, but I knew it was Gabe.

"For what?" I asked casually.

"For pis—making you mad. I know you can take care of yourself. I only worry because I'm fond of you."

"That makes two of us, dear."

"You're fond of me?"

"I'm fond of *me*. That's why it's two."

He laughed. Mozart tried to capture the sound and came close.

"Come on, fess up, Yoder. You're fond of me too, aren't you?"

"Okay, so I'm fond of you."

Freni tugged on my sleeve. "Ach, enough of this sugar talk, Magdalena."

"That's sweet talk, dear." I turned my attention back to Gabe. "Is that all you called to say?"

"No. I'm glad you asked. I want you to promise me you won't be doing any spying tonight."

"Gabe!"

"Promise, Magdalena."

I wanted to slam the receiver down hard enough to hurt his ear, but I knew he would just call again. If what I said next was a lie, it's only because I had my back against the wall.

"I promise," I said and then slammed the phone.

"Promise what?" Susannah asked.

Freni pointed to Susannah's dress. "She promises that she will not let you wear such a thing."

"Oh yeah? Well, she can't stop me. I'm a grown woman. I can wear anything I like. Besides, Melvin says that if I wear this, it'll attract more male voters."

I held up a quieting hand. "She's right, Freni. She's old enough to do what she wants—even make a fool of herself on television." I turned to my baby sister. "Remember to keep your legs crossed when you're on camera, and I'd ditch the dinky dog if I were you. A hairy black head emerging from your neckline may attract lots of voters, but they won't vote for Melvin, I can assure you of that."

Susannah cast Freni a triumphant look. Then in a gesture that defied those centuries of tradition, she grabbed me by the shoulders and gave me a quick peck on the cheek.

"Thanks for your blessing, Mags. You're the best."

I reeled, rubbing my face in confusion. It was the first time I'd ever been touched by a blood relative's lips. Don't get me wrong—my parents loved me, they just didn't equate smooching with deep abiding affection.

Finally I found my tongue. "I didn't give you my blessing," I wailed. "The Whore of Babylon wore more than that. I merely said you were old enough to make your own mistakes, and then gave you a few pointers on how to avoid the worst."

"Just the same, Mags, you didn't out and out forbid me, which in my book is the same as a blessing."

"No, it's not! Don't you be putting words in my mouth."

"Oh, Mags, you always pretend to be such a grouch, but deep down you're such a pussycat." Susannah fished in her purse, retracted a ring of keys, and tossed them at me casually.

Fortunately I have good reflexes. "What's this?"

"Your keys, silly. Melvin did just what he said he would. He had your car towed and three new tires put on."

"Thanks. Where is it?"

"It's sitting outside. Hey, which reminds me, I've got to go. My sweetykins is waiting for me in the squad car. I got to drive *that* over here." She giggled. "It was the first time I ever sat up front."

"Well, tell Mel—"

But Susannah had already skipped out of the kitchen, waving her dress in front of her like a flag.

I turned to face the inevitable music from Freni. She, however, was standing as rigid as an ice sculpture. Her lips appeared to have been hermetically sealed.

"I *didn't* give her my blessing," I said.

Freni blinked, but said nothing.

"Look, I know ever since Mama died, you've been a surrogate mother to both of us. We appreciate that more than you'll ever know, and we love you dearly, but like I told Susannah, you have to let us make our own mistakes."

I waited eons for Freni to say something, but she just stood there, blinking, looking for all the world like a squat lighthouse. She wasn't even breathing hard, and I began to fear she'd had some sort of a stroke.

"Say *something*, Freni. Say anything. Even an angry snort will do."

"I quit."

"What?"

"You heard me. I quit. Q-i-t. Quit."

"Just because of that stupid little dress?"

Freni began to move. Her stubby arms chopped at the air like a karate instructor. "I know when I am not appreciated, Magdalena. You don't have to hit me over the head with an ax."

"You mean a hammer, dear, and you've got it all wrong. I appreciate you immensely. I couldn't do without you."

Freni untied and removed the cooking apron she wore over her normal apron, which was really just a part of her outfit. She threw the garment on the table.

"So, now you will make supper for this bunch of English, yah?"

"No."

"This meat cake for the fat ones' anniversary is in the refrigerator." She lapsed into Pennsylvania Dutch. *"Grummbiere und Rubli—"*

"I don't care about potatoes and carrots," I wailed. "I care about you."

Freni ignored me, and continued to mumble the entire menu. Everything was basically ready, she said. I should remember to turn the oven from low heat to off after things were served, and if the more sensible English wanted something besides meat for dessert, there were two lattice-top cherry pies sitting on the counter. They should watch out for pits, however. The English were famous for their weak teeth.

There was no use arguing with the woman. She has quit eighty-seven times in the past. After a good night's sleep and a run-in with her daughter-in-law, she'd be coming back, wagging her tail behind her.

"You want a ride, dear?"

"I will walk through the woods."

"Suit yourself, dear," I said with perhaps just the barest hint of smugness in my voice.

"Ach! Do not think for a moment that I will be back like last time. I am an old woman, Magdalena. These insults I can get from my daughter-in-law. There is no need to cook for the English anymore."

"Have a nice walk," I said.

The kitchen door slammed behind her.

When I was satisfied she wouldn't return, I wrote a note of instructions for my guests and taped it to the icebox. For a mere ten dollars extra, I informed them, they could get their own supper. The privilege of washing up afterward would cost them fifteen, but when they got back to their respective cities, they could brag to their friends that they had lived an authentic Amish-Mennonite lifestyle.

Then I made myself three large cheese and tomato sandwiches (the bologna had all been consumed at lunch by you know who), poured myself a glass of fresh milk, and retired to my quarters, where I had several good books in progress.

In just a few hours I would leave my inner sanctum and crash an Amish party. While I would be missing out on the all-meat anniversary cake, I had a feeling, deep in my bones, that mine would still be a very entertaining evening.

23

At quarter to ten I sneaked from my room. It is the only bedroom on the ground floor and sits at the back of the house, between the kitchen and the parlor. The spring on the kitchen
screen door is rusty and squeaks, and if there were any guests
still in the dining room—perhaps trying their hand at quilting—
they would hear me, so that exit was not an option. Neither was
the front door, because to reach it I had to pass first through the
parlor, and then the lobby. The only safe way to leave undetected was my bedroom window.

I am a thoughtful woman, and as such had thought to hide a
step stool in the foundation plantings under my window. It was
a cloudy night, with no visible stars or moon, and I had chosen
my outfit accordingly. Navy blue dress, black cotton stockings,
ubiquitous black brogans (I own several pairs), and a black
shawl tied over my head to hide my pale face and light brown
hair.

Little Freni, bless her hairy hide, was sound asleep on my pillow. A clean little box, a fresh bowl of water, and a handful of
dry food awaited her. If only, I thought, I had someone to look
out for me like that.

Much earlier in the evening I had hung a DO NOT DISTURB sign
on my door. Now I locked it from the inside and turned off my
reading light. With that one flick of a switch, both my room and

the great outdoors appeared to be as dark as Aaron's heart the day he said "I do" when he had already done it with the woman up in Minnesota.

Backing out of my window cautiously, I felt for the stool with my right foot. Alas, it seemed not to be there. I could feel the top of a Japanese yew bush, and of course the wall, but nothing in between.

"What in tarnation?" I said. And then shocked at the swear word which had escaped my almost virgin lips, I begged the Good Lord to forgive me. "It's my guests' fault, you know."

"What's my fault?"

"Oh, not *your* fault, Lord. It's the fault of my English guests."

"Whew, then it's not my fault, because I don't have a drop of English blood in me."

That most certainly was not the Good Lord speaking. In my haste to see who it was, I slipped and fell backward out of the window and on to the flat sheared top of the yew bush. I suppose there are worse things upon which to fall—a bed of nails, shards of glass, jagged edge up, Mark Anthony's sword—but a yew is not comfortable, let me assure you of that. And it is also extremely difficult to extricate oneself from a large shrub without inflicting additional damage to one's person.

"Here, let me help you." A strong male hand grabbed my right one and began pulling.

"Wait a minute," I snapped, "my foot is caught on something."

At that, two strong male hands lay hold of diverse parts of my person, and with one strong yank, and a few yelps from yours truly, I was sprung from the trap. The person behind the hands set me gently on the ground.

Dark as it was, I could not identify him by his features until he smiled. The unnaturally white crescent that appeared suddenly like a light switched on could only belong to Archibald Murray.

"You do this often, Miss Yoder?"

Taking advantage of the blackness, I stuck out my tongue. My teeth, a pleasing shade of beige, would not give me away.

"Only on alternate Tuesdays."

"I believe it's still Monday."

"I'm trying to beat the crowd."

He laughed. "We filmed a scene just like this on my show, *Two Girls, a Guy, and a Calzone,* and I was the one who had to fall into the bush. But that bush was only a stage prop, and when the girls tried to get me out of the bush, it came right along with me. Ron—that's the director—thought that was really funny and left the scene in. It was our highest-ranking episode."

"That's nice, dear, but do you mind telling me why you were skulking around in front of my window? And was it you, per chance, who stole my step stool?"

"I wasn't skulking, Miss Yoder. I came outside for a smoke. You have this strict no-smoking policy inside."

"I'm well aware of my rules. Now answer my other question. Did you take my stool?"

"Stool?" He laughed again. "So you really were planning to sneak out of your own house?"

"You never know when religious persecution will rear its ugly head. Perhaps I was practicing my escape."

Please note that I said "perhaps." It isn't a lie unless you declare something in no uncertain terms. And anyway, even then the Lord will make exceptions if it's for a good cause.

"Maybe I can help you. I read for the lead role in a remake of *The Great Escape.*"

"But you didn't get the part?"

"I turned them down. They wanted me to crawl through an actual tunnel." The white crescent became a blur and I knew he was shuddering. "I would have gotten dirt in my hair. And spiders."

"Well, I don't plan to crawl through any tunnels. Now if you'll excuse me." I reached into my handbag, which I had not dropped, even in the bush, and extracted a small flashlight. I switched it on.

"You certainly come prepared."

I ignored his observation and shone the light along the foundation of my inn. There were no step stools behind any of the bushes. Had Freni found the stool and returned it to its rightful place in the pantry? Or could someone possibly have been out to thwart me? And could that someone be Archibald?

"I didn't take your stool, Miss Yoder," he said, as if reading my mind.

I shone the light at Archibald, not at his face, of course, but some inches lower. Imagine my surprise when I found myself staring at a well-muscled, quite naked chest. I made a quick sweep from chest to feet. He was wearing shorts, thank heavens, but the rest of him was as naked as a baby jay bird. I clicked the light off. Better to brood in the dark than lust in the light.

"Well, *someone* took it." I shone the light along the wall again, and of course finding nothing, turned to walk away.

"Where are you going, Miss Yoder?"

"That's none of your business, dear."

"Would you mind if I came with you?"

I stopped, but didn't turn. "Yes, I would mind. And isn't that a silly thing to ask? You have no idea where I'm going, or what I plan to do."

"Doesn't matter to me. I just want to come."

"What if I'm going to church?"

"Wow, what kind of church meets this time of the night?"

"Maybe mine does."

"That's cool. So, can I come?"

"Not dressed like that, dear."

He laughed. "Yeah, well, it's real nice out tonight, and I've never been too fond of clothes."

"Are you a nudist?" I asked in alarm. Heaven forfend he would divest himself of his shorts as well. Seeing the full Monty might be more than my ticker could take, and besides the batteries in my flashlight were old, and might die before I was ready to shut it off.

He laughed again. "Would that be so bad?"

"It's a sin, of course. That's why the Good Lord invented clothes."

"He did?"

"Certainly. He sewed animal skins together for Adam and Eve."

"But didn't He create them naked in the first place?"

I sighed. "I don't have time to argue theology, Mr. Murray."

"Just take me with you and I promise to shut up."

"You sound desperate."

"I am."

Short hairs bristled at the nape of my scrawny neck. "You sound like you don't like it here."

"It isn't that exactly. I mean, this place is really great if that's your bag."

"And it isn't yours?"

"I thought it would be. Hollywood's crazy and just about anywhere I go in the country I get mobbed. Here nobody even knows who I am. I gotta admit, it's kinda disappointing."

"You poor dear."

No doubt I need to work on my sarcasm skills. "So?" he asked, brightening. "Does this mean you'll let me ride along? Like I said, I don't really care where. Church is fine—hey, there wouldn't happen to be a video poker parlor nearby, would there?"

"Get dressed and we'll see."

"Great!" The crescent disappeared and I could hear him trotting off into the black night. The boy must have been weaned on carrot juice.

I turned my flashlight back on and made a beeline toward my car.

"As ye sow, so shall ye reap," the Bible says. This is true, of course, but sometimes I reap far more than I've sown. That night I had a veritable bumper crop. I may have misled Archibald when I sent him back into the house to put more clothes on, but Melvin out and out lied to me.

New tires indeed! Sure, the tires were new to my car, but they'd traveled more miles than Lodema Schrock's tongue, and I'd seen eggs with more tread than what was left on these three. On the plus side, they *were* round—basically—and almost the same size as my fourth tire. If I drove slowly, and steered clear of the Keims' driveway, I might make it as far as the old Berkey barn. But judging from the faint hiss I heard, I stood a good chance of having to bum a ride home with the Hamptons. They would, I'm sure, be as pleased as champagne punch to see my smiling face again.

"Nothing ventured, nothing gained," I said and climbed into my sinfully red BMW. I will confess that I am braver when driving on four good tires, and as a consequence, it took me longer to get to the old Berkey barn than I had anticipated. The dilapidated white structure—even cows are not permitted to be sinners in Hernia—sits well back from the highway, and is virtually hidden these days by a pasture that has been allowed to return to woods. By the time I arrived, there were already eight buggies and three automobiles parked behind the old structure, carefully hidden from even the most prying of eyes. In order to avoid detection by the teenagers upon whom I was spying, I had to park in an abandoned cornfield a half mile away.

It is no easy feat to walk across an overgrown field on a night as dark as Aaron Miller's heart. Thank heavens for Hostetler ankles. Mama was a Hostetler, you see, and every one on her side of the family—male and female alike, fat or thin—had ankles as big around as their waists. Susannah has them too, which is why, I'm sure, she wears those floor-length swirls of fabric. After all, there isn't an ankle bracelet that has been made that will encircle one of these babies, and belts don't count. But I'm not complaining, mind you. If it weren't for ankles as sturdy as marble pedestals, I most probably would have twisted one or both on corn stubble and ended up a temporary invalid. Instead, I was able to make good time over very rough ground. I didn't even have to use my flashlight, although I did turn it on for a few seconds every now and then, just to check the ground for snakes.

When I got close to the barn, I was afraid the horses might smell me and whinny. Of all God's creatures, they are the only ones high-strung enough to qualify as Yoders (surely God is not responsible for Chihuahuas!), and as such make good sentries. But the breeze was blowing toward me, and I got to smell them instead. Having just hosted a group of French tourists, I can honestly say there are worse odors.

I entered the barn via the milking room. It had a concrete floor, which I took as a sign that somebody, somewhere, was praying for me. Nonetheless, I crept carefully across the floor and peered into the great vault of the barn. There in the middle of the vast space, sprawled over bales of moldy hay, were nineteen Amish kids. Fourteen boys and five girls.

I gasped, and then clamped a hand over my mouth. So many! And so young. Elam Keim, who was indeed there, was probably the oldest.

Catching a deep, but almost silent breath, I studied the group more closely. I recognized seven of the boys: Elam Keim, of course, his younger brother Seth, Jacob Lehman, Christian Schmucker, Daniel Livengood, Gideon Fisher, and John Eash. Barbara Troyer was the only girl whose name I knew. There were no English present.

I can't describe the scene as a party, although most of my parties have been no livelier. Like I said, everyone was just lying there. Some even appeared to be asleep. A radio, the kind our young people refer to as a boom box, played softly in the middle of the room, and not only did I recognize the music—I use that term loosely—but I knew the recording artist. The Booty Hunter had once been a guest at my inn, but back in the days when he was a famous gospel singer.

Were the kids spaced out on drugs? I couldn't say for sure, having never used the stuff myself. But from what I had read, and from what little Susannah had shared of her life, I suspected that was the case.

So now what was I supposed to do? Sneak back through the milking room, trek across a pitch black field, and trust three bald tires, just to inform an incompetent police chief that something appeared amiss? Or was I to take the matter into my own hands?

24

There was only one dilapidated bright yellow Buick parked behind the barn. There had been no need to lock it—or so the
Keim boys thought. I opened the left rear door cautiously,
flicked on my light, and peered inside. The faux leather of the
seat was ripped in several places and there was enough hay
scattered about to feed a horse for a week, the consequence no
doubt of using a haystack as a garage.

Then I saw the mouse. It was all I could do not to scream. Lest
you think it silly that I should be afraid of such a small creature,
let me remind you that even elephants are supposed to be afraid
of them. According to legend, the tiny rodents have a penchant
for running up the inside of a pachyderm's trunk. This may, or
may not, be true. But since I have the Yoder nose, I wasn't about
to take any chances.

"Shoo!" I hissed. "Scat! Scram."

The little rodent looked calmly up at me with beady eyes.

"I'm coming in," I warned, "and you don't want to mess with
me. I may be a Mennonite through and through, but my paci-
fism does not extend to animals."

The mouse squeaked and skittered off beneath the front seat.
I climbed gingerly into the back. There I settled in for a long
wait. A *long* wait.

After an hour of intense alertness, I found myself getting

drowsy. To stay awake I recited Bible verses, hummed hymns softly to myself, told ghost stories to an audience of six—there was an entire family of mice living under the front seat—and even went so far as to make a mental list of my enemies and subsequently forgive them. In the end there was nothing I could do to keep awake.

When I awoke, the sky had cleared and there were faint remnants of morning stars. It would be dawn within the hour. I roused myself, brushed hay from my lap, and studied my environs through the open window. What I saw in the growing light gave me such a shock I nearly bumped my head on the sagging padding of the Buick's roof. The little improvised parking lot was all but empty. No horses and buggies remained, and there was just one other motorized vehicle, a sleek blue late-model car. Somehow I had managed to sleep through all that, whereas at home, a guest snoring, upstairs and three bedrooms away, can keep me up all night.

I was at a loss for what to do. Had the Keim boys discovered me and then hitched a ride with somebody else? Should I check to see if they were still in the barn? Should I count myself lucky and make a beeline for the cornfield and my red BMW? Or should I stick with my original plan?

The sound of two young male voices speaking Pennsylvania Dutch settled that. Plan A was on again. I settled back into the seat and sat as still as Lot's wife, *after* she'd turned into the pillar of salt.

Before clambering in, the boys needlessly stomped their shoes against the running board. A dead leaf or a few particles of dirt were not going to mess up their car any. I must say, however, that I was surprised and pleased to see them buckle their seat belts. I was even more surprised when Elam, the driver, didn't even glance in the rearview mirror, before starting the engine. I waited until he turned on to the highway before making my presence known.

"*Gut marriye*," I said in a loud, clear voice.

The car swerved and I, who was not belted in, got a good strong dose of side-to-side whiplash.

"What the hell?" Elam said in English.

"*Gotte en heimel!*" Seth cried.

"Indeed He is, but I'll thank you not to take His name in vain. And you," I said, poking Elam with a bony finger, "should not swear."

Elam slammed on the brakes and my head got a chance to shoot forward and back. "Miss Yoder, it is you!"

"As big as life and twice as ugly." It's all right to say that about one's self.

"What are you doing in our car?"

"Will you tell Papa?" Seth asked, his voice breaking into an adolescent squeak.

"I will do the talking," Elam said sharply to his brother. He turned to me. "*Will* you?"

We were sitting in the middle of the road, mind you. At any moment someone could have come along in a car and hit us. Sure it was still only daybreak, but by Hernia standards it was the top of the morning.

"Why don't you drive someplace, dear, and we'll discuss it along the way."

"Ach, but it is getting light. Someone will see us."

" 'Light has come into the world,' " I said, quoting from the third chapter of John. " 'But men loved darkness instead of light because their deeds were evil. Everyone who does evil hates the light, and will not come into the light for fear that his deeds will be exposed.' So that's what you're afraid of, right? Of being exposed."

Elam's dark face, originally just a blur, was acquiring features. "What is this exposed?"

It occurred to me that he might not be familiar with the passage. "Don't you read the Bible?"

"Yah, but in German."

"It means to be seen. You're afraid to be seen in this car because you know you shouldn't have it in the first place, and in the second—well, you know what you were doing in the barn is wrong."

"Ach!" Seth squirmed in his seat. "She knows, Elam!"

"I said to shut the mouth," Elam shouted.

"Easy," I said. "Just start driving down the road and I'll tell you what I know."

"Where do I drive?"

"How about Stucky Ridge? If you take Hershberger Road, there's less chance of being seen."

"Maybe we go back to the barn."

"I don't think so, dear. Not until you tell me who the owner of that blue Chevy is."

"I cannot."

"Somehow I didn't think so. In that case, press the pedal to the metal. The fuzz is still buzzing, if I know my brother-in-law."

"Miss Yoder," he said, still not cooperating, "you speak in riddles, yah?"

"Yah—I mean, yes—I mean, do I? Okay, let me put it another way. Drive fast because Melvin Stoltzfus, the Chief of Police, is still sleeping. You don't have to worry about getting a ticket, and if you drive fast enough, no one will recognize you."

"Yah?"

It was without a doubt the stupidest advice I ever gave a teenager. As far as I knew, the boys had just been doing drugs, and I knew for a fact that Elam had never taken a driver's education course. He certainly didn't have a driver's license.

I searched desperately for a seat belt as we careered and careened down Hernia's byways and then up the steep winding road that led to the dizzying heights of Stucky Ridge. Alas, there was no belt. Perhaps there had never been one, or perhaps the mice had eaten it. Immodest as it was, I lay on my back with my feet in the air. Should we crash, it was better that something sturdy went through the windshield first.

At the top of the ridge, Elam squealed to a stop in the picnic area parking lot. "We talk now, yah?"

"Not yet, dear. Drive *slowly* over to the Settlers Cemetery. We'll talk there."

You may think I was being picky, but allow me to explain. The picnic area is only occasionally used for the consumption of food. Instead, the young people of Hernia have turned it into an open-air den of iniquity. Kids have been known to go far beyond hand-holding. Intense osculation has been observed from time to time and—you may find this hard to believe—I heard that a few of these children have even gone beyond that stage.

Sure, Gabe the Babe and I were going to have our picnic up there, but that is a different matter altogether. We are mature adults, and know when to stop. But heaven forbid I give Elam and Seth the wrong idea. After all, I am an attractive woman, still in my prime. If I caused either of them to think lascivious thoughts, the sin would be on my head.

Besides, the cemetery gives me comfort. It is where my parents are buried, and their parents before them, stretching back six generations. Now I don't believe in ghosts, mind you, but if I really needed her, Mama would somehow come to my rescue. Papa too. But Mama is capable of producing earthquakes by rolling over in the grave, something which she does on a regular basis, whenever I say or do something which displeases her. Just how a woman who was squished to death under a milk tanker can manage to roll over is beyond me, but trust me on this one. She does.

Seth jumped at the word "cemetery." "Ach, not the English cemetery."

"It isn't just English who are buried there," I corrected him. "All the original settlers of Hernia were Amish, my people included. That all changed less than a hundred years ago."

Elam shrugged. "The dead are dead," he said and followed my instructions.

We pulled into the parking space closest to my parents' plots. "Okay, dears, now we talk."

"It is not Seth's fault," Elam said the second I closed my mouth.

"What isn't?"

"The drugs," Seth said.

"Shut the mouth!" Elam ordered.

The back of Seth's flaxen head disappeared as he slumped into his seat. It registered with me that the boys were hatless.

"Really, Elam, I'm surprised at you. Yelling at your brother like that! For your information, I know all about the drugs."

He turned so that I could see his dark, handsome face in profile. Not a drop of Yoder blood in that one.

"This is a trick, yah?"

"No trick, dear." So maybe it was, but it's okay to fib when you're intervening to save a young person's life.

"Ach, the drugs. They are a terrible thing. I know that now, but now it is too late."

"What do you mean?"

"They are like a bitch."

"I beg your pardon!"

He flushed. "The female dog is called that, no? When she is in heat, there is no stopping her."

"I only have a cat," I said dryly. "I wouldn't know."

"These drugs—it is too hard to stop. I have tried many times."

"What about you, Seth?"

Seth remained silent.

"I will speak for my brother. For him there is still time."

"Is that true, Seth?"

Silence again. I kicked the back of the boy's seat.

"I know you speak English, dear. I demand that you answer me."

Seth mumbled something unintelligible.

"Louder, dear."

"I think maybe it is hard for me too."

I kicked Elam's seat. "You see what you've done? You've gotten your younger brother hooked on something that could kill him."

It was light enough by then to see the tear that rolled down Elam Keim's right cheek. "Yeah, maybe."

"No maybe about it, dear. You heard what he said. And you the oldest child, for crying out loud."

I felt strangely betrayed by Elam. The oldest child gets inexperienced parents who experiment on her, and then she is supposed to toe the line, to carry on the family tradition. It is the youngest child, the pampered one, who gets the privilege of being the black sheep. Ask any psychologist or psychiatrist. Ask the Drs. Hanson. Or better yet, look at Susannah and I.

The oldest by almost eleven years, I did everything my parents asked of me. I attended Bedford Community College as a commuter when I really wanted to go away to school, to try my wings at the University of Pittsburgh. I stopped seeing Henry Blough at my parents' request because he belonged to the First

Mennonite Church of Hernia, which is a tad more liberal than Beechy Grove Mennonite Church.

But what did Susannah do? She barely even graduated from high school. In fact, she wouldn't have, had Principal Potter known that it was Susannah and her cohorts who put the dead opossum in the heating vent. And as for her choice of boyfriends, not only did my sister marry a Presbyterian right out of the gate, but since our parents' death has slept with more men than Rock Hudson. One, I think, was even a Catholic.

"Miss Yoder," Elam said somberly, "will you tell our parents?"

"I'm afraid I have to."

He turned in his seat to face me. "It will kill Papa."

"Your papa is stronger than you think. If you keep taking drugs, it will kill you. What you need is help—some kind of program. Your parents are going to have to know."

"Then I will tell them."

"When?"

He shrugged.

I leaned forward, bracing a hand on the back of his seat. "We can tell them together."

His face clouded. "Maybe."

I sat back. "Maybe won't do. They need to be told before I tell the police."

"Ach!" They both gasped, and although all the windows were open, I felt a surfeit of oxygen.

"Of course. Surely you know that buying drugs is against the law. Do you sell drugs as well?"

I don't think they heard me. "The police," Seth moaned. "The police."

I'm sure my critics would say I should have had more sympathy for the boys, coming from such a sheltered environment as they did. But I came from a sheltered environment too, and I'll tell you this, I still knew right from wrong.

"Look, guys, you are in serious trouble. It can go one of two ways. Either you fess up and come clean—er, I mean tell the whole truth—and *maybe* the law will go easier on you, or you can give me and the authorities a hard time, in which case, you'll get hard time right back." I chuckled at my little pun.

"Ach, Miss Yoder, you laugh?" Seth's normally pale face had been drained of any color, except for the blue tint of a myriad of tiny veins. He looked like the photo of a newborn baby from which someone had deleted the color red.

"I made a little joke," I explained. "I wasn't laughing at you. In fact, I feel very sorry for you."

"Then say nothing," Elam urged. "We will stop with these drugs."

"Yes, but you've tried, and it didn't do any good."

"I will try harder this time. And Seth, he is not—uh, how do you say?"

"Addicted?"

"Yah. So I will try, yah?" He sounded desperate to end the conversation right there.

"I'm sure you will, but from what I understand, that won't be enough. Besides, it's not just you and your brother. What about the other kids? Can you be so sure none of them are addicted? Or that maybe some of them are just so turned on by the whole experience, they'll just keep getting deeper and deeper into it?"

Seth was nodding his head. "Barbara Troyer, she has this problem."

"Shut the mouth, Seth!" Elam's dark eyes were flashing. He'd raised a hand as if to strike his brother, and then jerked it back.

"But it is true. You said so yourself."

"I have a fool for a brother." Since those are the harshest words an Amish boy can speak to his brother, I was not surprised when they brought a torrent of tears.

"Ach, what have we done? Poor Papa. Poor Mama."

"And poor you," Elam said bitterly.

I felt sorry for Seth then. He was not, as I saw it, as responsible for his actions as was Elam. He was also more contrite. But most importantly, he was willing to cooperate.

"Maybe you'd like to take a little walk, Seth," I said kindly. "Elam and I will work things out."

"Yah. Go, baby," Elam said.

Seth needed no further urging. He stumbled from the car and staggered into the cemetery like a drunk man. It wasn't the drugs that made him stagger—I was pretty sure of that—but the tears that kept flooding his eyes.

We watched in silence as he made his way slowly between the stones, finally selecting one upon which to sit. I must confess that this shocked me almost as much as the fact that such a sweet-looking boy would take hard drugs. I had been raised to never sit on a headstone, and in fact, to never even step on the ground above the actual grave. Once when we were visiting Grandma's grave, Mama brought that lesson home to me with the back of her hairbrush. For Seth's sake, I could only hope that it wasn't Mama's stone he was sitting on.

When Seth was settled, I gathered my skirts and climbed into the front seat. Just to be on the safe side, I buckled myself securely before turning to face Elam. I was not surprised to see that in the interim his smooth dark face had hardened, like maple sap on a cold day.

25

Zucchini Crepes

3 tablespoons chopped onion
4 tablespoons butter, divided
1½ pounds zucchini, sliced
½ cup chicken broth or water

1 egg
1 cup grated Cheddar cheese
½ cup fresh bread crumbs

Sauté onion in 2 tablespoons melted butter. Add zucchini and broth. Cover and cook for about 10 minutes or until zucchini is done. Remove zucchini and onions to a mixing bowl and mix until zucchini is broken up. Drain any liquid from bowl. Add the egg and cheese; mix well. Spoon the zucchini filling onto 12 crepes, fold them into desired shape. Mix remaining 2 tablespoons of butter and the bread crumbs and sprinkle over the crepes. Bake at 350 degrees for about 15 minutes.

26

"Well, well, well," I said. "It seems to me like you've got a problem."

He said nothing.

"I know it seems like an impossible thing to do—turning yourself in. I know you think it will hurt your parents. But look out there, it's already hurting your brother, and your parents *will* find out about this."

"Maybe not," he muttered. Lips don't move on a face that stiff.

"What do you plan to do, kill me?"

My words shocked him into pliancy. "Ach, not me!"

"Oh, so you plan to have someone else do it? You want that on Seth's conscience as well."

Elam softened further. "I love my brother."

"That's a hoot!"

"But I do."

"Then why are you willing to risk his life?"

"Ach, I would not do such a thing."

"Wrongo! Every time he participates in one of your little drug parties, his life is in danger."

"It is his decision," Elam said, gathering strength like a worn-out hurricane traveling back over warm water.

"Just out of curiosity, who started in on drugs first, you or him?"

"He asked." Elam's eyes were flashing again. "I did not push this on him."

"Yeah, well, I noticed you have some very little brothers. If one of them asked for matches to play in the hay barn, would you give them to him?"

"That is not the same."

"Bull." That is not a swear word, but a gender-specific term for the male bovine. "The newspapers are full of stories of people dying of drug overdoses and drugs laced with other dangerous chemicals. What makes you think your brother isn't going to get hold of some lethal substance one of these days?"

He shrugged sullenly.

"Don't think for a second that you can trust your supplier."

"I do trust him."

"Well, what's his name—" I let my voice trail off, hoping he'd be tricked into filling in the blank.

"Miss Yoder," he said instead, "I must be going now. It is light already. Papa will worry because we are not there to do the chores."

"I'm sure he is worried. Although I should think he'd be used to it by now. Anyway, before I let you go, I'm going to offer you a deal."

"Deal?" he asked in surprise. "Elam Keim never makes deals."

"He does now, buster, and here it is. You tell your parents what you've been up to, *and* you tell me the name of your supplier, and I'll do everything that I can to see that the law goes easy on you and your brother."

Elam laughed. "This you can promise?"

"I know Judge Greenburg up in Bedford, and he likes to give deserving kids a break, *if* he's convinced they're deserving. That's where I come into the picture. I can be very persuasive."

"I think maybe you talk like a sausage," he said, using an idiomatic expression I find particularly offensive. He leaned out the window. "Seth! Come now! We go."

"You don't sound convinced, dear. So, I guess I'm going to have to put a little more effort into this."

"You speak in riddles again, Miss Yoder."

I glanced at the Timex my parents gave me for a high school graduation present. It is my only piece of jewelry, if one can call it such, and has been more reliable than any number of friends. It's kept right on ticking, while I've taken a number of lickings.

"Six o'clock this evening," I said. "That's twelve hours from now. That's how long I'm giving you. If you haven't told your parents by then, I will."

Elam paled, his dark skin a sickly shade of beige. "It will kill them," he whispered.

"And you or Seth dying from an overdose won't?"

"Please Miss Yoder, Seth comes now."

I glanced out the window. "So? He's going to have to know. One way or the other by six o'clock."

"Please." For the first time I heard pleading in his voice. "I will do it my way."

"As you wish."

Seth was beside the car then. He peered in the window and seemed almost surprised to see me. Perhaps he had been using his time in the cemetery praying that I would disappear. If that was the case, I knew how he felt. The day after I discovered I was a bigamist, I refused to wake up to a world gone haywire. I'd open my eyes, willing everything to be the way it was a mere twenty-four hours earlier, and at the encroachment of the first painful memory, I'd close them again. Over and over I tried to manipulate reality this way. By the end of that day I had not stirred from my bed, but both my bladder and my eyes got a thorough workout.

Poor Seth didn't even get a second chance to wish me away. "Get in the back, Seth," Elam ordered.

"No." I opened the door, and jumped out. "Ride up front, Seth. I'm going to walk."

"Ach!" the boys squawked in unison.

"Well, it is a nice day," I said. "And I could use the exercise."

"But Miss Yoder," Seth protested. "You are—uh, you are old, yah?"

"Old, no!" I snapped. "I could walk circles around you if I wanted to."

Elam was stupid enough to take drugs, but not dumb enough to look a gift horse in the mouth for more than a few seconds.

"Have a safe walk!" he yelled, and the second his brother shut the door, Elam pressed the pedal to the metal. The ancient yellow Buick shot forward, spraying my poor, but sturdy, ankles with stinging gravel.

"Remember," I whinnied, "six o'clock!"

The car disappeared in a cloud of dust.

My intention was to initiate a couple of mountaintop chats before descending into the chaos of the world below. If I had to follow through on my threat to Elam, I was going to need a lot of emotional support. Dealing with the Keims was going to be one of the hardest things I'd ever done, of that I was sure. I may not know what it is like to be a disappointed mother (Little Freni brings me only joy), but I am the world's expert on disappointed sisters. Pain is pain.

At any rate, the first of these chats was with my Maker. I do this on a regular basis, by the way, and not just in church or on mountaintops. Okay, to be totally honest, these aren't so much chats as they are opportunities for me to demand answers, but you get the picture. At least I make an effort to communicate. The Good Lord, however, has never once bothered to answer me in an audible voice. This frustrates me to no end, and I've gone so far as to take up the matter with my pastor who, as it turned out, was not nearly as sympathetic as I had hoped. Pastor Schrock merely smiled and said that if the Lord ever did speak to me in an audible voice, I'd either die of shock, or shock treatments in a rubber room.

Maybe the Reverend is right, but I still think it would nice if God communicated more directly. If He would just give me a sign, a *single* sign, like He gave the Israelites of old, I would never ask for another. And I'm not talking about plagues, of course, but maybe a little handwriting on the wall, in a neat legible cursive. Or maybe a nice block printing.

So, not really expecting an answer, I demanded of God a very clear path to follow in the Keim case and asked whether or not anything would come of the blossoming romance between me and Gabriel Rosen. I reminded the Good Lord that Gabe was one of His kinfolk, and that I wouldn't be at all averse to Him shutting Lodema Schrock's big mouth, just like He shut lions' mouths for Daniel.

As usual, God did not answer, so I went over to chat with Mama. I don't pray to her, mind you, because that would be idolatrous. Instead, I inform Mama of everything that's been going on in my life, and allow her to vent. You might find even that notion sacrilegious, but you don't know Mama. Not only can I hear her responses in my head, but I see them with my eyes, and hear them with my ears. Unlike the Good Lord, Mama is not opposed to dispensing signs and wonders to the present generation of believers.

She didn't have much to say about the Keim kids, but she had plenty to say about Gabe. She was, if you'll pardon the pun, dead set against him. She made that clear by the brief down-pour that materialized out of an only partly cloudy sky and drenched me the moment I mentioned his name.

"But he's a doctor, Mama. A heart surgeon. That means he's saved many lives."

The sun appeared just as suddenly and warmed the back of my neck.

"But he's retired now. He wants to write mysteries."

The sun popped behind another scattered cloud and a chill wind blew across the top of Stucky Ridge.

"Writing is a worthwhile profession too, Mama. Isn't reading a better way to escape than, say, drugs or alcohol?"

Mama must have heard about the mimosas, because at the mention of alcohol, the wind picked up considerably. I huddled next to her stone.

"That was by accident!" I wailed. "You should know that. And I promise it will never happen again. If these lips of mine as much as touch a drop of alcohol, I'll tell everyone I know that you were absolutely right about everything we disagreed about, and I was wrong."

Immediately the wind abated and the sun shone warmly all over my body. Steam rose from my clothes. Still, I had been chilled to the bone and, despite the sudden increased tempera-ture, sneezed.

"Bless you."

Mama's voice was deeper than I remembered, but perhaps the grave does that to one.

"Thank you, Mama."

"I am not your mother."

"You mean I was adopted?" I asked hopefully.

Mama laughed. "Magdalena, you're such a hoot. Have I ever told you that?"

I whirled. Mama would never call me a hoot.

"Gabe!"

He grinned. "Who else?"

"But—but—" I struggled to my feet. I was tempted to make a run for it. Thanks to the rain, I was a mess. My hair, which I normally wear in a very neat bun, was wet and stringy, and only the mere remnants of a bobby pin–encrusted lump remained, clinging precariously to the left side of my head like some horrible growth. My white prayer cap was nowhere to be seen. My dress clung to me like a second skin, and underscored in embarrassing detail the sturdy underpinnings of a pious, albeit small-bosomed woman.

"You're something else," he said, the admiration in his voice unmistakable. "I bet there's never a dull moment living with you."

"Well, you'd bet wrong." I clawed wet hair away from my face and tried to fluff the bodice of my dress. At least the bra was thick enough to hide the fact that the wetness had created mountains where only molehills had been.

"Aaron Miller was a lucky man. A fool, of course, but lucky nonetheless."

I crossed my arms over my chest. "What on earth are you doing up here?"

"I came up to see the view I missed the other evening." He chuckled. "You were right, it certainly is beautiful."

"How did you get here? Where's your car?"

"I parked it over on the other side, by the picnic tables. I've never been up here. Thought I'd explore around a bit, see the view from both sides, and voilà, there you were, talking to a gravestone."

"I *wasn't* talking to a gravestone."

He grinned again. "I've got good ears, Magdalena."

"Then you should know I was talking to my mother, who incidentally disapproves of you."

The grin widened. "Because of my religion?"

"That, and the fact you're now a writer. More specifically, a mystery writer. Mama never read a book of fiction in her life. 'What's the point?' she'd say. 'It's all made up.' "

He laughed. "She sounds like a hoot too."

"*Shhh!*" I held a bony finger to shriveled blue lips. "Talk about good ears," I whispered, "she can hear a toad belch in China. She wouldn't approve of being compared to me."

"I see." His gorgeous brown eyes were still laughing. "Mrs. Yoder," he said in a loud voice, "you are incomparable. I wish I could have met you. I'm sure we would have gotten along very well."

As Gabe is my witness, that very second the sun hid its face behind a thimble-size cloud. Dr. Rosen the mystery writer was alone in the shadow.

"You see?" I said. "She doesn't like you."

"That's just a coincidence. Mrs. Yoder," he practically shouted, "if that's really you, then I'm disappointed. I thought you could do better than that."

Gabe had barely closed his mouth when we were deluged by a gully washer of a rain. We made a dash for the nearest tree, but the second we reached it, the sun came out brighter and hotter than ever. Already the offending cloud was a mere cotton puff on the horizon.

"Just another coincidence, dear?"

"It certainly is weird, I'll grant you that."

We stepped out into the warm sunshine. "Frankly, dear, you got off easy. Mama can be as mean as a snake. Why once when I—"

The floodgates of Heaven opened yet again. This time a bolt of lightning hit the tree we'd just been standing under. There was a second loud crack as a large limb crashed to the ground, obliterating one of the tombstones.

"Now do you believe?" I demanded.

"I believe it would be stupid of us to keep standing here."

Gabe grabbed my arm. "Come on, we'll be safe in my car. I've got a towel in my trunk. You can dry off with that."

I went with him willingly. "I don't suppose you have any food too?"

That was perhaps a silly question, but I was ravenous. Even a breath mint would be gratefully accepted.

"As a matter of fact, I do. How does a bagel with lox and cream cheese sound?"

"Well—"

"And if that's not your shtick, I have both cheese and raspberry Danish. Oh, and I couldn't remember if you like coffee, so I brought a thermos of hot chocolate as well."

I wrenched free of his grasp. "Wait just a minute! How did you know I was up here?"

"Call it a hunch. I went over to the inn first thing this morning. I wanted to invite you up here for a breakfast picnic. Anyway, your car wasn't there, so I was hoping you'd somehow managed to read my mind." He grabbed my hand. "I guess you did."

I freed myself again. Romantic as that notion was, it didn't fly. A man who didn't believe in ghosts, even when he met one, face to bird droppings, wasn't going to drive up a mountain on a hunch.

"What if I hadn't been here, then what?"

"Well, then I guess I would have eaten alone."

I sneaked a peek at my Timex. "It's not even seven o'clock. What were you planning to do, wake me?"

"Give me a break, Magdalena. You're a farm girl. You're used to getting up with the chickens."

We rounded the copse of trees that separates the picnic area from the cemetery. I gasped when I saw the sleek blue car ahead.

"Is that your car?"

He laughed. "Do you see another?"

"I didn't know you had a new car," I managed to say calmly. My heart, by the way, was pounding like a madman on an xylophone. You wouldn't believe the crazy thoughts that were flitting through my brain.

"It's not a new car," Gabe said. "It's the same one I've always had. Are you okay, Magdalena?"

I slowed, forcing him to follow my pace. "Speaking of cars, dear, you don't see mine, do you?"

He glanced around. "I guess not."

"You *guess* not? What kind of an answer is that?"

"Okay, I don't see it."

"Then how come you're not even the least bit curious about how *I* got up here?"

"I am. I figured you'd tell me all about it over breakfast."

I tried not to panic as the thoughts began to gel. "Show me the food." If the coffee is hot, I'll believe him, I told myself. There was no way Gabe could have followed the Keim car up the mountain from the Berkey farm, and then dashed home to make breakfast.

"Well," Gabe said, "if you're that hungry, why do you keep slowing down? Would you like me to carry you?"

Perhaps he meant it as a joke. Perhaps not. For all I knew he wanted to carry me to the nearest cliff and throw me over.

"Most definitely not."

Gabe stopped. "Magdalena, what's wrong?"

I tensed, ready to run. "You tell me."

He shrugged. "It's damn hard to figure out any woman, and you're twice the woman of any one I know."

"I'll thank you not to swear," I said. One must demand good manners, even in the face of death.

"That's my Magdalena, always prim and proper."

"I am not *your* Magdalena."

It was the first time I'd seen a full-fledged frown on that handsome face. "Okay, enough of this horsing around. Out with what's bothering you."

I stepped well out of reach. "So, you want the truth, do you?"

"Nothing but."

"Then you asked for it, because I saw your car last night parked behind the Berkey barn."

Gabe didn't even have the decency to blink. "I was home all evening."

"Are you calling me a liar?"

"I'm saying you're mistaken."

"Oh, is that so? Am I mistaken about the fact that you called yesterday and begged me not to spy on those Amish kids?"

"I didn't beg," Gabe said quietly. "I certainly didn't use the word 'spy.' "

"That's exactly what you said! I couldn't figure out why then, but now it all makes sense."

"What does?"

"You're from New York, aren't you?"

"So?"

"The big city," I said. "Drug pushers. I may not watch television, Gabe, but I read the papers."

He gaped at me, frozen in time, like one of those fossilized people they found in Pompeii.

"You might want to be careful of flies, dear."

Gabe came to life, slapping his forehead with a broad palm. "So that's it! You think I'm a drug pusher just because I'm from New York. From the outside."

"If the shoe fits."

"There are other outsiders," he growled. "Like the Hamptons."

"*They* didn't try and stop me from doing my job. *Their* car wasn't parked behind the Berkey barn. And—"

"It wasn't my damn car!"

"And," I said, my voice rising, "you still haven't explained how you found me up here—unless you'd been following me."

"I said it was a hunch." Each word was spit out like a nail.

I smiled sardonically. "Men don't have hunches."

"The hell they don't!"

"I'm not putting up with your swearing any longer." I turned and headed for the road.

"Magdalena, come back!"

"When pigs fly."

"You'll be sorry."

I kept walking.

"You're not going try and walk all the way down this mountain, are you?"

"Why not?"

"What about the rain? You could get hit by lightning."

"As if you'd care," I said childishly. I looked up. There was no longer a cloud in the sky. Mama was undoubtedly pleased with my decision.

"Magdalena, be reasonable."

"That's exactly what I'm doing. And anyway, for all you know, I walked up here. Walking back down should be a piece of cake."

"Enjoy your cake," he said. I could tell by the sound of his voice that he was no longer following me.

27

I am a healthy woman, still in my prime, but it was adrenaline that propelled me down Stucky Ridge and into town. Well, to be truthful, I guess I could have rolled down the mountain—it's that steep—but from the bottom of the incline I had to walk a good quarter of a mile until I hit Slave Creek, and then another quarter mile into town. From there it was two point two miles to the PennDutch, but I wasn't about to walk that far on an empty stomach.

Thank heavens Yoder's Corner Market was on my side of town and opened early. I am also eternally grateful that no one drove by as I straggled up Main Street looking like something the cat dragged in.

That's exactly what Sam said when he saw me. "Is that you, Magdalena? For a second there I thought it was something the cat dragged in."

I grimaced. "I thought you were going to start *buying* your meats."

"Very funny. What happened to you?"

"Mama."

Sam nodded. He's my first cousin and knew Mama. No further explanation was necessary.

"So what can I help you find today?"

"Your restroom."

Sam nervously brushed a lock of phantom hair back across a bald forehead. "I don't have a restroom."

"Yes you do. It's that little room in the back off the store-room."

"That's for employees only. They're liable to complain if I open it to the public."

"You're the only employee, Sam."

Sam sighed. "Use it. But put the seat back up when you're done."

I left the seat down. In fact, I weighted it down with the heavy ceramic lid of the tank. On top of that I stacked the plunger, the wastebasket, *and* a stack of *Playboy* magazines. Alas, Jacob Troyer had been telling the truth.

I also took my time sprucing up. My clothes were mostly dry by then, and a tug here and a tug there did wonders. So did Sam's comb, which was lying on the sink and hadn't been used in decades. When I emerged—except for my missing prayer cap—I looked quite presentable.

"For shame, Sam," I said, surprising him in the canned fruit section.

He flushed, from neckline to neckline. "A Lodge buddy gave them to me. I didn't buy them."

"Don't be so embarrassed, dear," I said, enjoying every second of his discomfort. "I'm your favorite cousin, remember? We played post office together when we were six."

His color deepened to that of Freni's beet-pickled eggs. "You aren't going to tell Dorothy, are you?"

"Your wife's a Methodist, dear. I'm sure this kind of thing won't surprise her at all. I was, however, thinking of mentioning it to Lodema Schrock."

Sam's pale gray eyes bulged beneath frosty lashes. "You wouldn't! She'll tell her husband and then I'm off the Mennonite Buddies Bowling League for sure."

"In third grade you dipped my braids in the inkwell," I reminded him.

"They no longer had inkwells when we were growing up, Magdalena. I put gum in your braids."

"Same thing. Mama had to cut them off. My hair was still

blond then and for weeks everyone called me Little Dutch Boy."

"The Bible says to forgive seventy-seven times."

"I stopped counting at one hundred. That was the time you put the live toad in my peanut butter sandwich."

"I only did it because I liked you."

"What?"

"I've been crazy about you for as long as I can remember. If we weren't first cousins—well, I even thought of asking you to run away with me to South Carolina. We could have gotten married there."

If my mouth had hung open any wider, I could have swallowed pigeons as well as flies. Not that there are that many of the former in Sam's store.

"What's the matter, Magdalena? Cat got your tongue?"

I shook my head vigorously, dissipating some of the shock. "Maybe the cat does have my tongue. After all, it dragged me in."

"Come on, Magdalena. Admit it. You liked me too, didn't you?"

"I detested you, Sam," I said politely.

"Ha-ha! You're such a teaser. That's one of the things I've always liked about you." His face grew pensive. "You don't think it's too late, do you? I mean, you're not married and as for me—well, Dorothy's a strong woman. She can take care of herself."

"Forget it, Sam. I wouldn't marry you if you were—well, the third or fourth last man on earth."

Alas, that seemed to give him hope. "We wouldn't have to get married. We could just—well, you know, be close."

"You mean have an affair?"

Sam nodded hopefully.

I gasped. "Samuel Nevin Yoder! I'm not only shocked, I'm disgusted. Adultery is a sin! And just the thought of doing the horizontal hootchie-cootchie with a cousin—"

"So your answer is 'no'?"

"Is your produce fresh?"

He may as well have dyed his face red. "You're not telling *this* to Dorothy, are you?"

Perhaps it's because I have big feet, but I can think fast on them. "Not if you sell me a buggy full of groceries—my choice—at cost."

"Done!" he said, too eagerly.

"*And* give me some information."

"Okay," he said slowly. The red flags that went up matched his complexion. "What sort of information?"

"It's about Gabriel Rosen, you know, that retired doctor who bought Aaron's farm."

As Sam relaxed his color lightened two shades. "Oh him. What do you want to know?"

"How well do you know him?"

Sam shrugged. "He comes in just about every day. Buys a little of this and that. Never even looks at the prices." Sam chuckled. "Yesterday he bought anchovies. Said it was for a picnic. That can has been sitting on that shelf for almost eight years. I know, because I ordered them special for Lily Bontrager when she was on her pizza-making kick, which was the year Pete Hershberger dropped his bowling ball on my toe and broke it. I had to back out of the finals on account of that. Anyway, Lily read the recipe in some magazine, but when she came in to pick up the anchovies and saw that they were little fishes, she changed her mind. I forgot to look, but I wouldn't be surprised if the tin had expired."

"How could one tell?" I asked wryly.

He chuckled. "Beats me. Never eaten the things myself. Special orders like that I usually pitch after ten years."

"How considerate of you. But back to Dr. Rosen, does he seem suspicious to you?"

"How do you mean?"

"Does he talk too much? Ask too many questions?"

"He's not as bad as you," Sam said without the hint of a smile.

"Remember, dear, I'm still in the catbird seat. What Dorothy and Lodema don't know *yet* could hurt you."

"He seems like an okay guy," Sam said quickly. "Not like some of the other folks from the coast—the kind that stay to themselves. Claim they have to shop in Bedford where they get more choices."

"Like the Hamptons?"

Sam spit on his own floor. I paid close attention to where the globules landed.

"*They* should have stayed in the big city. Did you know they had the nerve to laugh when I told them the only kind of asparagus I carry in the winter comes in cans?"

"City slickers!" I snorted. "So tell me, Sam, did Gabe—I mean, Dr. Rosen—ever mention drugs to you? The illegal kind, of course."

Sam shook his head vigorously. At least he didn't need to worry about messing up his hair.

"Magdalena, Magdalena, Magdalena."

"That's my name, don't wear it out."

"Always jumping to conclusions, aren't you?"

"It's the only form of exercise that doesn't make you sweat," I said defensively.

"You think the doctor had something to do with Lizzie Mast's death, don't you?"

"Don't put words in my mouth, dear."

"What's the matter? Your foot taking up all the room?"

"Very funny, coming from someone who is about to be famous—or should I say, infamous—for keeping dirty magazines in his bathroom."

Like I said, he could have saved his skin a whole lot of trouble by staying red. "Those magazines," he said, studying the canned pears, "were given to me by the same man you're so clumsily trying to investigate. From what I hear, Magdalena, the two of you are sweet on each other. Why don't you just interrogate him?"

"*Gabe* gave you those?"

He nodded. "We got to talking one day. Mentioned he had them. Said he was throwing away his entire collection now that he'd met a *real* woman. I hinted that I might like to take a peek at them—you know, read the articles—before he trashed them. Next thing I knew he showed up with the magazines. Maybe fifty of them. I didn't keep them all. Spread them around to guys in my bowling league."

"What? You spread smut to the BMs?"

"That's MBs, Magdalena, but hey, now that you mention it, I've got nothing to hide. If I get dropped from the church team, so do Elmer Reiger, Orville Weibe, and Walter Sawatzky. If that happens, Reverend Schrock will have your head on a platter just like John the Baptist's."

Sometimes it's wise to get while the going is good. "But we're still on with the buggy full of goodies at cost, right?"

Sam smiled. "I think you just talked yourself out of that."

Sometimes it's necessary to paddle faster. "Okay, so maybe you've single-handedly contaminated the church's bowling team, but you're the only one who has propositioned me. If I re-call correctly, it was Dorothy's father who set you up with this store and it's in Dorothy's name. A few well-chosen words to her and you're out on your ear like last decade's anchovies."

"Okay," Sam growled, "you win. But they have to be big items. Say bigger than a grapefruit. No filling up the buggy with spices. Those cost a fortune. Even I have to pay through the nose."

"Deal. Now, may I use your phone?"

Same shook his head.

"I'm not calling for help," I said. "I don't want to use up my free spree today. I'm calling for a ride."

"It doesn't matter. My phone's out of order."

"Give me a break."

"Come here," he said and led the way to his cubicle of an of-fice. I followed, gingerly picking my way over the spittle. "See," he said triumphantly, showing me the cracked remains of an an-cient princess phone. "Dropped it last week."

"That's your only phone?"

He nodded.

"Why don't you get a replacement?"

"I will—*sometime*," he added with a sly smile. "Not having one keeps Dorothy off my back. Anyway, why don't you use the public phone on the corner?"

"It's back in order?"

Sam frowned. "Never been out of order, far as I know."

"That's funny. Jacob Troyer said it was out of order. He stopped at the PennDutch to use mine."

"Jacob Troyer, the good-looking Amish man?" That may seem like a silly question to you, but I know of eleven Jacob Troyers in this county. Five of them are Amish, but none comes close to being as handsome as the Jacob I meant.

"That's the one. Said his sister-in-law was giving birth to twins over in Ohio."

"She's originally a Mast, isn't she? They're always having twins. Sort of a two-for-one special going on in that family."

"Ah, that reminds me! What if, during my spree, I put an item in my buggy that's part of a two-for-one special. Does that mean that after the spree I still get the second item free?"

"You get what's in your buggy, Magdalena, that's all! In fact, maybe I was being too generous. I think I'll just—"

"Hold that thought!" I said and skeedaddled out the door while I was still ahead. Sure, I had something on Sam, but he was a Yoder, remember? As one, he was capable of cutting off his nose to spite his face, and still have plenty of proboscis left.

28

The phone on the corner obviously worked. When I got there, Catherine Gingrich was giving her married daughter over in Lancaster County canning instructions. This is worse than carrying coals to Newcastle, if you ask me, since every Amish girl over six knows how to put up preserves. But Catherine is a compulsive talker, and had only recently discovered that the telephone expanded her audience. This was, of course, somewhat of a relief for her husband—until she talked him into the poorhouse—but was surely bad news for the daughter, who had no doubt moved away to escape the constant verbiage.

I could have interrupted Catherine, but I didn't want to have my ear bent for half an hour, during which time someone else would probably have come along to use the phone anyway. Besides, Freni does all my canning. Preferring to walk rather than to listen, I steered clear of that corner and hoofed it all the way back to the PennDutch. By the time I got there, my dogs were barking so loud I could barely hear myself think. Hertzler Road always has *some* traffic, but that morning it had none. Halfway home I was so desperate for a lift I would gladly have accepted a ride from Lodema Shrock.

There was no way, in my weakened condition, I was going to hoist myself back into my bedroom, so I reluctantly tried the kitchen door. Just in the nick of time I heard Freni's voice. That she was back at work didn't surprise me in the least. What surprised me was the patience in her voice as she tried to explain to Keith Bunch that meat-flavored ice cream was just not doable.

"But can't you put some ground beef in the cylinder along with the cream and sugar?"

"Ach, it is Magdalena's freezer. She will—how does one say in English—blow her stack if I do this thing."

"You've got that right," I muttered as I slunk around to the front door.

It is a sad state of affairs when a grown woman has to sneak into her own house, but believe me, it beats having to sneak out. Not that I've done much of the latter, mind you. I was always an obedient child, dare I say "perfect" even. It was Susannah who went to bed fully dressed and then, because Papa had the windows nailed shut, learned to pick the front door lock with a twisted coat hanger.

At any rate, there was nobody in the lobby or the parlor, and I was able to make it to my room unnoticed. The first thing I did when I reached my sanctuary was dig into my stash of Three Musketeers, which I keep in my top drawer under some clean unmentionables. (Lest you find it odd that I hide candy in my bedroom, let me explain that my guests have been known to rifle the pantry and kitchen cupboards for midnight snacks.) Since I always find one of these fluffy, not stuffy bars a great pick-me-up, I ate two. That gave me the strength to stagger into the bathroom and fill the tub with hot water and plenty of bubble bath.

Susannah gave me the bottle of bath salts for Christmas. It's called *Midnight Pleasures,* and much to my surprise, I took an immediate liking to it. Its not so subtle fragrance is not something I would want detected on me in church. In fact, Lodema Schrock would have conniptions if she got a whiff of it. Still, I imagine something akin to this scent was worn by *the* Mary Magdalene, after whom I am ultimately named, and bathing in these sensuous suds always makes me feel womanly.

Mama used to say it was a sin to loll about in a tub during daylight hours, but then again she never staked out drug-using

Amish teenagers, or walked down from Stucky Ridge. For Mama, one bath a week, on Saturday night, sufficed. Heaven forfend you should enjoy it. So in memory of Mama I turned the spigot open all the way to create the maximum number of bubbles, and stepped in with a defiant grin.

I lolled until the water got cold, refilled the tub, and lolled again until I was as wrinkled as a sunbathing California chain smoker. Then just to be really wicked I got a third candy bar and ate it in the tub. That, unfortunately, was not such a good idea because the suds on my hands gave the chocolate a funny taste. Still, there is nothing like frolicking in the froth to fill one with felicity. Which is not to say I only had fun in the tub; I did some serious thinking too. In fact, some of my best thinking is done while immersed up to the neck, which leads me to the following conclusion: a woman should be President.

After all, it is we women who take the long therapeutic soaks in the bathtub, while most men prefer a shower. And where, pray tell, do men spend most of their bathroom time? So whom would you rather have for President, an introspective prune like myself, or some man who made his decisions of state while sitting on the pot? Enough said.

I was debating on whether my skin could tolerate yet another water change when the door to my inner sanctum was flung open unceremoniously. Apparently in my fatigue I had forgotten to lock the doors behind me.

"I quit!" Freni said without a preamble.

Refreshed as I was, I could afford to smile benevolently. "I know, dear. You made that quite clear, yesterday."

"Yah, maybe, but this morning I un-quit."

"Whatever. Now be a dear and close the door. There is a definite draft coming all the way from the hallway."

"Yah, I will close the door. But this will be the last time."

My sigh pushed a flotilla of bubbles halfway across the tub. "There, there, I'm sure that whatever it is, we can work through it. Anyway, I was just thinking it was about time to give you a raise."

"Ach, I do not—" Freni's dark eyes glittered behind the thick lenses as my words sank in. "A raise. This means more money, yah?"

"Absolutely."

"How much is this raise?"

"You name it," I said blithely. I mean, how much money could an elderly Amish woman possibly want?

"Double my salary," Freni said without a moment's hesitation.

I sat up abruptly, losing some of my sudsy cover. Fortunately, since I don't have much to hide, the few remaining bubbles sufficed. Besides, Freni practically raised me.

"*What?*"

"You heard me, Magdalena. I want twice what you pay me now."

I slapped my forehead as the truth dawned on me, getting soapy water in my eyes. "Oh, I get it now! You want the money to bribe Barbara."

Beady eyes blinked. "Barbara?"

"Don't play innocent with me, dear. You know very well whom I mean."

"Ach, is it a sin to build your daughter-in-law her own house?"

"Her *own* house? You mean a separate house?" Like most Amish families, the Hostetler household consists of several generations living together. In most cases, upon reaching retirement age, the oldest generation relinquishes the main house to a married son or daughter and moves into especially built quarters adjacent to or nearby the main dwelling. This little apartment is called the Grossdawdy house, or grandfather house. There the retirees live the remainder of their lives, still independent, but close to the bosom of their loving families. In this case, however, it appeared as if Freni intended to fly in the face of tradition and reverse the order. Even worse, Barbara would be banished by herself to the grossdaddy house, and Freni would live happily ever after with her husband Mose, their son Jonathan, and the adorable triplets.

Freni hung her head which, because of her stubby neck, wasn't very far. "She could visit the babies whenever she wants." She thought a second. "Once a week should be plenty, yah?"

"For shame," I said, and then scooted back down into the water. The air in the room was considerably cooler than my bath, and Shasta and Everest, as I mockingly call my female embellishments, were gaining elevation. "Freni, if you don't watch it, one of these days Barbara is going to pack the children and move back to her people in Iowa. If that happens, I wouldn't be surprised if Jonathan went with her."

Freni gasped. "Ach! Such a thing could never happen!" She gulped for air. "Could it?" she asked, in a much weaker voice.

"You bet your bippy, dear. Where do you think Jonathan would rather live? With his wife and children, or with his—now how do I say this kindly—controlling mother?"

Freni turned the color of her own candied apples. "But the Bible tells the son to honor his mama, yah?"

Thank heaven for my strict Mennonite upbringing and all the scripture verses I'd been forced to memorize as a girl. I repeated for Freni the passage I'd quoted to the Hamptons in my inadvertently inebriated state. You know, the one about a son leaving his parents to cleave unto his wife.

The red left Freni's face as she muttered something so shocking that to this day I still can't believe my ears. If I heard correctly—and I pray that I didn't—she intimated that the Good Lord was no expert on marriage, having never been married Himself. And He certainly wasn't, according to Freni's tongue, an expert on daughters-in-law.

I cringed, fully expecting Freni to be struck by lightning, or at the very least turned into a pillar of salt. Since I was sitting in a tub full of water just inches away from the sinner, I wished for the salt. After all, it wasn't me who had blasphemed, so why should I get electrocuted? Besides, we get a lot of snow here in Hernia, and good rock salt for the driveway doesn't come cheap.

Okay, I must confess that when nothing happened to Freni, I felt a trifle disappointed. I didn't want her to get hurt, mind you, but you have to admit that her salinization would have been an exciting thing to observe. It certainly would have given Lodema Schrock something to talk about for a while.

"Count yourself lucky," I warned her as I wagged a long slender finger. "You could have been fried to a crisp or turned into salt."

Freni nodded. "Yah, but the raise, you will still give it?"

"I most certainly will *not*. Instead, I will buy a heifer for each of your grandchildren, and will pasture them here if you like. By the time the triplets get married, they'll have their own little herds going. But in the meantime, you get back to work."

My cook loves her grandchildren as much as she despises their mother. The idea that each of them would someday have their own dairy herd pleased her to no end. Her face lit up like a Coleman lantern and she scurried from the room before her tongue had a chance to undermine my generosity.

"Shut the door!" I yelled.

I don't think Freni even heard me.

I had just pulled the plug—with my toes, of course—when Darlene Townsend bounded into my tiny bathroom like a Great Dane on steroids. I couldn't help but shriek in alarm.

"Oh, don't mind me," the big gal said, and sat on the edge of the tub just as naturally as if I'd offered her a seat in the parlor. "I'm a gym teacher, remember? I've seen it all."

I thrashed at the water frantically to create a few new suds. "Get out!"

"Don't tell me you're embarrassed, Miss Yoder."

"I said, 'get out'!" The water was draining rapidly and I was forced to lie flat on my back to stay covered.

She didn't budge. "You really have no reason to feel that way, if that's the case. The human body is a thing of beauty."

I briefly entertained the idea that my body was beautiful. *Briefly.* I may as well have imagined that I liked calf's liver and mashed turnips.

"You sound like Gingko Murray," I said as I placed my hands over strategic areas.

"Please, Miss Yoder! That woman gives me the creeps."

"She may be an egg shy of an omelet, dear, but she has yet to invade my bathroom."

Darlene seemed to have selective hearing. "She's a crackpot, all right. L.A. will do it to you. I have a friend who spent six months out there and—"

"I don't mean to be rude, Miss Townsend, but if you don't leave by the count of three, I'm going to splash you. *One*—"

"I saw Betty Quiring," Darlene said quickly.

"What?"

"You know, Hernia's physical education teacher. You said she likes to pull ears."

"That's true. *Two.*"

"But I pulled her ears instead."

"Look away!" I barked. I grabbed my towel on the rack beside me and yanked it into the tub. "Now, dear, you did *what?*"

"I pulled her ears. I went over to see her, like I said I would, and she was really very nice at first. She invited me in. Even served me a glass of cranberry juice."

"Get to the point, dear."

"I am. You see, I can be clumsy at times and I accidentally spilled a drop of cranberry juice on Miss Quiring's white rug. A *drop.* I mean that literally. Anyway, the woman went crazy and started pulling my ears, and yelling at me like I was a little kid. So I pulled back."

"You go, girl!" I said, mimicking my sister Susannah. I know ear pulling is unhealthy, and violence should never be condoned. But this was Betty Quiring we were talking about!

Darlene smiled. "I thought you'd like to hear that."

"What happened next?" I asked breathlessly.

"Well, I guess what I did kind of took her by surprise. Then we both started laughing. We got along really well after that."

"Oh." I didn't bother to hide my disappointment.

"She's a nice woman, Miss Yoder. Just a little bossy. Anyway, I asked her if she knew of any girls who were good at the game—basketball, I mean—and she suggested Dorothy Mitchell and Anna Lichty. Do you know them?"

I frowned. "Dorothy Mitchell is a Presbyterian."

"What does that mean?"

"Well, they're almost as bad as Episcopalians. They're allowed to drink beer. In fact, I've heard rumors that some of them even bathe in beer."

"Really?"

I nodded. "The Episcopalians, of course, bathe in wine."

She laughed. "I'm an Episcopalian, Miss Yoder, and I don't drink at all."

"Well," I sniffed, "perhaps you're the exception to the rule. At any rate, I know *of* Dorothy Mitchell, but I don't know her personally. Her parents own a dry-cleaning store over in Bedford. Anna Lichty I know quite well. She was in my sixth grade Sunday School class four or five years ago. Even then she towered above all the other kids. Come to think of it, she was almost as tall as me."

"How tall is that?"

"Five ten."

"Miss Yoder, that isn't exceptionally tall by today's standards."

"I know, but I see Anna almost every Sunday. She's grown since then. Now she's a veritable giantess. Why, she's almost as tall as you." I bit my tongue, for having let that slip out.

Darlene merely smiled. "Do you think her parents could be persuaded to let her attend St. Daphne's in Philadelphia?"

"I rather doubt it. We Mennonites shy away from saints."

"Why is that?"

"Praying to all those statues, well, that's the same as idol worship."

Darlene laughed. I'm almost positive I heard the Bontragers' donkey down the road bray in response.

"We don't pray to any statues at St. Daphne's. In fact, I don't even know who St. Daphne was."

"Well, in that case, you might stand a chance. The Lichtys are very reasonable people and proud of their daughter. But I have to warn you, they don't have a lot of money."

"Oh, that doesn't matter. If Anna qualifies, I'm prepared to offer her a full scholarship."

I sighed. Where were the Darlene Townsends of the world when I was sixteen? I'd have given my eye teeth to get away from Hernia and—well, let's face it—Mama.

"You're very generous," I said. "Now, if you'll excuse me, I'm getting cold sitting here."

She remained sitting, as still as my faucet. "Would you be willing to call ahead and introduce me? Miss Quiring would, but apparently she pulled Anna's ears one too many times. Supposedly the girl hates her."

"Okay!" I practically shouted. "If you'll get out of my bathroom."

"Certainly." She took her time unfolding her long limbs. "I tried to ask you last night, but you weren't here."

"Don't be silly. Of course I was here. I just went to bed early." There was some truth in that.

She looked down at me, her eyes unblinking as a cow's. "No, you weren't here. I got in late from seeing Miss Quiring. It was just after ten, and as I came up Hertzler Road, I thought I saw your car driving the other way. I took a chance and knocked on your door."

"I didn't hear you," I said. *That* certainly wasn't a lie.

She smiled. "I knocked really loud. And your car wasn't in the driveway. Where were you?"

The nerve of the woman! There I was, naked except for a towel, and she was quizzing me like I was her teenage daughter.

"Out!" I shouted. "Out, out, out!" I grabbed my bottle of Suave moisturizing conditioner and waved it threateningly.

Darlene ambled slowly out of the room. "Let me know when you get the introduction set up, Miss Yoder. This morning would be best but—"

I threw the bottle of conditioner, causing ten generations of pacifist Amish and Mennonite ancestors to turn over in their graves. Fortunately I didn't hit her, and the tremors caused by all those rolling relatives ceased by the time I got dried and dressed.

The day was definitely off to a rotten start.

29

Freni made me cinnamon apple pancakes. After gorging, I went back to my room, hung a DO NOT DISTURB sign on the door, *locked* the door, and took a good long nap. When I awoke two plus hours later, I felt both ravenous and bloated. I also had a splitting headache. Most importantly, however, at some point during my truncated sleep cycle I'd had a dream, one which, upon awakening, still made sense. A lot of sense. Call it an epiphany if you will. The first piece in solving the puzzle of Lizzie Mast's incongruous death by drugs had suddenly fallen into place. But in order to see if the piece did indeed fit neatly, I needed my car.

Since I can just as well be sick away from home as I can at home, I gave Susannah a call. She answered just as her machine picked up. Apparently she was giving herself an avocado facial in preparation for her first TV appearance. She sounded as if her jaws were wired shut.

"Susannah, dear," I said cheerily, despite my pounding head, "do you still have the keys to Melvin's cruiser?"

She hesitated. "Technically it isn't against the law," she finally said. "The law says the cruiser is supposed to be used for official police business, but I'm Melvin's wife. And what's more a Police Chief's business than his wife?"

"Nothing, dear."

"Cool, Mags, I think you're finally loosening up. Hey, you want to go for a spin sometime?"

"Absolutely. How about now?"

"No can do."

"Of course you can, dear. I just want you to drop me off at the old Berkey barn. I seem to have left my car there."

Susannah wasn't the least bit curious. "It's a mask, Mags. I have to leave it on for an hour, and I just started."

"Avocados are meant to be eaten, not worn," I said patiently. "But since you insist on putting it on your face, instead of into it—well, it doesn't bother me."

"But it will bother me. If I go out now, I'll look like a Martian."

"I can't believe you care," I said bitterly.

A good deal of the cleansing hour passed in silence. "I do care," Susannah finally said. "I've turned over a new leaf. I now have a reputation to uphold."

"You do?"

"Look, Mags, I know you don't like Melvin, so—"

"Oh, but I do," I said. My nose itched fiercely.

"Give it a rest, Mags. You think he's an incompetent nincompoop. You've said so a million times."

"Well, I take some of that back. If Jesse Ventura can be elected as Governor of Minnesota, there is no reason Melvin couldn't be President. He could even ask Dennis Rodman to be his running mate."

"You mean that?"

"Truer words were never spoken."

"Because I've been doing a lot of thinking about what kind of a First Lady I'd be. I mean, should I be a fashion plate like Jacqueline Kennedy and reintroduce elegance to the White House, or an environmentalist like Lady Bird Johnson and—"

"Susannah," I said softly, "don't you think you should wait at least until after Melvin wins the councilman's seat before you install yourself in the White House?"

"Don't be silly, Mags. Now is the time to start planning. And I've already picked my pet project." She giggled mysteriously. "Don't you want to hear about it?"

"If it will make you happy, dear."

"You're a pal, sis, you know that?"

"I try to be." The truth be known, there was no way I would have listened to a woman who was unable to move her lips tell me her plans for the White House, had I not needed a favor.

"Well, I've decided that my number one priority will be doggy diapers."

"*What?*" I quickly jiggled a pinkie in my phone ear to make sure it was in working order.

"You know, canine nappies. Poochie Pampers. And tougher leash laws. I plan to spearhead a national drive to make every dog owner responsible for cleaning up after his or her pet."

"That's what I thought you said. What about cat diapers?" I asked guardedly. Little Freni was, at that very moment, taking her own bath in the privacy of my brassiere.

"Naw, cats are different; they cover it up when they're through. But whenever I take Shnookums for a walk around our neighborhood, I have to be careful not to step in these huge piles left behind by bigger dogs. Shnookums, of course, always wears the little diapers I make for him from Melvin's old T-shirts. It isn't fair what the other dog owners let their dogs get away with."

I nodded. That was certainly a cause I could get behind.

"I'll contribute a thousand dollars to Melvin's campaign."

"Really?"

"You've got my word. Now hurry on over with the cruiser. I need to retrieve my car."

It is undoubtedly hard to whine through an avocado mask, but she did a pretty good job. "Mags, I told you I can't do that."

"I'll make that two thousand dollars then."

"I'll be right there," she said and hung up.

Susannah showed up ten minutes later, even though she lives a good fifteen minutes away. Somehow she had found the time to cut eye holes in a brown paper grocery bag, which she wore over her head. Why she didn't find *that* embarrassing is beyond me.

She chatted the entire way to the old Berkey barn, but the combination of mask and bag made it impossible to decipher a single word. I nodded and smiled at regular intervals and that seemed to keep her happy. To my knowledge she didn't even ask what I was up to, but her muffled cry of joy when I said good-bye made me a tad nervous. Two thousand dollars was as much as I was willing to contribute to Melvin's hopeless campaign.

At any rate, I was relieved to find my car exactly where I had left it, and in the same condition. I patted my Beamer lovingly—a sin, I'm sure—and spoke aloud to Little Freni.

"Ready to take a spin, dear?"

Little Freni purred. She loves my car almost as much as I do.

We got in and, after carefully negotiating the stubble in the field, pulled out on the highway just behind, of all people, Lodema Schrock. I will confess now that what I did next was purely of the devil, but I must hasten to explain that I have long since repented for the error of my ways. At any rate, just to irritate my clergyman's meddling wife, I inched my car as close as I could to her rear bumper without actually touching it. One tap on her brakes, and our vehicles would have kissed, but I knew Lodema would never allow that to happen. She was, after all, a control freak. Besides, we at Beechy Grove Mennonite Church don't believe in overpampering our pastors, and I knew that Buick meant as much to her as my Beamer meant to me.

Sure enough, when Lodema saw what I was doing, she floored it. Unfortunately for her, the pastor's old Buick has about as much oomph as a satiated man, and I was able to maintain my distance. From what some of my guests have told me, drivers in both Carolinas would have been proud.

Lodema was livid. She turned to look at me, her face as white as a Longhorn's breast. I could see her lips moving, but thanks to the roar of her engine, I couldn't hear a word. How blessed, I thought, to go through life being unable to hear one's enemies—or in Susannah's case, a money-siphoning sister.

Finally, when I thought both she and the old car were about to blow gaskets, I dropped back and, when the gap was right, passed her with as much ease as I might have passed an Amish buggy. Of course, I couldn't resist looking back with a gloating grin. Who knows, I may even have stuck my tongue out at her.

Perhaps it was Divine retribution but I noticed my turnoff in the nick of time. I had to do some fancy steering to get my Beamer on to Augsberger Lane in one piece. The pinging of gravel against my newly waxed finish was like a volley of stones striking my soul.

"Darn!" I said, which is as bad as I can swear. "Darn, darn, darn!"

Lodema Shrock leaned on her horn as she passed on the highway behind. No doubt the Mennonite Women's Sewing Circle was in for a few chuckles at my expense.

Needless to say, thanks to my headache and a pockmarked car, I was not in the best of moods when I pulled into the Troyer drive. Therefore, I prayed for a Christian tongue. If the Good Lord did not see fit to give it to me—well, then it is really His fault, isn't it?

Gertrude Troyer was on her hands and knees in her front yard weeding her dahlia bed. The Amish may be plain people, but they have an appreciation for the beauty of creation. Still, kneeling in a flower bed seemed a little too fancy to me.

She looked up suddenly, startled to see me, and for a second I thought she was going to bolt. Had she, I would have been flattered. After all, a fierce reputation is better than none. But Gertrude quickly composed herself and continued to weed as if I weren't there.

I got out and approached her. "Your husband anywhere around?"

She pulled a dandelion out with its root intact, a feat which impressed me. "Do you see him?"

Her caginess impressed me even more. "That isn't the question I asked, dear. Is he around?"

She refused to answer.

"Fine. I'll find out for myself." I trotted off in the direction of the barn.

"Miss Yoder!" She was a spry little thing and caught up with me after I'd gone only a few yards. "Miss Yoder, it is not right that you should—ach, what is the word—barge, yah? Barge into our farm. It is illegal, no?"

"No. I'm not barging into anything. I'm merely looking for a neighbor."

She grabbed my right elbow with her dirt-stained hand. "But the barn you will not go into."

"Says who?" I said as I started for the barn.

She grabbed my arm with both hands and tried to restrain me. She was surprisingly strong, but not nearly as devious as I. A hard kick to her shins and I was free and running.

"Jacob!" Gertrude yelled. "Jacob!" Fortunately she has a thin high voice that didn't carry at all well.

I raced for the barn, ignoring the horse and buggy parked outside the closed main door. The horse whinnied as I approached, and it was only then that I realized Jacob must have company. Why hadn't I noticed the horse before? Jacob, like any Amish man, would never leave a horse hitched unless he was intending to go somewhere momentarily. Besides, the buggy didn't belong to the Troyers. Not that it mattered now. Magdalena on the warpath is as unstoppable as a German panzer, if I may be permitted to use a very unpacifist analogy.

The barn door was not locked, but it was heavy. I've been opening barn doors all my life, and I knew to throw my shoulder into the act. It slid open smoothly, so smoothly that I took Jacob by surprise. In fact, I caught him right in the act of taking money from another man. It looked to be an enormous amount of cash.

I gasped, not at the size of the wad—I've seen bigger before—but upon recognizing Jacob's companion. It's hard to say who was more surprised, the men or I.

Needless to say, I found my tongue first. "Benjamin Keim! What are you doing here with Jacob Troyer?"

Elam and Seth's father looked as pale and rigid as Freni might have, had the Almighty chosen to smite her for blasphemy. His arm remained extended, his hand still clutching the cash. Only the blinking of his eyes convinced me I wasn't looking at a statue.

As for the drop-dead gorgeous Jacob, he recovered the instant I said his name. He turned to me, just as calmly as you please, his full lips arranged in the most seductive of smiles.

"Good morning, Magdalena." His voice was like that of a cat purring, not out of contentment, but from a need to be fed. "It is good to see you."

"I wish I could say the same," I snapped.

"You look upset, Magdalena. Is there anything I can do to help?"

I laughed bitterly. "Well, you could come right out and confess. That will save me oodles of time. Maybe even a few gray hairs."

"What should I confess?"

He smiled again, and just seeing that smile made *me* feel a need to confess—if you know what I mean. It took all my inner strength to look at his shoes while I spoke.

"You can confess to supplying the young people in this county with drugs."

As you well know, I don't swear, but if I did, I'd swear that even Jacob's shoes smiled. What's more, the man seemed to read my mind.

"Ach, such an imagination! And what is this you say about drugs?"

"Don't play stupid with me, buster. That's drug money passing hands right now."

"If you must know, Magdalena, the money Benjamin is giving me is for a horse. A plow horse. Is that not right, Benjamin?"

"Ach!"

I had no trouble looking above Benjamin Keim's shoes. He had too much Yoder blood cruising through his veins to jumpstart my hormones.

"Benjamin," I said sternly, "at least have the decency to admit to your crime. Buying drugs for your sons is horrible enough. Don't add a lie to your sins, it may break the camel's back."

His blue eyes thawed, becoming the pale watery pools I was used to. "Elam was right. You speak in riddles. What is this camel's back?"

"Forget camels!" I shrieked. "Just admit that you are buying drugs from this creep!"

Benjamin hung his head but said nothing more.

"Well, Miss Yoder," Jacob said smugly, "you are not so right about things as you think."

I studied his laces. The left one had a knot.

"So straighten me out."

"Well, from what Benjamin tells me, his sons came to him this morning and told him that you had given them uh—uh—"

"An ultimatum?"

"Yah, maybe that is the word. So now Benjamin comes to me and wants to give me this money so that I stop selling these drugs to his sons."

I looked up, too angry to lust. "So you admit it! You do sell drugs!"

For the first time I could see that what I had once thought of as a seductive smile was nothing more than a smarmy smirk. I could stare now straight into Jacob's eyes, and not feel the slightest quiver in my loins.

"Yah, I sell drugs," he said almost casually. "There is much more money to be made with drugs than with farming. And do not think I keep all this money, Magdalena. I give very much to the widows' fund, like a good Christian, yah? But the farming, I must do a little so the people do not become too suspicious."

"Shame, shame, shame! And you call yourself a Christian!"

He blinked, and had the nerve to look crestfallen. "But I am a Christian."

"True Christians," I shrieked, "don't corrupt teenagers! True Christians aren't drug dealers."

He shook his once handsome head. "Ach, but I take care of these kids. I make sure that the drugs I sell them are pure."

"And *that's* Christian?"

"Perhaps you don't understand, Miss Yoder. The world has come to Hernia. These children, they will take drugs anyway. So I protect them. I buy the drugs they want from a good source, and I myself test them."

"Well, bully for you! Maybe we should erect a statue in your honor."

"Ach, no!" He may have been a drug dealer, but he was still Amish enough to be horrified by the very thought of a graven image.

"That was sarcasm, dear." I stepped confidently forward. "You know I'm going to have to turn you in."

"But my boys," Benjamin cried, "you will turn them in too?"

I turned from Jacob to face Benjamin and nodded reluctantly. "Yes, but I promised them that if they cooperated—which they obviously did—I'd do everything in my power to see that the law took it easy on them."

"You have such powers, Miss Yoder?"

I smiled encouragingly at the boys' father. "I'm not saying they won't go unpunished, but I will make it clear to the judge that they cooperated and were instrumental in Jacob's arrest. I'm sure some sort of plea bargaining can be arranged."

"What is this plea bargaining?"

"Well, it's like this," I said, and fell flat on my face in the straw at Benjamin's feet.

30

Lemon Crepes with Raspberry Filling

Crepes

2 eggs
dash of salt
1 cup flour
1½ cups milk

2 tablespoons sugar
1 tablespoon cooking oil
1¼ teaspoons grated lemon
zest

Place all ingredients in a blender and mix until smooth. Drop about 2 tablespoonfuls of batter onto a hot, greased 6-inch skillet, tilting pan until batter covers the bottom. Cook one side only until brown.

Filling

1 10-ounce package frozen
raspberries, thawed
⅔ cup water

1½ tablespoons sugar
1 tablespoon cornstarch
2 tablespoons water

Drain the raspberries and put the liquid in a saucepan with ⅔ cup of water and the sugar. Bring to a boil. Dissolve cornstarch in 2 tablespoons of water and add to the boiling mixture, cooking and stirring until mixture thickens. Carefully add the raspberries. Makes about 1½ cups of filling. Also a great pancake topping.

31

Fortunately I can't remember the fall, or that it was caused by Jacob hitting me on the back of the head with a pitchfork handle. The next thing I knew I was waking up in utter blackness. At least I *thought* I was waking up. I wasn't sure, you see, because it occurred to me I might have died and gone to Hell.

I know that might be hard for some of you to understand, since we Mennonites, like many mainstream denominations, believe that one can pretty much be assured of salvation by repenting and believing in the saving power of Jesus's blood, but I seemed to have done an inordinate amount of sinning in recent days. Let's face it, I had told more lies than Pinocchio, I had lusted after a married man, I had been greedy numerous times, and if memory served me right, I might even have spoken sharply upon occasion.

Now, I read my Bible on a daily basis, and it doesn't say a whole lot about Hell, but I know it is a place of extreme discomfort and hot as well—Hell. My environment at the moment, however, was not exceptionally hot, and while I ached all over, it felt more like having the flu than anything else. I briefly entertained the notion that, thanks to my kinship with Susannah, I'd been relegated to Presbyterian Hell. You know, Hell "Lite." For Episcopalians, I've been told, Hell is having to use paper napkins at a sit-down dinner.

Of course, one can always pinch oneself to see if one's awake, so I reached down to where my leg should have been and gave it a real hard tweak. Much to my surprise, I could feel my flesh with my fingers, but not the other way around. I might as well have been pinching a meat loaf, if you get my drift. Anyway, even though I couldn't feel myself being pinched, I heard, quite distinctly, a low guttural moan.

Again, while I could hear the sound, I couldn't feel myself making it. Perhaps, I thought, this was simply a characteristic of Hell. Perhaps I, the spirit, was torturing Magdalena, the body. To test this theory, I grabbed a big hunk of flesh and dug my nails in deep.

"Ouch!" I yelled in a loud deep voice, even though I hadn't even opened my mouth.

I willed my heart not to beat through the bony walls of my chest. The Bible gives us some of the horrors of Hell, but it doesn't necessarily list all of them.

"Mama?" I wailed. "Mama, are you here too?"

Please don't get me wrong, I loved Mama dearly, but when I was a girl, even the thought of spending an eternity with my mother was a Hell of its own kind. To be absolutely honest, back then I often fantasized that Mama and I would end up in separate places—if you know what I mean. That isn't to say that I was a totally selfish daughter, and consistently chose Heaven for myself in these fantasies. To the contrary, many was the time I was willing to dance with the devil, just to get Mama off my back. Rest assured that since her death—squished between the milk tanker and semitrailer loaded with Adidas shoes—I have stayed clear of these fantasies. For the most part.

"Ach, Miss Yoder, it is only you!"

"Benjamin!" I gasped. "Benjamin Keim?"

"Yah, it is me. Why do you pinch?"

"Sorry about that, dear. It was an honest mistake. You see, I thought I was dead and—well, never mind that now." Little Freni was scrabbling about in the depths of my bosom, which settled that question once and for all. Scripture makes it very clear that animals do not have souls. If my pussy was stirring, I wasn't dead. It's as simple as that.

"Miss Yoder, are you still there?"

"As far as I know. But look, dear, I think you should call me Magdalena. Miss Yoder sounds awfully formal under the circumstances."

"Magdalena," he said slowly, as if trying my name on for size, "are you hurt?"

I frisked myself which, under the circumstances, was not at all pleasurable. "Remarkably not. But the funny thing is, this morning I woke up with a horrible headache, and now it seems to be gone. How about you?"

"Ach, my head. Young Jacob hits very hard with a shovel."

"Is *that* what he did?"

"With you it was a pitchfork. The handle, yah? With me the shovel."

"Was there a scuffle? Did you put up a fight?"

"It is not our way," he said quietly.

"But it isn't Jacob's way either," I wailed. "So what did you do, just stand there and let him whack you?"

"Ach, I am a man of peace, Magdalena. Not a jackass. I was running to my buggy, for to get help, when Jacob hit me from behind. I did not wake up until now."

"Then how did you know it was a shovel, and not the pitchfork?"

"He had to hit me twice." He laughed, choking on the pain. "I have a hard head, yah?"

Little Freni had not taken well to my frisking and was determined to crawl out of the safety of my bra. "Stay, girl," I pleaded. "Stay."

"Magdalena, who do you talk to?"

"My kitten. She wants out."

"Ach, is this another of your riddles?"

"I wish." One of these days I was either going to have to get the tyke declawed, or figure out another mode of transportation. "Benjamin, do you have any idea where we might be?"

"Ach, no. Do you?"

"For a second I thought I did. I thought I was in Hell."

Benjamin's laugh surprised me. "Ach, so funny, Magdalena. Do you see English tourists?"

"No."

"Then this is not Hell."

"But I don't see anything. Do you?"

"It is as dark as the time I fell into the grain silo and was buried by the corn."

"Ah, yes." Benjamin Keim's one claim to fame was the aforementioned incident. It made the headlines as far away as Cleveland and Newark. It even made the *National Intruder*—not that I read that rag, mind you. What caught the public's interest was not the fact that an Amish farmer fell into his grain silo, but that by the time the rescue team dug the suffocating man out, he had somehow managed to become separated from his clothes.

"I did not take them off," he said, as if reading my mind. The Amish, it seemed, were remarkably good at this.

"Whatever you say, dear."

His ears, unused to sarcasm, didn't hear it. "Are you afraid, Magdalena?"

"A little."

"Just a little?"

"I'm sure I'll be terrified at any minute, dear. It's just that I'm still so relieved I'm not in Hell. The question remains, however. Where *are* we?" I felt around me with my free hand, taking care not to feel in Benjamin's direction. I was sitting up, that much I could tell, and on a relatively smooth, hard surface. "Perhaps we're in a cave," I said in answer to my own question. "A *deep* cave. There are lots of limestone caves in the area, you know."

"Yah, there are many caves."

"Any on Jacob Troyer's farm?"

"I do not know of any. But the Schrock farm is next door to Jacob's, yah?"

"So?"

"So, Jonas Schrock has a deep cave on his farm."

"He does? I never knew that." I've always had the hankering, but not the guts, to go spelunking.

"Even Jonas did not know until this spring when his new heifer disappeared. Jonas looked all over the pasture, no heifer, and all the fences not need mending. Finally, Jonas found the cave. By then the heifer was dead."

"That's too bad. How did they get it out of the cave?"

"They could not. The cave is too deep, and the heifer too heavy."

I gingerly smelled my hand. It didn't smell like dead heifer remains. It did smell familiar, however. I took another deep whiff.

"Coal."

"Yah, it is cold," Jonas said sympathetically.

"I'm not talking about the cold," I said, perhaps a bit irritably, "although that should have been the big tip-off that this wasn't Hell. I'm talking about coal. C-O-A-L. We're in a coal mine."

"Yah?"

"Rub the floor and smell your hand. It's slightly greasy and the smell—well, it's like our old furnace room used to smell like before Papa installed gas."

I heard Benjamin sniff. "Yah, it is coal. But there are many abandoned coal mines in this county, Magdalena. We could be anywhere."

I sighed. "Isn't that the truth."

"So, what do we do now?"

"I haven't the slightest idea. What about you? What do you think our plan of action should be?"

"Maybe we should pray."

"It certainly couldn't hurt, dear. Why don't you pray first?"

We Mennonites and Amish are used to praying aloud, and in each other's company. The Bible assures us that when even just two people share their prayers, God hears them. Fortunately the Good Lord knows High German as well as He knows English, because that's the language Benjamin used.

While I know some Pennsylvania Dutch words and phrases, none of them are prayer words. High German is certainly beyond my ken. Not only did I not understand most of Benjamin Keim's prayer, but it was interminable. Sometimes I think we Mennonites get carried away with our ecclesiastical verbiage, but the Amish really take the cake. Their church services last more than three hours and Benjamin, I remembered belatedly, sometimes preached in his. Therefore, I cannot be blamed if my mind wandered just a bit.

From infancy up, I'd been taught to pray with my hands folded and my eyes tightly closed. That is how one should pray. However, it was so dark where we were that I didn't bother to close my eyes, and as for my hands—well, in my defense, I started out with them folded. Can I help it that Little Freni started fussing again? What else could I do but unfold my hands and put her in my lap?

Alas, the feline furball was not content to stay put. Much to my horror, she wiggled free of my restraining grasp and got completely away from me.

"Little Freni," I whispered desperately, "Little Freni! Come back to me. *Please!*"

Either Benjamin didn't hear me, or he thought I was praying for Big Freni. At any rate he droned on as if I hadn't said a word.

"Little Freni!"

I felt the playful bat of a padded paw against my arm. The sweet little dear was trying to engage me in a gentle game of boxing. I batted back with an unseen finger.

Benjamin prayed while Little Freni and I played. Every now and then, just to be polite, I threw in an amen. Who knows how long the man would have prayed, had not Little Freni suddenly stopped playing by the rules and sunk both teeth and claws into the palm of my hand. I shook her off, but she was on me again in a flash, her fangs sunk even deeper.

"Stop that!" I waited in genuine pain.

"Ach!"

"Not you, Benjamin. My cat!"

"This cat," he said skeptically, "I cannot see it. And I do not hear it. How do I know it is really there?"

"Just like God," I said.

He gasped.

"I don't mean to be sacrilegious, dear, but it's true. Have you ever seen God?"

"No. But I feel God. In my heart."

"You can feel Little Freni too." I fumbled around until I had the troublesome little waif by the scuff of her neck. Then I dropped her in what I hoped was the general direction of Benjamin's lap.

"Ach, you do have a kitten! One with many teeth and sharp claws. But where did it come from? I did not see one with you in the barn."

"I have my secrets."

"Yah."

We sat in silence for a moment, which was a big mistake. What is irksome in broad daylight can be downright terrifying in utter blackness.

"Did God speak to you?" I asked just to hear the sound of my voice. "Did He tell you how to get us out of here?"

"No. Maybe now you pray."

"*Me?*"

"Yah. Mennonite prayers are good too."

I gave it my best shot. I began by begging the Good Lord to forgive me all my sins, both known and unknown. Then, the slate wiped clean, I implored Him to show us the way out of the coal mine.

No sooner had I said amen than my prayer was answered.

32

"I see light!" I cried.

"Where?"

"Straight ahead!" I pointed in front of me. "There!" Okay, so maybe "light" was the wrong word. What I saw was a smudge of darkness that was less black than its surroundings.

"I do not see anything."

"But it's there! And it's getting stronger all the time."

"How is it you see this light, Magdalena, yet I see nothing?"

"Because I cheated," I wailed. "I had my eyes open during both our prayers and I've been staring straight ahead. Your eyes haven't had a chance to focus yet. You'll see it in a minute."

"Ach! You pray with the eyes open?"

"Not usually, dear. And anyway, my prayer was answered, wasn't it? Now look straight ahead."

"But what if we are not looking in the same direction, Magdalena?"

"Good point. So stick out your arm," I ordered.

"Yah, it is out."

I felt around until my fingers found his forearm. Rest assured, they found nothing else along the way. Still, Benjamin squawked like a hen which had just laid an egg.

"Don't be silly," I chided gently. "I'm just going to point your arm to where I see the light." He was about as plastic as a lamppost, but I managed to orient him in the general direction. "There, do you see it now?"

"Ach, no."

"Well, it's there. Look harder."

"But I see nothing. Is it moving?"

"No, but you can bet your bippy we're going to. Give me Little Freni."

The kitten was not happy about being transferred again and mewed pitifully. Her tiny claws all but shredded my hands. Mercifully she settled down when I tucked her back inside my bra. No doubt she found the small space comforting.

"Stand up," I ordered, doing the same.

"Yah, now I am standing."

"Give me your hand."

"My hand?" He sounded as nervous as a bride on her wedding night, and I'm speaking from personal experience.

Benjamin was not cooperative, but I managed to grab his right hand, which felt like a large pineapple with five smaller pineapples extending from one end. I pitied the cows he milked.

"This way," I said and pulled him along.

It was not as easygoing as I had hoped. The light at the end of the tunnel was still just a smudge, and I still couldn't even see my feet. Whereas the floor of the tunnel where we'd been sitting had been smooth, I soon discovered that there were chunks of coal and even rock scattered everywhere. I had to feel my way along, my toes acting as sensors. I repeatedly banged my tootsies painfully, and every now and then I flat out stumbled. If it hadn't been for Benjamin's strong grip, I might well have fallen all the way to the ground and broken something. Probably my probing proboscis.

"Magdalena," Benjamin said, after pulling me upright for the umpteenth time, "how did you know Jacob Troyer was the one selling drugs?"

"There were clues, dear."

"Clues?"

"Signs. I barely know the man, but ever since Melvin asked me to help him investigate Lizzie's death, Jacob Troyer has been popping up like a jack-in-the-box. His scrawny little wife too."

"What?" he asked in alarm.

"Like gophers in a flooded field," I said, switching to an analogy he might understand. "Plus Jacob lied to me. He stopped by the inn and asked to use my phone. He said the public phone in Hernia was out of order—well, it wasn't! Besides, I figured the English had to have a go-between to reach the Amish kids. And what better choice than Jacob Troyer? He's so—so—well, so charismatic."

"Yah? What does this mean?"

"People like him. They find themselves drawn to him."

"Yah, you think this way?"

"Well, you have to admit, he's mildly attractive."

"I do not see it. But then, it seems I see very little. Ach," he choked back a sob. "I turn a blank eye to my sons."

"That's blind, dear."

"Yah, blind. This is what I am. My sons, they take drugs, and I think they are normal boys. They look like normal boys, yah? Maybe they act a little strange, but I think it is the age. 'It is just the rumschpringe,' I tell Catherine. 'They will get through it. They will get baptized. You will see.' But drugs are dangerous, Magdalena, yah?"

"Very. And addictive. I'm afraid times have changed, Benjamin."

"Yah. We did not have this problem when I was a boy."

"Nor when I was a girl." To my knowledge, Hernia had been drug-free in those days. The most shocking thing the kids I knew did on a regular basis was to hang out behind the janitor's shed and smoke cigarettes. The tough boys wore their trademark pegged pants, the tough girls their boyfriends' rings sized to fit with multiple wrappings of mohair yarn. *I* was not among them. True, Norah Ediger got pregnant her junior year, but that was just a onetime thing, and she was promptly expelled.

"I have trusted too much," Benjamin said, his voice cracking again.

"And I have trusted too little."

"Yah? How is that?" It sounded like his misery needed company.

"Well," I said, obliging him, "to be honest, Jacob wasn't my first suspect. I thought sure the supplier was one of the English that moved here from the outside. New York, in particular."

"Like the Hamptons?"

"You know them?"

"Yah. They are such good people. They take my Catherine to the doctor whenever the little ones get sick."

"Don't forget your blank eye," I reminded him gently. "Remember, appearances can be deceiving. Besides it wasn't just the Hamptons I suspected. I suspected Dr. Rosen as well."

"Ach, he is a good man too."

"I know!" I wailed. "I don't know what got into me. I kept thinking about the big-city angle and, well, I guess I just jumped to conclusions."

"Yah, you—"

"Look, before you say anything else, I already know what I did wrong. What I don't know is how to fix it. Gabe—I mean Dr. Rosen—will never want to speak to me again."

"But Magdalena—"

"And spare me the lectures, please. What I need now is advice. Not that I'm expecting you to come up with any pearls of wisdom, mind you, because I doubt if you've ever been in my shoes."

He wisely said nothing.

"But you don't have to be silent either, because it's awfully creepy here in the dark."

"Say you are sorry," Benjamin said quietly.

"I beg your pardon?"

"Ask Dr. Rosen to forgive you. That is my advice."

I thought hard and, while doing so, stubbed my toe. "Darn!"

"Magdalena, are you all right?"

"Fine and dandy, dear. I'll probably limp for the rest of my life, but otherwise I'm okay."

"This is a joke?"

"Yes. Now back to what you said. Do you think Dr. Rosen can forgive me for thinking he was a drug dealer?"

"Yah, I think so. Like I said, he is a good man."

"And so are you," I said.

*   *   *

We had gone about a hundred feet when Benjamin, too, saw the light. By then I was able to pick out dim shapes in front of me and our progress picked up considerably. Soon it was Benjamin tugging on my hand and leading the way.

"Look!" he barked suddenly. "There are boards."

"The entrance!"

He let go of my hand and surged forward. I stumbled after him. Little Freni hissed or mewed with each new jolt. But the closer we got to the entrance, the more light there was, and soon we were leaping over piles of debris like gazelles over savanna bushes. Benjamin's legs may have been slightly longer, but he's less sprightly, and I was able to keep up. The last fifty yards we raced neck and neck. He won, I'm sorry to say, but only by a nose.

"It isn't even sealed," I said, gasping. "Look, this board is loose. We can get out."

Benjamin ripped the board away and threw it out the opening. Another board followed a few seconds later.

"Ladies first, yah?"

"Yah," I said and slipped carefully into the blinding sunlight.

Before me loomed the silhouette of a tall figure. I couldn't see the features, but its stance was warm and welcoming. It occurred to me that I was indeed dead after all and had merely been moving through that proverbial tunnel. This meant—my heart began to pound—I was in Heaven. I'd made it after all!

"Lord, is that you?" I asked, my voice high and shrill with excitement.

"Magdalena?"

"It is I, Lord."

"Magdalena, are you all right?" My eyes adjusted to the light as my ears adjusted to the voice.

"You're not the Lord, at all," I wailed. "You're the giantess Darlene Townsend."

"Magdalena, what happened to you? You look awful. And who's this?" The gym teacher pointed at Benjamin, who truly did look awful. He was covered in coal dust from head to toe and looked more like a chimney sweep than an Amish farmer.

I looked at my hands, and then down at my clothes. No doubt I looked the same.

"We were—well, it's a long story. You wouldn't happen to have a cell phone with you?"

She shook her massive head. "No, I was just out for a walk and I heard something in the bushes. I thought it might be a deer."

"A *walk*? Where are we? How far are we from the inn?"

She shrugged, altering the skyline. "I'm not sure. Maybe two miles."

"Which direction?"

She indicated an area broad enough to include half of Pennsylvania. "Are there more of you in there?"

"Only Doc, Grumpy, and Sneezy. Snow White took the rest with her to lunch."

She strode past me and peered into the mine shaft.

"They'll be along soon," I said. "Doc stopped to tie his shoes."

Darlene straightened. "Miss Yoder, I don't know what to make of this."

Neither did I. It seemed an unlikely coincidence that she would just happen to show up at the mine shaft. Come to think of it, she'd been popping up as often as mushrooms after a warm summer rain. And hadn't she been there when Jacob Troyer showed up at the inn that day? I decided to give her a little test.

"Like I said, Miss Townsend, it's a long story. I'd be more interested in learning what you're doing tramping around through strange woods. Aren't you supposed to be off interviewing high school girls for St. Agnes?"

"Didn't I tell you? I saw both of those girls we talked about this morning. You were right. They were both pretty tall—but it doesn't matter anyway. Both sets of parents said they wouldn't dream of sending their daughters away to school. The Mennonite couple practically shuddered when I mentioned St. Agnes."

"Oh. Is that so? The name really freaked them out, did it?"

"Different strokes," the giantess said and smiled in resignation.

I turned to Benjamin. "Would you hold Little Freni, please?"

"Yah," he said with surprising eagerness.

I reached in and extracted the recalcitrant mite. When I finally got her out, I nearly dropped her in her surprise. My poor pussy, a purebred Chocolate Point Siamese, was now as black as a Halloween cat.

"You poor, poor dear," I cooed. "Mama didn't know there was coal dust when she put you down. Mama's sorry. *Sooo* sorry." I thrust the kitten at Benjamin. "Here, take her."

He took her in a hand just as black as she. "Is something wrong, Magdalena?"

"I have to visit Doc and the boys for a second."

"What?"

"I think she has to tinkle," Darlene said, and forced a giggle.

"That's right. Catch you guys in a bit." Then as casually as if passing from room to room in my own home, I stepped back into the old abandoned coal mine.

My eyes seemed to adjust faster this time, and almost immediately I found what I was looking for. Rocks. Lots and lots of little rocks. Coal lumps too.

I said a brief little prayer for courage and guidance and quickly slipped out of the upper half of my dress. Then it was my bra's turn to come off. This wasn't an easy thing to do, mind you, since that garment has never been removed outside the privacy of my home or doctor's office. But off it came.

Then I pulled my dress back up, buttoned it securely, and gathered up the stones. It's none of your business, of course, but in the days before Little Freni, I wore a smaller model, since space was not an issue. But lately, what with growth spurts— Little Freni's, not mine—I now sported a bigger bra. It may surprise you just how many golf ball–sized stones and coal lumps can fit in a forty, double D cup. You also wouldn't believe the weight.

As I armed myself, I could hear Darlene and Benjamin conversing. Their voices got progressively louder. What a foolish woman that Darlene Townsend was. We Mennonites don't put much stock in the concept of saints, but if we did, we could at least remember the right name. St. Agnes, indeed! Agnes was my fifth grade teacher, the one who paddled my skinny bottom with her tennis racket because I couldn't do long division. If she was a saint, then so was I. The voices outside were clearly arguing now. Finally only one voice, Darlene's, could be heard.

"Magdalena," she yelled, "get back out here."

"Coming," I called cheerfully.

"Now, Magdalena!"

I held my homemade sling behind my back and stepped back outside. Darlene Townsend was pointing a gun on poor defenseless Benjamin.

"Well, it's about time," she said. "I was just about to shoot your friend here to get your attention."

"Benjamin is an innocent man," I said calmly. "You don't want to hurt him. You want to hurt me."

"Actually, I was thinking of shooting that ugly little kitten of yours. That way I get two birds with one stone."

That did it. That hiked my hackles.

"Speaking of stones!" I cried, and like David the shepherd boy, I whipped my loaded sling from behind my back and let the stones fly.

They didn't all hit their mark, of course—one or two somehow managed to hit me, and I know a couple pelted Benjamin—but the majority of my launched missiles found their target. Given her size, how could they not?

Darlene staggered, perhaps more from shock than impact, but unlike Goliath, did not topple to the earth as I had planned. However, I had just enough time to grab one of the boards Benjamin had thrown on the ground, and harnessing all the anger I could, from every hurtful thing and injustice visited upon me in my long miserable life, I whacked the so-called gym teacher on the kneecaps.

She dropped the gun, and the rest is history.

33

"So," Gabe said, "this gives new meaning to the phrase 'over the shoulder boulder holder.' How incredibly inventive of you, Magdalena."

I flushed with sinful pride. "You work with what you are given—or not."

"And the board to the knees. Ouch, that had to hurt."

"You bet. Melvin says she's never going to walk again without limping."

"And this makes you happy?" I heard admiration in Gabe's voice.

"I know it shouldn't, but I'm limping now too. My poor tootsies really had a workout. Anyway, think of all the lives she's ruined. Lizzie is dead—and oh by the way, it was Gertrude Troyer who killed Lizzie."

"It *was*? How?"

"Crepes," I said. "Crepes of Wrath. The Masts knew too much, thanks to the carelessness of the Keim boys. Joseph wasn't a credible witness, but Lizzie was. She told the boys she was going to the police if they didn't straighten up. She actually gave them a two-week warning. Anyway, they passed that bit of information on to their supplier, who was not amused."

Gabe whistled. "I didn't think the Amish had it in them to kill."

"They're only human."

"But still! I mean, *murder*?"

"It was all that mousy little Gertrude's idea," I said. Somehow it was easier to be forgiving of the handsome Jacob. "Gertrude had heard that Lizzie was an awful cook. She figured the two of them would be desperate for something palatable. She laced powdered sugar with enough Angel Dust to kill a horse and rolled the crepes in it. Kind of clever for a simple Amish woman, huh?"

Gabe whistled again. "How did Gertrude keep from having to eat the lethal crepes herself?"

"She claimed to be diabetic and hadn't taken her insulin that day. That's something Lizzie understood. She never suspected a thing."

"What about that note? Was that the diabolical Gertrude at work as well?"

"You bet your bippy. She cut those words out of *The Budget*."

"The what?"

"It's the largest Amish newspaper in the country."

"So how do you know all of this stuff, Magdalena, if the Troyers are still on the lam? Because as I understand it, that Townsend woman refuses to plea-bargain."

I smiled. "You promise not to tell?"

"I swear."

"No need to swear, dear," I said with just a hint of disapproval in my voice. I had my work cut out for me if I was going to train the man. "You see, I uh—well, I sort of broke into the Troyer house."

"You what?" The admiration in his voice was palpable.

"Well, Melvin was going to get a search warrant and he didn't want me tagging along. He wanted all the credit for himself. What else could I do?"

"What else indeed?"

"Anyway, it was all there in Gertrude's diary. She may have been a very bad Amish woman in some respects, but she was typical in others, and they love to keep diaries. Funny, but Gertrude seemed especially fixated on Lizzie's inability to cook."

"Well, from what I hear, Lizzie had a good heart, even if she couldn't cook." He held aloft a glass of wine. "May she rest in peace."

"Yes, in peace," I said and raised my milk.

We drank in companionable silence for a few minutes. Finally Gabe spoke.

"I hear that one of your guests is taking partial credit for your success in solving this case."

"That would be Gingko," I growled. "She was only partly right. True, Lizzie was murdered, but I most certainly didn't die in a cave—it only felt like it. Besides, it was a coal mine, not a cave."

Gabe winked. "Hey, take it easy. I was only pulling your leg."

I sighed. "Sorry. It's just that the woman drives me nuts. Now she's predicting that I'm going to marry Jacob Troyer! Claims she saw it in a vision. Can you imagine anything as ridiculous as that? As if that mousy little wife of Jacob's would ever divorce him."

Gabe grunted. "She better not. But if she did—would you be tempted?"

"The man is a criminal!" I wailed. "A murderer!"

"Rumor has it they fled to relatives in one of the Midwestern states."

"Yes, Kansas, I think. Despite all her supposed powers, Gingko is unable to pinpoint where."

Gabe smiled. "Do you think the Troyers are likely to resume their life of crime there?"

"Gertrude maybe. But her handsome husband I'm not so sure of. I think he got a lot more than he bargained for. He was supposed to kill us—Darlene's orders. But after knocking us out, he couldn't even bring himself to tie us up. And of course he left the mine unsealed. Clearly he just wanted time to get away from the whole mess."

Gabe shook his head. "I don't get it. Why is it the police can't pick up a pair of Amish fugitives? How fast can a horse and buggy go?"

"Oh, didn't you hear? They stole the Keim brothers' car. Jacob is going have to live with a whole lot of guilt. Sooner or later, wherever he is, he's going to confess, if not to the police, then to the elders. He'll eventually spend time behind bars. I can almost guarantee that. Now that mousy little wife of his—"

Gabe chuckled. "Whom you clearly don't like."

"Well—"

"It's all right. But what about the bogus gym teacher? What happens to her?"

"She's being charged with first-degree murder for running down Thelma Hershberger. She would have gotten away with it, since the car was barely damaged, but poor Thelma left behind just enough of her DNA on the bumper. The arraignment is tomorrow. Melvin says we're lucky to try her in Bedford County on the drug charges. She's wanted in three other Pennsylvania counties and at least one in Ohio. She's the ringmaster and chief supplier of a whole network of church and youth group–related drug rings. Thank heavens this was the only Amish one."

"Any Jewish?" Gabe asked.

I shrugged. "Melvin was sparse with the details. He and Susannah are off to a fund-raiser tonight."

Gabe smiled. "I know. I donated to their campaign."

"You *what*?"

"It was only a thousand dollars. I figured it was worth it to get him off your back for a while. I made him promise not to bring you his hard cases for two weeks."

"Thanks!" I took a swig of my cow juice. "You've really forgiven me?"

He sipped his wine. "How could I not? You've apologized a million times. Besides, the first words out of your coal-blackened lips were 'I'm sorry.' I want you to know, Magdalena, that really got to me."

"I must have looked a sight!" I wailed.

"You still do. And I mean that in the nicest way." We were sitting on his Italian leather sofa—well apart, mind you—but he patted the spot next to him seductively. "Magdalena, I've been thinking. I'd like to take this relationship to another level."

My heart raced and my hand shook so hard the milk in my glass turned to butter. "You what?" I asked in a strangled voice.

"Put your feet in my lap, Magdalena. I'd like to give your poor tootsies a nice long massage."

It was then that I *knew* I'd died and gone to Heaven.

34

Cheese Blintzes

(In honor of Gabriel Rosen,
who gives one heck of a foot massage.)

Batter

½ cup flour
⅛ teaspoon salt
2 eggs, beaten

⅔ cup milk
1 tablespoon melted butter

Filling

½ pound dry cottage cheese
2 egg yolks
½ teaspoon cinnamon

2 tablespoons sugar
dash salt (optional)
butter, for frying

Batter: Sift flour and salt together; add rest of ingredients and mix until smooth. Drop about 3 tablespoons batter onto a hot 6-inch skillet. Tilt pan to cover bottom. Cook one side only until brown.

Filling: Put cottage cheese through a sieve. Discard liquid. Add the rest of the ingredients to the cottage cheese and mix well.

Assembly: Place a tablespoon of filling in the center of each blintz on the brown side. Fold both sides over the filling; then fold over the bottom and top, forming a tight pocket. Fry in butter until both sides are golden brown. Or you can bake blintzes in a greased baking pan. Brush the tops with melted butter and sprinkle with cinnamon and sugar. Enjoy!